UPON MY WORST ENEMY

by Mike Wellins
illustrated by Colin Batty

A Freakybuttrue Publication
Portland, Oregon, USA

No part of this publication may be reproduced in whole or in part, or stored in a retrieval system and transmitted in any form or by any means, electronic, mechanical, photocopying, recording or otherwise without written permission by the publisher.
For information regarding permission,
email info@freakybuttrue.com.

ISBN: 978-1493683536

Text copyright © 2014 Mike Wellins
Illustrations and graphics
copyright © 2014 Colin Batty
Cover illustration copyright © Colin Batty
Edited by Lucy Vosmek
Design and Layout by Lisa Freeman
All rights reserved.
Published by Freakybuttrue, Portland, Oregon.

This is a work of fiction. Names, characters, places and incidents either are products of the author's imagination or are used fictitiously. Any resemblance to actual events or locales or persons, living or dead, is entirely coincidental.

Printed in the USA
www.freakybuttrue.com

*But the most dreaded instrument,
In working out a pure intent,
Is Man -- arrayed for mutual slaughter,
Yea, Carnage is thy daughter.*

—Wordsworth

1.

Out of the roaring storm, came a thundering crash of water and metal that shook the terrain and shattered the night. Seven hundred tons of iron ground along the rock as the nose of the battered German U-boat slammed through the breakers with a towering spray of water as the submarine ran aground onto a tiny faceless island in a remote corner of the vast ocean.

November 1944, somewhere in the North Atlantic. Before running aground, the crippled submarine, the U-494, had been foundering for two days, after a tangle with an American antisubmarine plane that had dropped two small bombs, damaging the sub's superstructure, destroying its antenna array, and disabling its rudder.

During the brief, one-sided battle, the U-boat dove below the surface to hide from the circling aircraft and, after a panicked thirty minutes, was miraculously able to surface again. Once on the surface, the crew was relieved to hear that the plane had gone, but their relief was short-lived, as one calamity followed another. The damage from the bombing was more extensive than the crew had figured, and without major repairs she'd never dive again. In fact, she was lucky to be afloat.

The captain and crew tried to steer the damaged boat by throttling the two giant Mercedes engines up and down. The technique worked somewhat, but once the U-boat was hit by the vicious winter storm, it became pointless. Unable to dive and get below the storm, the boat was at the mercy of the wind and waves. None of the crew had ever experienced such a ride. The submarine, when fully functional, always dove for cover from the storms and enemy alike. It was the submarine's most lethal weapon. Now, stuck on the rolling surface, the boat pitched up one side of a mountainous wave, crowned out, and then dropped down the backside with an excruciating crash, followed by another and another. When surfaced, the broad flat side of the sub and the conning tower, or the sail as it was known, behaved exactly like a sail, an excellent catch for the driving wind and currents.

Most crewmen were violently seasick and vomiting, so hanging on for dear life proved difficult. Worse yet, when a huge wave struck broadside, the boat would roll completely sideways. Only the huge amounts of ballast seawater and the fact that she was mostly airtight would right her again after the wave had crashed over the crippled craft.

Ensign Vogel didn't get seasick. He faithfully manned his post in the nose of the foundering sub. He'd improvised a few places to hang onto and braced himself as the ship tossed and turned. Vogel received very little information about their dire situation. A few messages from the bridge came over the squawk box, but mostly other sailors whispered information down the line. What Vogel did know was that they'd been attacked by what was rumored to be an Allied aircraft. It was hard to tell time in his sealed-in world, but it had happened about two days ago.

Early in the war, the submarines worked in groups, the wolf packs, and hunted the North Atlantic with near impunity, sinking ships in massive numbers. But that was three years ago now, and the Americans had proven far more resourceful than the German navy had ever imagined. Now, the subs were fair game, and the Americans were uncanny in their ability to find and sink their dwindling enemy. Little did the Germans know, but by that time, the Allies had cracked the "unbreakable" radio codes and knew the missions of every single German sub.

In battle, running underwater was a sub's best escape, but running underwater required turning off the air-breathing diesel engines and switching to the huge array of lead-acid batteries to power the electric motor. The huge, bulky batteries, given how many there were, ran for a surprisingly brief amount of time before the sub had to surface again, run the diesel engines, and recharge the system. Worse yet, when the lead batteries met with salty seawater, they often exploded, creating clouds of toxic gas, the final insult.

Many of the newer U-boats were fitted with a snorkel of sorts that allowed the engines to run and breathe fresh air while the boat was submerged.

There had been rumors that the 494 was to return to base to be retrofitted with a snorkel, but first the sub was ordered to attack until it depleted its cache of torpedoes. Then and only then could the U-boat return to the submarine base in Saint-Nazaire, France. This, Vogel guessed, would now never happen. Sadly, the 494 had only one remaining torpedo when the fateful run-in with the American plane occurred.

Vogel knew that the sub had taken a hit, maybe two. The boat had dived, and was barely able to surface a half hour later. He gleaned that the crew was trying to take care of two wounded men. Everything seemed to be going OK—when they were hit by the storm. From his estimation, they'd been in the storm for twenty or twenty-five hours, and Vogel was sure that the ocean would tear the sub apart as it pitched up and down and rolled side to side. Then an electrical short caused a fire to erupt in the engine room. In a panic, the engine room was sealed off. Frantic whispers revealed that sailors had been trapped in the engine room when it was sealed. Others nearby heard screaming and pleading as the trapped sailors were asphyxiated or burned alive.

To compound their hopeless situation, when the engine room was sealed off, the engines were running wide open, full power. There was now no way to control them since the link to the bridge had been severed by the initial attack of the American airplane.

The sub was out of control and running at full speed when she ran aground on a nameless island in the North Atlantic. Sixty-knot winds and huge waves only added to the sub's forward momentum as she smashed headlong into the barnacle-covered boulders.

Nineteen-year-old Vogel, a tall, skinny boy, was at his station in the forward torpedo room when the ship ran aground. Unbeknownst to him, the first impact was in less than ten feet of water as the submarine slammed across the rocky bottom. On impact, huge rocks tore into the hull while the forward inertia launched the bow of the ship up and out of the water. The boat continued up and onto the surface of the volcanic rocks for another thirty feet.

Vogel had already thought he was dead several times in the last two days. When the first hit threw him to the deck, he grabbed onto anything he could, but he again knew it was certainly futile, for he was sure he was all but dead. The boat seemed to crash forever, shaking and buckling violently as metal snapped and bent everywhere simultaneously. The lights went out. After another violent hit, a loud cacophony shook Vogel's skull and exploded in his ears. The noise was so deafening that Vogel was sure that he would be deaf. That didn't matter, however, because he was certain that he was just seconds away from dying.

In those drawn-out seconds, it all seemed to him to be leading up to something dreadful, a massive explosion perhaps, something to finally kill him, to viciously finish him off. But after the last crunch, the ship seemed to roll to starboard about twenty degrees and stop. As debris continued to rain down inside the boat, it was obvious that they'd definitely stopped moving.

Vogel felt something jabbing into his back, but he hung onto the pipes and waited for more. Did they hit bottom? How deep were they? Then ice-cold water began to cover him in a fine spray, and he tasted the salty ocean. He almost wept with fear. Now they'd sprung a leak. The hull was breached, and water was pouring in. The horror of drowning gripped him, and in adrenaline-fueled panic, he opened his clenched eyes and sat up.

Thick, rolling clouds. Gray clouds with dark ribbons and wisps of white filled his vision. It was unmistakable. It wasn't smoke; it was sky. And the spray wasn't a leak; it was rain. Vogel, who hadn't seen daylight in thirty-six days, now climbed to his wobbly legs, staring at the sky and the land. A hole from ceiling to floor looked out onto the rocks as the frothy ocean washed around either side. The wind howled and whistled through the wreck.

The bow of the sub was ripped away. The nose of the ship was at a forty-five degree angle to the rest of the boat. Vogel was shaking as he climbed up and looked at the incredible scene in front of him. Hanging above the huge hole, splashed by rain, was the shiny nose of the sub's remaining torpedo, just four feet from the rocks.

Vogel heard a voice behind him, from deeper in the damaged ship. "We've run around! I think we've run aground!"

Somewhere in Vogel's confused mind, he caught the irony of the comment as he stared out at the rocks. Yes, he thought, We've run aground. He simultaneously giggled and wept with a strange giddiness. He trembled with fear, panic, and relief, and he vaguely noticed the telltale warmth from urinating on himself at some point. But now he was on land. Somehow, he was on land. The one thing he had begged for, prayed for, dreamed of for almost four months was now before him at his feet. Just moments before he was sure that all was hopelessly lost, that he was all but dead. But now he was somewhere, anywhere, just not out in the middle of the ocean in that awful submarine. Surveying the damage, he was sure of one thing: he'd never be going out on that boat again. He was terrified and euphoric at the same time.

A huge wave pushed at the back of the sub, and she listed more to the side, rolling in the surf and grinding on the rocks. The metal sections twisted against each other as Vogel hung on and dodged falling debris.

Then the calls came.

"Abandon ship! Abandon ship! She's breaking up! He could hear the wail of the siren inside the ship. There was power somewhere on the boat but nothing near him.

With pleasure, he thought. He walked forward and effortlessly stepped onto the boulders that had split the

hull. An enormous, toad-shaped rock was scarred with deep gouges but had survived the entanglement no worse for wear. As he climbed up on the rocks, the excitement of being alive was tempered by the reality of the situation. Vogel was blasted by ripping wind that swirled around him and pelted him with rain.

In a matter of moments, he had gone from the stifling, stale air of the torpedo room, which hovered at around 103 degrees, to just above freezing, but he still breathed the icy fresh air deep into his lungs and welcomed the swirling winds that pushed on him. Still, Vogel realized that the cold would soon be a problem. His navy-issued coat and hat were back in his bunk at the other end of the destroyed ship.

Vogel climbed back into the torpedo room and looked around. He spotted a heavy welder's jacket and a fire suit and put them on. He found a pair of boots and put those on over the fire suit's booties. He looked around the torpedo room for things he'd need. He grabbed a flare and a soggy loaf of brown bread and stuffed them into his fire suit.

He filled his arms with whatever else he could carry.

From the creaking wreck, Vogel heard the clanking of someone opening the bulkhead. He thought of going back to help them, but he decided to deposit what he was carrying and then go back. He climbed out of the nose of the sub and stood looking back at its long, dying body, half out of the waves, spread across the tiny beach.

The sub seemed not yet dead but perhaps in the final throes of involuntary jerks and twitches prior to death, as it rolled slightly in the waves. Against the dim daylight, small figures were emerging from the crippled sub. Many came out of the hatches, now parallel to the water, and flopped into the surf, dazed by the shocking cold. Some were injured. Some started swimming. Others just pawed at the surging waves.

Still others dropped beneath the water, their wet clothes and gear weighing them down, drowning them just a few feet from other oblivious, struggling sailors. Some wore life vests; most didn't. A few shuffled through the waves and headed toward the beach. Vogel was flabbergasted by the spectacle. He stepped across rocks to see if he could make any order out of what he was seeing.

But the cruelty of the ocean and the storm wasn't complete. A huge wave, slammed against the backside of the sub, spraying over the top of it. As water poured over the hulking wreck, the sub resisted briefly and then rolled hard starboard. With a metal shriek and a massive splash, the sub crushed down on several of the floundering crew. The conning tower smashed against the rocky beach just past the water line as men scrambled to get out of the way. Two were swatted dead in the rolling sea as pieces of periscope and antennas smashed into the water in a spray of white foam.

Vogel numbly watched the disaster. Above him, a piece of steel plating from the underside of the boat had come loose and flopped up onto what was now the top.

One final rivet popped, and the sheet of steel broke loose. It slipped off the bow, catching Vogel, completely unaware, from behind. The inch-thick sheet of rusty steel swung free and slammed into the back of his neck, instantly breaking it and crushing his spine against the jumbled, unyielding rocks.

No one who survived that day would ever know that Vogel had come ashore. They would assume that he had died, like most of the crew, in the explosions or the fire or the crash or the rolling sea.

Prior to his death, Vogel had begged, prayed, and bargained with fate and with what he thought of as God. He had endured so many excruciating hours in that sub, so terrified, so desperate. So many times, Vogel had wished to be off that boat, to stand again on solid ground and to breathe fresh air. That had been his overarching desire, to simply be on land and to breathe free. Vogel ultimately got his wish, but only just. Unlike anyone else who set foot on that remote rock, he died a happy man, deluded into believing that, for him at least, everything was going to be OK.

2.

"What the shit was that?" A squad of American seamen on the west side of the small island stopped, each standing motionless in the field of smooth, wet boulders. They searched each other's faces for some clue to what had caused the screech and rumble that reverberated through the rocky terrain as the submarine grounded not eight hundred yards away, just over a small hill of more featureless rocks.

"Sir, what was that?" asked one of the men.

"I have no idea," Lieutenant Brenner growled, slightly annoyed at the question suggesting that he had some secret knowledge of strange sounds off in the distance.

Brenner looked out at his nine men amidst the rocks. To him, they looked like mushrooms, their ponchos nestled between the rocks and topped by their shiny helmets. Each man had stopped what he was doing, frozen, holding gear, carrying lumber, or opening wooden crates. The men stood motionless, their eyes glued on Brenner.

"Sir, that wasn't a natural sound. No way."
"Agreed. Murray, Walters, grab a rifle and take a look."

The rest of the men stopped what they were doing. Chief Petty Officer Steele, noticing the lack of activity, barked at them. "The rest of you keep that equipment moving. If that gear isn't up off the rocks, the tide will wash it out to sea. That is unacceptable."

Lieutenant Brenner commanded a squad of naval engineers known as Seabees, the front line of engineers for the US Navy in World War two. Their name was derived from the initials CB in Naval Construction Battalion, a powerful arm of the military conceived when the specter of war loomed on the horizon in 1941.

After the attack on Pearl Harbor, the secretary of war activated the Seabees as the backbone of military construction operations around the globe. The Seabees were well known for building airfields on South Pacific islands long before the Islands were cleared of the enemy. Harrowing accounts of construction feats accomplished under enemy fire were common. A powerful force in the war against the Axis, the Seabees and the Army Corps of Engineers built thousands of miles of roads and trails, bunkers, buildings, dams, and other installations all over the world.

This group of Seabees, a squad from the Second Battalion, was commanded by Lieutenant Alex Brenner. Brenner had plenty of combat-construction experience and was a fully qualified engineer. The lashing wind and high seas were nothing compared to enemy fire, and Brenner was relieved that they were on what he believed was an uninhabited island. This kind of assignment wasn't new to him; he had done this exact job twice before—in Nova Scotia and in Maine.

Brenner and his team were on this strategically located rock to build and install a radio-repeater station.

Why it was strategic wasn't Brenner's concern. He didn't need to know, and he didn't care, because the radio station's purpose had no bearing on anything that was required of him and his men. Still, it didn't take a military strategist to figure out how important communication was to the Allied forces.

He and his men had been dropped off by the USS Hardison, a Naval Construction Brigade ship. After dropping anchor offshore of the tiny island in the pouring rain and pitching seas, the ship quickly unloaded several huge crates with its large booms and hoists.

The cargo was ferried crate by crate by smaller boats onto a narrow strip of gravel beach surrounded by the black boulders. The landing crafts dropped their front loading gates, and the huge crates were rolled onto the gravel just above the water line. It was then up to the men to get the material further, using their backs and, for the heavier stuff, a come-along winch.

The ship was gone as quickly as it had arrived, leaving the ten men on the rocks to sort out their supplies, equipment, and tools from the heap. That was three days ago, and it hadn't stopped raining or blowing since.

The island was really nothing more than a conglomeration of hundreds of thousands of rocks without even one flat area to pitch a tent. The lieutenant and the chief petty officer conferred. The first order of business was to install wooden-plank platforms to which Arctic-type tents could be attached. They would erect a larger tent and platform to serve as the workshop, where the parts to the radio tower could be assembled and where they could do anything else that needed to be done out of the weather.

They had four tons of cement to make a solid base for the tower and lumber and girders to make the frame of the antenna, as well as what they would need to construct a little radio shack to house the electronic equipment and the generator. Everyone had specific jobs that adhered to a very specific timetable.

In ten days, another ship would return at a specific time. Brenner and his men were expected to have completed the construction and to be waiting in rubber boats beyond the breakers. If that didn't occur, a chain of shit would rain down on him and his commander, and he was damned if he would let that happen.

Brenner never spoke about it, but, like so many others, he felt a deep, lingering guilt because friends of his, including his brother and cousin, were fighting and dying in Europe and in the South Pacific at that very moment. He felt it and never spoke about it. With that guilt hanging over him, the least he could do was build a rotten radio station.

There was no calling back to command to say that the island wasn't an island but instead an impossible pile of boulders in the middle of the ocean. No one really cared what it was or what it was like. All anyone cared about was getting the job done, period. As men stumbled around on the rocks, moving the unsealed cargo to various locations, others scanned locations for building. The real construction hadn't even begun, and they were already way behind.

The ground proved so tough that they'd barely gotten up the platforms and tents to house themselves by the first night. They fought not only the weather but also the rugged terrain. The boulders were either slick with algae or savagely sharp with razor clams and barnacles.

As the rain continued, they had just finished the platform that would hold the work tent when they heard the terrific crunch and screech and felt the grinding noise that reverberated through the island and up into their soaked boots. Brenner sent Murray and Walters to take a look. The rest of the men, struggling in their drenched ponchos and thick coats went back to work.

In World War II, the first activated Seabee units were sometimes comprised of men twenty years older than the average rank-and-file GI. The US military, early on, had few age requirements for skilled engineers, valuing their experience more than their vigor. Toward the end of the war, the Seabees recruited younger and younger men because the engineering training they provided had proved successful enough for any fit sailor. Brenner himself was thirty-six, and Hank O'Connor was forty-one. The oldest man on the island was Chief Petty Officer Martin Steele at forty-three. There were youngsters of course. Walters was nineteen, and Murray was twenty. Brenner had just sent them on their first reconnaissance mission—ever.

Murray and Walters cautiously left the makeshift camp, climbing over and around the slimy boulders.

"Hey, Walters," Murray said, "I heard you saw combat in the Azores."

Walters continued to move along.

"Not really. I was shot at by some Japs in the Aleutians, not the Azores. And the Japs were way off. I couldn't even see 'em, really."

Walters was skinny but tall. He had a tiny face on a big head. He had a nervous look about him, but in this place, that was expected.

"Sounds like combat to me," Murray said.

In reality, Walters had been working on a bridge over a river in the Aleutians. He had been there just two days when the construction site and his squad were in danger of being overrun by Japanese who had invaded the

island and come down off a ridge.

Walters was down in the valley with the heavy equipment.

He watched as Marines rushed past him and up into the hills. He and his squad were ordered to stay with the equipment. They fired their rifles but were simply too far away to have any effect. They were worried they might hit the Marines instead. It was little more than an exciting distraction.

A few rounds whizzed by them as they stood around in a muddy lot beside a fast-moving river in the freezing mountains. Eventually, enough rounds plinked off the heavy machinery that they casually decided to take cover. Ultimately, the Japanese were repelled, the bridge was finished, and Walters was shipped back east for another bridge. Then he wound up with Brenner and his company building this radio installation.

Murray was almost the opposite of Walters. He was short and stout and looked as if he came from a long line of Irishmen. He had bright red hair, pale eyes, freckles and a big overbite. This was Murray's first deployment. Besides training with the Seabees, he had only worked in his father's auto garage in Olean, Illinois, and had turned out to be a virtuoso with machinery. When the Japanese attacked Hawaii, he tried to join up immediately, but his mother wouldn't hear of it. As time went on, however, he sold her on the idea of being a builder, not a sailor, far away from the enemy lines.

She never really bought the story, but she had to give in. She cried and cried when he went off to the train depot.

Murray, of course, had no intention of staying away from the action. He wanted to kill the Japs and the Germans with his bare hands. But Uncle Sam didn't agree. After a battery of tests and the revelation of his aptitude for machinery, the government found him a spot with the Seabees.

But now fate had spun everything around, and was he going to get his chance at some action. But now he didn't want it; he wanted nothing to do with it. Murray hated boats, he hated the sea, he hated the cold, and he hated being ordered around. What a fool he'd been. He hadn't been drafted; he might never have been drafted. Instead, he joined up. And now he was prowling around an island devoid of anything but rocks and rain. He hated it. Still, he must do his job. He must be a man. What would his dad think of his cowardly thoughts? As he and Walters moved through the landscape, he tried to shake off his thoughts and focus on the task at hand.

Murray and Walters debated which way the sound had come from and settled on their route. After several hundred yards, Murray grabbed Walters and stopped him, signaling him to be still. They listened. They listened beyond the patter of the rain. They listened so hard they could hear their own heartbeats. Faintly, off in the distance, they heard voices.

They looked at each and drew their rifles in front of them. The two men, draped in dripping ponchos, wound silently between fifteen-foot-tall rock walls. They inched forward until they could identify distinctly German voices—lots of them.

Walters tugged on Murray's poncho, silently pleading with him to retreat, but Murray jerked his arm free, signaling that he had to get a visual of what sounded like the enemy.

Hunched over, Murray continued, as Walters reluctantly crept along behind him. Together, they peered around the corner of a jagged rock and looked down into a small cove. Their view was limited, but from between the rocks they could see at least a dozen Germans—probably more—hauling gear, milling about, and talking loudly. They weren't infantry; they looked like sailors.

Walters swallowed hard, silently agreeing with Murray's shaky signals. They turned back, sliding around the boulders, disappearing into the rain and wind.

Hudson Preston was a fit, all-American boy from Texas, drafted in early 1943. He had met up with Mark Hammond in boot camp. Hammond was a handsome fellow from Nevada. He was a wrestling champ and knew all about construction. Preston and Hammond struck up an immediate friendship, partly based on their common understanding of the absurdity of what they'd been pulled into. Their friendship helped them both. The two joined the Seabees wanting to do their part but not necessarily get killed in the process.

When they heard stories about heroic soldiers or sailors fighting valiantly but dying, Preston would lean over to Hammond and whisper in the gravelly voice of General Patton, "The point of war isn't to die for your country, but to make the other poor son of a bitch die for his." This was the two friends' secret agreement: they'd do their part, but they'd also stay alive. On this tiny island, however, they weren't so sure. They weren't so sure at all. The constant wetness was the least of their discomfort, but it gnawed at them. They stopped and stood, panting for breath.

Hammond and Preston were bringing up lumber to build the frame for the concrete. They carried stacks of two-by-four posts, stumbling and slipping across the rocks.

"You know what it could have been? It could have been some sort of sea junk. You know. An old buoy thrown around by the wind," Hammond suggested.

"Why'd we hear it only once then and not again? If it was being tossed around by the waves and all that, I think we'd still hear it," Preston argued.

"I don't know. Maybe it got stuck or sank. I mean, what else could it be? Sounded like metal breaking or something. Maybe a ship or something came ashore."

Preston looked over and across the small cove and set down his end of the load. He pointed as Murray and Walters came scrambling back from their reconnaissance trip.

"I don't know, but they don't look to me like they've seen a buoy."

Lieutenant Brenner and the other men gathered around Murray and Walters. Murray was panting for breath. Walters did the talking.

"Dorothy, we ain't in Kansas no more. Krauts, for sure, sir. We got a visual. Sailors, I think. I didn't see any of the helmets and the boots and all that."

The men collectively gasped. No one said a word; no one needed to.

"Must've come in some sort of boat, I guess. I couldn't see. There was all sorts of men, doing stuff, gear maybe. Maybe there was an injured guy, I think. All sorts of activity. More than a dozen easily, sir."

Murray nodded in agreement.

"And, Lieutenant," he said, "they all have beards. Some have big long ones." It was irrelevant, but Murray had to add something to the debriefing.

Brenner produced a map of the island, and the two men pointed out roughly where they thought they'd seen the German landing.

"That noise must have been them coming ashore," said Buchanan, a tall man in his mid-twenties. He was smart, sturdy, and intense. Like everyone else, he was bundled up in his arctic clothing underneath a poncho.

Brenner studied the map.

Hank O'Connor was Brenner's second in command.

"Lieutenant," he said, "the Navy said this island was clean. Apparently they were wrong."

"They might have been right when they looked six months ago, but the situation has obviously changed."

O'Connor studied Brenner.

Without hesitating, Brenner snapped orders to the men.

"All right, listen up. For anyone who's got mud in their ears, there's goddamn Krauts on this rock. Stop what you're doing, and secure any sensitive equipment. Take up defensive positions in a three-point perimeter with the sea to our backs." Brenner indicated three spots around their encampment. "You see German uniforms, you fire. You two, up on those rocks as lookouts. You two, keep the equipment moving. Get it up and behind those rocks before the tide comes in. You get something too heavy, then signal one of these two." He pointed. "They'll help you with the heavier stuff. And I want absolute silence."

Each man knew exactly what to do and moved into action.

"What do you think, Lieutenant?" O'Connor asked.

"I don't know what they're doing here, but they'll find us one way or another. And it's not like we can go ahead with construction with a squad of Krauts a half mile away. It sounds like they've got us outnumbered—and probably out gunned." Brenner stared off toward the enemy, running scenarios in his mind.

"Well, dammit, Navy said this area was clear, so

naturally we've got minimal weapons. Snafu," O'Connor said.

Brenner started another cigarette, but a fat raindrop found it and soaked the tip. He tore off the wet paper and lit it again.

"What are they doing here? We're out in the middle of goddamn nowhere," O'Connor pondered.

"If this place is strategic for us, it's strategic for them," Brenner said flatly.

O'Connor nodded.

"We could wait to try and ambush a few that wind up finding our camp. But that would give our position away. No question." Brenner was thinking out loud.

"And we'd have to wait until they decide to come looking. We're on a timetable," O'Connor added.

Buchanan was loading his rifle nearby, and spoke up.

"Sir, what if we radioed for help? Told them what we've got. They could send artillery to that side of the island."

"That's an idea, sailor," Brenner answered. "Except we haven't assembled the radio yet. Just load your weapon and get up there with Cassidy."O'Connor thought about it. "What if we sent a small force around to that side of the island and attacked them from their right? Make them think we're off to the south of the island. Then we outflank them when they go to defend to the south."

Brenner burned through his cigarette and tossed the butt to the wet ground. A few more ideas were tossed around.

"Those all sound like hairball ideas. Damn! We've got so few men and so few weapons. I need to see for myself. First thing. Murray, you're going to take me back there. The rest of you sit tight until I get back. Secure anything you can. And be ready to fight." The lieutenant struggled to get his arms free from under his poncho.

"Ahhh, I can't move in this damn thing," Brenner griped. He peeled off his soaked poncho. His coat underneath instantly started to get wet. Brenner stepped into the tent, grabbed his pistol and holster, and strapped them on.

"Lead the way," he said as he and Murray, tramping purposefully around the rocks, were quickly out of sight.

Brenner was an old-looking thirty-six. He had a hard expression, a big nose, and sharp eyes. His leathery skin suggested that he had spent much of his life out of doors. He rarely smiled, and when he did, it didn't seem to fit his face. He was all business. He was a Seabee and proud of it. But this, this was new to him. Being afraid and in charge was new to him as well.

Brenner was a builder, but in order to build, he must be a killer first—and a clever one at that. Otherwise, he would certainly be killed himself. Brenner had been on some of the most battle-torn islands in the South Pacific. When he was wounded in the side by an exploding Japanese mortar, he had been evacuated back to the Construction Battalion Recuperation and Replacement Center at Camp Parks in Shoemaker, California, with malaria, dysentery, shrapnel in his ribs, and combat fatigue.

He spent six months recovering there. Even though the war was still raging, Uncle Sam required no further involvement from the aging Alex Brenner, but Brenner refused his honorable discharge. His superiors were pleased with his commitment, and he was reassigned to a completely different climate and job up in the North Atlantic. It wasn't supposed to involve combat, but that had suddenly changed. Brenner didn't welcome the change, but he would do whatever it took.

Oddly, for as much battle as Brenner had experienced, he'd never fired a shot. He was wounded in a bunker after running off a half-built airfield during a strafing by a Japanese plane and a pounding by mortars. The closest he'd ever come to participating in combat was when he and another injured man drove a bulldozer over a Japanese machine-gun crew. But he'd seen fighting close up, and it had been absolute chaos. This, however, was different.

Nothing could be as bad as the South Pacific, he thought. And inside, for some strange reason, there was a tiny part of him that wanted—almost needed—to go back to that insanity again. He didn't know why, perhaps to have a chance to do things differently, to act more quickly, to fight harder. It was irrational, he knew it, but as much as he tried to deny it, down deep he wanted it again on some level. Now he was going to get it, and fear was welling up in him.

Brenner followed Murray back toward the Germans over the uneven ground. He had to reholster his pistol because he needed both hands to maneuver through the slippery rocks.

The men walked and climbed for another twenty minutes. Murray gave a signal and slowed down, crouching low. Brenner followed suit. He heard the unmistakable noise of men and activity. Even with the continual pattering rain and blowing wind, they could discern a hub of activity ahead.

Murray silently directed Brenner to look over a large rock. Brenner lay down on the smooth surface of the boulder and slid across on his stomach, inching up to the edge. He eased up and peeked through a narrow crevice. The rain was driving so hard that the splatter made it hard for him to keep his eyes open. Lifting his head further, he peered through the narrow gap and saw, unmistakably,

Germans on a small gravel beach. Men passed through his field of view carrying odd items, all sorts of what looked like mangled parts and debris.

Brenner craned his neck to see more, when suddenly something moved in the periphery just a few feet away. He froze. A German sailor stepped from between two rocks. The German was definitely a sailor, with a gun of some sort slung on his back. Oblivious to the Americans, he unbuttoned his pants to relieve himself. Neither Brenner nor Murray moved. Brenner's sidearm was still in his holster, and if he made a move for it, he knew he'd give himself up. Just six feet away, the sailor hadn't seen Brenner's face or helmet. The sailor must have been cold. Brenner could see that he was shaking and trembling. Although he couldn't see the sailor's face, Brenner could hear the faint sound of the man crying as he urinated.

The sailor finished but stood with his head down, quietly sobbing. Someone called to the sailor, undoubtedly his superior because he snapped to, wiped his face, and called back in submissive tone as he trotted off.

Brenner relaxed and finally pulled out his pistol, annoyed that he hadn't pulled it out before. He turned back to Murray and motioned for them to return to their camp.

Back at the camp, the men had all but stopped working. They squatted in the rain. Some nervously whispered, their weapons at the ready, as they waited for Brenner and Murray to return. After almost an hour, Brenner and Murray came sliding across the rocks. The men gathered around Brenner.

Brenner lit up a cigarette. O'Connor had been with Brenner for a year and knew that Brenner had seen some real action in the South Pacific, but the look on Brenner's face concerned him. Brenner smoked and stared at the ground, deep in thought. The men waited, and Brenner said nothing for an agonizingly long time. Finally, he spoke up.

"All we have is the element of surprise. There's plenty of them. That's for sure. Hank, your idea sounds less hairball now that I think about it."

The lieutenant flipped through a few soggy maps. He found a map of the island.

"Like you said, we circle around their landing site, and we attack them from all sides, kill as many as we can, and then fall back. We'll give them a chance to surrender. Buchanan, you speak German, right?"

Buchanan nodded cautiously, his helmet hiding his terrified eyes.

"Good."

Brenner fished a pencil out of his pocket and tore off a corner of the map. He jotted down a message and handed it to Buchanan. "When the time comes, you read this. I'll signal you."

"Yes, sir," Buchanan answered. He studied the little note.

"Now, if they don't surrender, then they'll regroup and try to counterattack. We hope they'll pick the wrong direction. We'll hit them again—in their flank—pinning them against the sea. But first we've got to have a fix on their numbers. If they've got a boat or come from a larger ship out at sea, they could have tons of weapons.

"Cassidy, I want you to circle around, follow the water. See if you can make out their ship or a landing craft or whatever. We're going to sit tight until you tell us what you see. Go—double time! We need to strike now. I want you back here in less than thirty minutes."

Cassidy barely had time to take it all in before he was up and scrambling over the slick rocks. He simplified the order in his mind: "See what kind of craft the Krauts have. Get a count. Don't be seen. Be quick."

Cassidy was scared, but he knew how to follow orders. After a year at a junior college, he had worked at a hardware store. Short and solid, he had built cabins and roads with his uncles and was a fair builder. As a teenager, he'd played in the woods with his brothers and neighbors in Washington state. He felt at home out in the wild. He was glad to be sent on this mission alone because he was comfortable with himself and knew he could do this as ordered. He wasted no time. He circled behind the piles of equipment and disappeared over the rocks.

Brenner addressed the pensive men. "We've got to get this thing built, and these Germans are in our way. Our orders are to build that radio, and there's no way we can do that unless they're no longer a problem." He motioned toward the Germans. "Kill or capture," he said solemnly.

One of the men groaned, echoing everyone's thoughts. He wasn't even aware of it until it came out.

Brenner dismissed it and continued. "The rest of you, as I said, defensive perimeter. No noise. Treat this like a combat mission until told otherwise. We're engineers, but we're soldiers first. Got it?"

"Yes, sir." The reply was muted but enthusiastic. The men moved into their assigned positions.

"And another thing in our favor. I don't think they're here on purpose. I think they ran aground. They don't seem like any elite landing team. There was no order to what I saw. O'Connor, rally over by the equipment. Let's assess what weapons we have and what sort of attack we can mount."

O'Connor swallowed hard and shuddered. An icy rain soaked his thick coat and uniform, but underneath he was sweating. It was the rare feeling that only a soldier gets when he knows that he'll have to go into battle to get through the day. This truth made him tremble, and made his teeth chatter.

"So we are attacking?" O'Connor asked Brenner.

"We've got no choice, Hank," Brenner said as they climbed up to the equipment.

"Geez, we're going to have to kill all those guys then," Walters said flatly to no one.

The thought sunk in. Everyone hunkered down in the pouring rain and wind, waiting for Cassidy to return. Two men finished covering their supplies with a tarp and tied it off.

The air had turned colder. A few mushy snowflakes mixed in with the curtain of rain. But no one felt the chill as adrenaline worked through their veins.

After an agonizing forty minutes, a lone figure ducked in and out of the rocks. Cassidy came back out of breath. He was pale, and his hands shook as he fished for his soggy cigarettes. Someone handed him a lit one.

"It's a sub, Lieutenant. They ran aground. It's a U-boat, I think. It's all beat to hell and crapped up."

Brenner extended the map, and Cassidy tapped on the paper where the sub was.

"I also saw a couple of bodies in the water."

The men listened intently.

"No one saw me. There must have been some wounded because I heard someone calling for a medic or something. Hard to get a count because of the rocks, but twenty or more—easily."

The figure horrified the men.

"Twenty?" O'Connor whispered.

"Or more," Cassidy added nervously.

Brenner spoke up. "All right, get all the ammo you

can find. And all weapons. We meet over by the tent in two minutes to form up an attack plan. I want anything we can use. Got it? We can't give these guys time to get dug in and organized. Now is the time, gentlemen. I show almost 1600 hours. We can't let them hide in the darkness, and that's just around the corner. We jump off in less than ten minutes."

The men snapped into action. Cassidy stood still, fiddling with his pistol. Brenner picked up on it.

"Something else, Cassidy?"

Cassidy fidgeted with the gun.

"There are sharks out in the water, sir. Big ones."

"Possibly. Probably. What's your point? We're not going for a goddamn swim," Brenner said.

"I saw one, sir. A big one. Eating the body of one of the Krauts floating in the water."

Brenner pulled out several clips of ammo and stuck them into the thigh pockets on his trouser legs.

"Swell," he said. "We can use all the help we can get."

Brenner moved across the camp with the men in tow. Their camp wasn't much of a camp yet, just gear and crates, with two polar tents lashed to hastily made platforms perched between the boulders.

Steele barked orders. "You two, secure all that equipment. Put everything under that tarp and secure it with rope. You three, take up defensive positions."

Three men moved into guard positions, their rifles aimed at the horizon behind the team.

The rest took stock of their weapons. Each man had a rifle, and Steele had a Thompson submachine gun. Several also had a sidearm pistol. Two unopened crates contained additional ammo for all the guns.

Brenner had balked when their weapons were

originally loaded in Rhode Island, as per Navy regulations, but now he wished he had more. In a firefight, ammo would go so quickly. What appeared to be a lot was really very little, barely enough for a real attack. He'd learned in the Pacific that you never had enough, that you always ran low. One glance told him that they were already very low. They also had one crate of twelve grenades, twelve smoke grenades, and twelve flares. If necessary, they also had two cases of construction dynamite and a dozen drums of gasoline that had been floated ashore. The gas was for the small generator, still secured in its shipping crate, which would power the radio installation they were charged with building.

Brenner took out his soggy map of the island as the men huddled around him like a football team. The few who had been to the opposite side of the island conferred over the wet map with Brenner, laying out where they thought the enemy was, the position of the sub, and their respective routes. The Germans were holding up on a small gravel beach wrapped with boulders—like the rest of the island.

Brenner laid it out: It would be a turkey shoot. They didn't have enough ammunition for anything else. If the battle turned into a slugfest, they would surely run out of ammo. No, he had to force surrender immediately or decimate the German's force so deeply that his men could easily kill or capture the rest. This was a horrible choice, but it was the only one he had.

Brenner's plan was ruthless. They would move into positions surrounding the group. In a semicircle with the ocean on the other side, they'd have the Germans completely covered. They would go on a killing spree for three minutes and then retreat and demand surrender.

He hoped his men would kill most of the enemy.

Whoever was left would counterattack, dig in, or give in to their surrender command. He hoped, with the attack coming from all directions, the Germans wouldn't have a clue where they'd come from and would be so shot up that they'd surrender. What kind of weapons did the Germans have? What were they able to salvage from their sub? How well armed was a sub? A thousand questions raced around in Brenner's head.

Brenner also had no idea how many men they might be facing. He thought he remembered reading that the standard U-boat held about forty-four men and officers. Cassidy had seen a couple of bodies, and it stood to reason that a few were injured or dead after the wreck. But as many as thirty-five men might be left, easily out numbering Brenner's squad—three to one.

In spite of this ruthless ambush plan, Brenner knew that things never went the way one expected when the actual killing started, and men, with their lives on the line, had miraculous ways of surviving, dodging bullets, finding an escape. More importantly, most of these men, the fighting Seabees as they were known, had done little actual fighting.

Except for himself, O'Connor, and Walters, who'd been in a brief firefight with the Japanese in the Aleutian Islands, no one else had any real combat experience. The last time any of them had fired a rifle or a machine gun was during basic training. He hoped that having the enemy in this fishbowl would eliminate the need for much actual aiming.

Brenner decided to keep his grenades in reserve in the event the Germans were able to mount a formidable counterattack. He assigned each man to a point relative to the semicircle of the little beach. "Watch your crossfire. Keep it low. Pick your shots. Don't waste ammo."

Each man listened while reaching into the crates of ammo and filling his pockets.

"After two minutes, retreat back. Steele, you've got the Thompson. Keep harassing fire for another minute. Then we wait for two more minutes. Then, Buchanan, you demand surrender."

"I know the words, but I don't know if I'll know the response," Buchanan said.

Brenner mused, "Oh, we'll know the response. Everyone set? No one fires a shot—no matter what—until I fire. Clear? Remember, conserve your ammo."

Each man nodded or murmured solemnly as he got his assigned position. The group stood for a moment, looking at each other, expecting something else, expecting someone to say something.

Brenner studied their faces. He breathed a few deep, quick breaths and said, "OK, let's go."

Hank O'Connor stopped and grabbed Brenner's arm.

"Wait a minute, Lieutenant. I need to talk with you."

Brenner stood up and studied O'Connor's face, his square features, his strong jaw, his prizefighter's nose, his honest blue eyes.

"What is it, Hank?" Brenner asked.

"I think we should give them the chance to surrender before we open fire," O'Connor said loudly.

"Screw that," grumbled the men. "They didn't give Poland a chance, or France. I say we let 'em have it."

Brenner looked O'Connor straight in the eyes.

"I considered that, Hank. And then what? We've got maybe forty German prisoners. Ten guys watching forty prisoners *and* building a radio station? And what do we feed our German friends? Where do we bunk them? If they're our prisoners of war, we're required to give them basic treatment," Brenner noted.

O'Connor shook his head.

"We can't just kill them because it's inconvenient to have to deal with them."

The men stirred.

"Oh yes, we can. It's a goddamn war. We've got a mission. These guys alive with us guarding them is just as good as them shooting us. Either way, we don't complete our mission. We don't finish the goddamn build." Brenner was getting agitated. "Better yet, we have two guys watch maybe thirty men while the other guys take their load. How long do you think thirty Germans are going to wait before they try to overtake us? Maybe we can make them slaves, and they can build the base for us. They can catch fish and live off the goddamn sea."

The men glanced at each other with varying levels of concern at Brenner's outburst.

"I don't know. It just doesn't seem right not giving them a chance to surrender. It seems wrong."

A couple of the men nodded. Others looked at them with disdain.

Preston scoffed. "This is bullshit. Those guys wouldn't hesitate to shoot a ship right out from under us. There wouldn't be any flare. There wouldn't be any radio message that said, 'Hey, you stupid American bastards, we're going to shoot your boat out from under you, so you'd better get to the lifeboats, and keep them handy because when another ship comes to rescue you, we'll sink that honey, too.' Lieutenant, I say we—"

Brenner stepped into Preston's face.
"I don't remember anyone asking your opinion, sailor. I said silence, and I meant it. O'Connor, your objection is noted, but we proceed. We take out as many as we can.

Now move."

Brenner called back to the men who stayed behind. "Worst possible scenario. You men destroy all of this. Destroy the equipment. Scuttle the whole site if we don't come back."

With that, he turned and signaled the men to follow him up into the rock field. With their hasty plan in place, the seven men, lead by Brenner, worked their way around the island, climbing and sliding up and down the lumpy landscape.

Three men remained at the camp, hidden and ready to defend their equipment and supplies if necessary. Now, however, they were more concerned that they might have to destroy it all if the lieutenant and the rest didn't return.

A half hour later, the seven Seabees neared the German wreck site. They moved slowly and silently. The patter of the rain and the howling of the wind were now a comfort, another level of concealment. They moved on until the signal to halt came down the line. They sat. They could hear, unmistakably, the voices of the Germans up ahead.

Brenner signaled the men into formation around the cove. Two groups peeled off in opposite directions, moving into their positions. Draped in slick ponchos over thick winter clothing, they looked like toy men, chunky, slimy clay figures as they moved with stealth into a semicircle around the beach.

Hammond found a good spot, a narrow ravine that he stepped through to get a clear view of the beach and the Germans. He adjusted his position and eased forward between two rocks. His heart felt as if it would explode, and his lips were numb. He could see them, plain as day, twenty yards away. There they were, those bastard Jerries, right there. In his sliver of a view, he could see three

Germans across the beach as a few others passed by.

He raised his M1 rifle and lined up the three German sailors as they sat under a shallow outcropping. Hammond was more nervous than he'd ever been. He was about to shoot unarmed men, who were just sitting there trying to keep warm, lucky to be alive. He gently moved his rifle from man to man. One, two, three, that's how he would go, left to right, once the first shot was fired.

The gunfire would be shockingly loud. They would be startled, but it would be too late. He'd kill them before they even thought to move for cover. Then he would move up and pick new targets. He would do it as soon as the shooting started. He would do it. He would kill these men. These men were the enemy. These sad, wet, feeble men were the goddamn reason he was out here in the first place. If they hadn't started this thing, he'd be home doing construction, building houses in sunny Florida.

These were the same men, feeble looking or not, who had now taken over most of Europe and who had almost starved out the British. He knew he could have no pity or remorse because if the tables were turned, they would kill him without question.

Hammond justified his actions in his mind. His friend Preston wasn't just whistling Dixie back at camp. These were the German scum that had killed so many, left so many to drown out in the middle of the Atlantic. They looked pathetic. They were easy pickings. But that was just Hammond's good fortune.

To Hammond's left, Petty Officer Lawrence Temple had squeezed between two rocks and aimed his shaking gun down into the cove. He had four or five easy targets below him, where a group of Germans was sift-

40

ing through a pile of debris. He couldn't believe that, in a matter of a few hours, he went from opening wooden crates to now planning to kill as many men as he could. He would do it; he had to do it. His life probably depended on it. Still, the absolute surprise of moving to such an extreme put him into a kind of shock, as if he were on autopilot, going through the motions, his body readying for the attack, finding his targets, while his brain wallowed in the gravity of their predicament.

Temple had been pretty lousy on the shooting range in basic training, and he now felt unprepared. He searched his mind to find some bit of knowledge that might aide him. All he could remember from his drill instructor was the command to squeeze the trigger without jerking it. Nothing else came to mind, and he found that advice almost totally useless.

Across the cove, two more sailors had slipped in above the Germans. Walters slid into a crevice, and Steele followed him, sliding down and stomping on Walters' foot. Walters pulled his foot free without making a sound. He expected some look or gesture of apology, but Steele made no acknowledgment. He just peered over the rock. Walters looked at Steele's unshaven profile and was amazed to see the stub of a lighted cigarette poking from Steele's taught lips.

Yes, Walters had been in that minor battle with the Japanese in the Aleutians, but it was nothing like this, nothing so close and personal. He was terrified as never before, but his brain was stuck on the cigarette, trying to fixate on anything other than what was about to happen.

He stared at the glowing tip of Steele's cigarette under the brim of his helmet. Rain dripped from the brim, less than an inch from the orange tip. How did this guy do it? How was he able to keep his smokes dry and even light a cigarette in all of this?

Walters noticed for the first time that Steele was much older than the rest. He looked as if he could be forty-five, maybe older. To Walters, he looked like a high school PE teacher, with a rough complexion and a tight, flat-featured face.

Steele had been almost invisible during their trip on the USS Hardison. But as soon as they landed, he became an organized taskmaster and tireless worker. He took his orders from Brenner and O'Connor and administered them precisely. He kept everything moving even in the miserable weather. But there was no chitchat, no chatter, no "when I get home" nonsense. He wasn't there to make pals; he was there to work. He was all business. Now, seconds before battle, Walters wondered who this old man really was.

Steele puffed on the butt between his lips and checked his watch. He felt the eyes of Walters on him. He glanced at Walters, who was stunned to see the look on Steele's face.

Steele wasn't scared. He wasn't scared at all. He was excited. He was actually excited to be doing this. He was calm and still, just smoking his cigarette as if he were waiting for a train. Steele threw Walters a sly smile, confirming Walters' suspicions. He wanted this; he wanted to fight and kill these guys. Steele locked eyes with Walters, and they instantly knew each other's feelings. Steele smiled more broadly, more confidently. He actually winked at Walters.

The smile made Walters feel profoundly better. Steele's confidence was unmistakable. Walters tried to return the smile but couldn't. Mustering all his effort, Walters was able to whisper in a trembling voice, "So how many times have you done this?"

Steele stared straight ahead.

"Never." He checked his watch again and then cocked his Thompson submachine gun. He wrapped the strap of the gun around his forearm and held the weapon with a firm grip. He steadied his body and shifted his stance, preparing to stand.

Time slowed down, and Walters felt his face go numb as he knew what was about to happen. He watched as Steele's steady hand squeezed the handle and his index finger eased down across the gun, slowly wrapping around the trigger.

3.

Captain Otto Fessenden, commander of the U-boat, kept focus on the tasks at hand, although, in the back of his mind, failure was smashing down the door. He played the whole scenario over and over, from before the sub was initially attacked until now, and he could not think of anything he could have done differently that might have helped.

In front of him was the most outrageous scene he could have ever imagined and he vaguely wondered what advice his superiors would have for such a situation. To his left, was the beached carcass of his submarine that was now almost completely upside down half in and half out of the roiling waves.

The thirty-two-year-old captain rubbed his stubbly chin. Lean, with thinning light hair under his battered hat, the captain had a narrow face with long features. Dark circles were etched under his light-brown eyes, a visual record of the weariness he'd endured.

He had been thrown to the deck of the U-boat several times as it pitched in that seemingly endless storm, and he, like everyone else, had been forced to find a cramped space to brace himself and avoid being killed by being flung back and forth between the thick metal valves and pipes. Several men had died that way, and the captain had watched helplessly as the lights flickered and the sub rolled like a rock tumbler.

That now seemed like another time. The captain reached up under his soggy hat across his balding head and touched the gouge on the side of his skull. It had seemed so deep at first, but now it was just a curiosity that he gently, mindlessly touched with his fingertips.

On the beach, there was no order. It was, at the moment, every man for himself. As some men dragged themselves from the frigid water, others pulled bodies of dead comrades out of the waves. Haggard men brought salvaged items from the wreck site. Dazed men staggered around, covered in the oil and grease that was now strung along the tops of the rolling waves.

The captain had given orders to Heinz, his deck officer. Heinz checked on the men, determining who was OK. Depending on their level of injury or exhaustion, he assigned them tasks, from "Get yourself dry" to "Help anyone still moving in the water" to "Go see what you can salvage."

The small armory on a U-boat, the pistols, rifles, and machine guns, was secured in a simple locker in the conning tower, which was now splayed open and broken on the beach. Two sailors, sifting through the pieces, were able to open the locker and retrieve most of the weapons and ammunition, but it was an afterthought. What they all were desperate for and what they all knew in their hearts was going to be a real problem was food.

A group of men was slogging through the breakers around the wreck. One sailor fished a flare gun out of the water, but the flares were long gone.

Another pulled up a machine pistol, undamaged, and displayed it to his mate, who was digging through the metal sheeting. "Let's see you put that between two pieces of bread and choke it down," he muttered.

Anyone who was still thinking straight knew that they were already starving. Most of the rations they'd had on board were now feeding the fish.

One shivering sailor found a working waterproof flashlight. He turned it on, and it came to life. He quickly switched it off.

"Now there's something we can actually use," said another through chattering teeth.

The process continued. All had assigned tasks, but their weariness couldn't be hidden as they plodded about as if stuck in mud.

The sub was rolling and far too dangerous to enter, too dangerous, in fact, to even get near, but the tide was coming in, and, within hours, the sub would be almost completely underwater.

The captain conferred with his lieutenant. Lieutenant Kruger was good. He had been with the captain since they had left France. He was young, but he was smart and missed nothing. For the first time, Captain Fessenden heard real panic in Kruger's voice and saw it on his face.

"We could be anywhere within five hundred miles of our last known position." He glanced skyward. "We have no compass. I doubt we'll see any stars. We have no way of knowing anything. I think we should send out two teams in either direction to see if they can figure out where we are. Maybe there's a lighthouse or some visual landmark. This could be northern Canada, maybe Iceland or even Greenland. It's anyone's guess."

"Or it could be a rock in the middle of nowhere," the captain said, looking around.

"What makes you say that?" Kruger asked.

"It doesn't smell like the coast," the captain said, sniffing the air. "And there are no birds here. There are always sea birds when you're near the coast."

Kruger couldn't deny the logic. "But we should look."

"We should look," Fessenden agreed. "but we need to get this situation under control first."

There were a variety of minor injuries—scrapes, cuts, bruises—and two men were badly injured. The ship's cook, Liebe, was tending to them as best he could.

The rain showed no sign of stopping as men fished floating debris and anything useful from the gravel and shallow water. Some tried to ignore the bodies of their shipmates deposited at the water line. Others, panting for breath, dragged the bodies out of the waves and dropped a piece of tarp or an odd uniform jacket over their staring faces. The captain tried to get a head count to see how many of the forty-two men who had shipped out were still alive.

Night was coming. With only one usable flashlight, it would be important to try to get a fire going.

Lieutenant Caspar, a navigator, walked over to the captain and held up a large MG 42 machine gun covered in thick storage grease. He was a strange looking man—short and blond with a round head, a puffy, pink complexion, tiny eyes, a flat, wide nose, and a wiry beard.

"Sir, we were able to salvage this and two cases of ammunition."

The captain, with all things considered, didn't see the need for a machine gun. He was busy salvaging unopened cans of rations from tangles of seaweed. Most were twisted and torn, their contents ruined by the sea.

"Well done," The captain said absently to Caspar. "Go and tend to the injured. Then let's figure out a place for us to get shelter so that we can see who is alive and who is dead and who is dying. Get me a list of the dead and missing."

He glanced around, grasping for ideas, as he held back the panic that everyone must have been feeling. Above them, about twenty feet up was an outcropping of boulders.

"Better yet, Caspar, go up there. See if we can get out of this weather up there."

Caspar snapped a hard salute. Fessenden couldn't believe it. It seemed as if the little bastard was enjoying this.

"Captain, it's good that we insisted on greasing the guns. As soon as we're settled, I'll get this up and working." Caspar trotted off.

Second Lieutenant Werner, wrapped in a heavy tarp, approached the captain.

"Captain, sir, my count is twenty-eight men alive, two of whom are seriously wounded. Ensign Kasser has a deep wound to his abdomen. He's unconscious. Ensign Berg has a severe head wound, and Mr. Liebe says he won't survive. His…his brain is damaged." Werner motioned to his head to illustrate and then stood at attention waiting for a response.

Werner was a passable officer, but he questioned and commented on everything. He seemed pretty full of himself. The captain didn't care for Werner's constant questioning. But at the moment, Werner wasn't saying much at all. He didn't need to. He appeared to be on the verge of tears.

"That's fine. Thank you," the captain said. "Assist

the men salvaging supplies."

The young lieutenant saluted. The captain half-heartedly saluted back.

"Captain, what are we going to do?" Kruger whispered in a panic. He sat next to the captain, trying to keep warm. "No one knows our position, including me. We foundered for almost two days. There's no telling where that storm put us. The radio went down with the boat. We have no way—" He stopped in mid sentence. "Captain, do you smell that?"

The captain was suddenly overtaken with exhaustion. He just wanted to sleep. He just wanted Kruger to stop talking. His eyes fought to stay open as he listened to Kruger's panic. He would try his hardest to get them out of this mess—but not just now. He hadn't slept in over four days, and now he had hit a wall of exhaustion. The captain's brain was losing its wrestling match with the desire for sleep. Captain Fessenden was overwhelmed by a thought of simply going back to his cabin, turning down his clean, white sheets, and sliding into his bunk. He'd pull the curtain and fall deep asleep, lulled by the hum of the engines and the other equipment. He would sleep for days. Kruger was a good man. He could take over the ship for a day or two.

The captain shook the waking dream away and forced his eyes open. He looked at Kruger. Kruger was like a dog now, his head cranked hard, sniffing the air.

"Look, we need to rest. Then we'll sort it out," The captain offered.

"There, can you smell that? It's cigarette smoke," Kruger said.

The captain thought for a minute that perhaps Kruger was delirious. Then he too caught a faint whiff. It was cigarette smoke, but it was different. It smelled like expensive cigarettes. He and Kruger looked at each other, puzzled.

Suddenly, Kruger's face jerked. His jaw and the side of his head seemed to peel away in a spray of red mist. A deafening crack followed. The captain jumped as Kruger tumbled over onto the rocks. A thick splash of blood poured from the side of his mangled head.

Shots exploded from everywhere, and rounds ricocheted off the rocks in every direction. The beach erupted into pandemonium, as men ran screaming and diving for cover, only to be gunned down as they ran. The savage crossfire tore the sailors apart.

Two sailors managed to get at their recovered weapons. One stood to return fire with a rifle, but the gun wasn't loaded. Three enemy bullets found their mark, marching up his chest, kicking him back with each hit until he dropped, collapsing on his rifle.

Caspar, having reached the top of the hill, had flung himself between two slabs of stone. He peeked out and saw through the rain the shape of an enemy helmet. But he was forced to duck as bullets zipped and hissed on the rocks just inches from him.

The captain scrambled around a boulder as bullets ricocheted everywhere, sparking and zipping off the stones. He looked back at the faces of the men that he could see. They wore expressions of shock and confusion. He saw two men running for cover, gunned down.

The volley died, but someone with a machine gun kept up the pressure on anything that moved. When the machine gun finally stopped, the sounds were replaced by the wails of men in anguish.

The surviving Germans bounced back. They jumped up, shooting at the places where the enemy had been, but it was far too late. Still, they had to feel that they'd done something.

"We've landed in hostile territory," the captain said, still hugging the ground. The captain was in shock. He couldn't bring himself to look at the body of Kruger, not three feet from him, with his head unfolded.

Hans Burman crouched behind the captain. Burman was the chief mechanic. He had been lucky enough to be on the bridge when fire engulfed the engine room, killing his four men. How lucky Burman was feeling now was anyone's guess, the captain thought.

Burman now looked profoundly old, his eyes darting around, crazy with fear. He'd been grazed and had blood on his neck.

"We foundered for so long. Perhaps we've come ashore in America or Canada," Burman suggested.

"I suppose it's possible," the captain said.

"Gather all weapons and wounded and head for that embankment up there. You two, keep cover as they do it."

The captain took Kruger's pistol and his spare clips and tucked them into his coat. He grabbed Kruger's watch and his wallet. He managed to think of Kruger one last time. "I'll get these to his wife someday. I will."

The two designated sailors cautiously limped into action. They vaguely covered where the enemy had been, which was everywhere. They spun around with their rifles aimed, looking for movement. Werner ran back and crouched with the men near the captain.

The smell of gunpowder still floated in the air, and the cries of the newly wounded continued. The captain watched as a shocked sailor staggered around in a small circle. The man was so covered in grease and blood that the captain couldn't recognize him. Another poor boy lay alone in the middle of the gravel beach. He'd been was shot in the abdomen and the leg. He wailed in pain and yelled for help. Nearby, hidden among the rocks, other sailors pressed into crevices, terrified to move.

"Who is that?" someone asked.

"I think it's Schmidt," another answered.

"Schmidt is dead. He died in the engine room."The Captain closed his eyes. He could not believe what he was in the middle of.

"Someone go to him and shut him up," Burman ordered.

"We've landed in America. That's what happened. They're Americans."

Two cowering men stepped over the dead and pulled the wailing man behind a thick wall.

"Why don't they just get on with it, finish us off?" another weary sailor blubbered.

"That tells us a lot," the captain said softly. "They must have a small force. If they didn't, they would done just that. We are like a fatted calf in a pen."

"Maybe they're toying with us. Perhaps they're provoking us into a counterattack to draw us out," Heinz suggested.

"Why would they want that? Where are the tanks? Where are the mortars?" Burman asked.

"We can't stay here," Werner blurted out in a panic. "We're setting up for the slaughter. We've got to move out of this spot."

"To where?" Burman snapped. "The only direction we're sure they aren't is out there." He pointed out to sea. "And we are short on seaworthy vessels. We've got cover, and we've got weapons. We're ready now. Let them come."

"Perhaps we're in Canada, and we've run into a coastal patrol, and they're waiting for reinforcements," another sailor suggested.

"If that's true, then we should attack before their friends come," Heinz said. "We can resupply, take whatever they have, which is more than what we have now."

Werner agreed with Heinz and nodded emphatically.

The captain thought he might vomit. What next? What could happen next? Every time he tried to form a plan, every time he tried to take stock, something else happened. He was overwhelmed with this idea, wondering why he was being tested like this and what he had done to deserve being in this position. He never wanted war. He never wanted to be clever enough to get his own U-boat. He never wanted to shoot at anyone.

A call in broken German echoed through the rain and rocks. The battered crew instinctively hunkered down at the sound of this distant voice. It was obviously someone reciting rehearsed German, for the pronunciation was all wrong. But the message was unmistakable. "You're surrounded by Allied troops. Surrender and you will be well treated. Otherwise, you will be annihilated."

The captain listened as everyone else did. The announcement was repeated over and over. Captain Fessenden never thought he'd consider surrender, but if they were on Allied soil, they had no chance. More than half his crew was dead or wounded. They had no provisions, no radio, and no plan. He looked from his hiding spot to the faces of the men, so weary, so beaten, so utterly wiped out. They all shivered with cold, and their eyes seemed to be permanently begging, begging for anything better than where they were at that moment.

The captain, with his luger in hand, slid out on his knees and peeked around his rock. Across the cove, flattened against a rock wall, he could see Caspar. Caspar was passing potato-masher grenades down a line of three men. When he finished, he shouldered a rifle and crept from his hiding place.

Waving frantically, the captain tried to signal Caspar, but Caspar was too focused. Finally, the captain shouted through the rain in a hoarse whisper, "Caspar! Caspar! Get back! Get back!"

Caspar was fully aware that the captain was calling to him, but he didn't care. He pretended not to hear. To Caspar, the captain was weak, the cause of all their misery. The mighty captain was, in the final analysis, a coward, a weak-willed coward. All of their predicaments were the result of the coward's moronic decisions.

Caspar knew no fear. He was proud to be a German and, more importantly, proud to be a Nazi and part of the greatest race that had ever set foot on earth. His devotion was complete, and he'd never felt so sure about anything as he felt about his devotion to the Führer and the Third Reich.

Caspar had long given up on the captain's leadership, but he would not overtly disobey orders. That was mutiny, and although it was well deserved, he wasn't about to be mutinous against the Fatherland. If they were in Greenland or Iceland or some other Allied land, then they were hopelessly outnumbered. But that didn't matter. If he had to die, then so be it. The Reich would live forever, and in a way, so would he. Someday he'd be hailed as a hero, even if no one ever really knew what happened to him. He would not, however, be taken prisoner. This he swore to himself.

It would take twenty of them to take him down, and he would never disgrace the Fatherland by surrendering or giving up. He would fight until his blood had completely drained from his body.

He crept around a big mound toward the shouting voice. As the voice repeated the surrender demand again, Caspar rose up and fired a shot. He hit his mark. Caspar saw the man's helmet fly off as a chunk of the back of his head dropped away and his silhouette folded to the ground.

The invaders started firing again, but this time the Germans were ready and had managed to find safe spaces in the boulders. Three of the Germans flung potato mashers as the shooting Americans gave up their positions.

Two German sailors returned fire with their machine pistols. Another blast from the enemy machine gun ripped through their cove, and the sailors plastered themselves against the rocks as the bullets ricocheted in a thousand dangerous directions. Then it was quiet again, save for the occasional moan of a dying or hurt man.

Captain Fessenden looked out across the beach, and his first impression was that everyone was dead. Besides the few lined up on the wall with Caspar and the men huddled behind him, everyone else had been killed. Then he saw movement as a few men rolled over. Some even stood up and darted away. Another, shot in the leg, limped away. But the captain knew that the rest were as dead as the men that they'd pulled up out of the water.

The moaning began again, the whimpers and cries for help. The enemy was silent. No more shots or calls for surrender came. The men, soaked, hungry, and beaten, had to hang in a limbo, for hours, until darkness finally intervened.

Once it was dark, the captain sent out the men near him. They would regroup above, where they had discovered a shallow cave that seemed somewhat protected and gave the best possible vantage point of the area. With whispers and grunting, the German's worked through the night while three men with rifles and machine guns stood watch, expecting another attack at any moment.

The captain's deck officer, Hugo Heinz, whom he'd known since joining the Navy, was solid and determined. The captain was happy to have him. Heinz saw to things. He delegated tasks to Werner so that the group was pulled together. The wounded were treated, if possible, and moved from the potential line of fire. Usable material from the sub was collected and packed around the cave, along with strategically placed rocks, the one thing the island had no shortage of.

The moon was nearly full above the clouds. Occasionally, breaks in the fast-moving cloud layer would give the men a vivid view of their predicament. When this happened, each man, regardless of what he was doing, froze, knowing that he was completely exposed, his dark uniform set against the gray gravel and the white caps of the breakers beyond.

Werner established a rotation of guards and assigned a few tasks. Caspar found a dry corner and, using sheets of shredded life jackets, worked feverishly to clean the thick storage grease off the tripod-mounted machine gun. When the enemy returned, Caspar thought, they would get a wonderful surprise.

Heinz was able to keep a few men busy with specific tasks. Limping and staggering, the men complied. The remaining men made their way into the shallow cave, crammed tightly together, barely able to escape the weather.

Once all the men were accounted for, the captain was horrified to find that only nineteen men were still alive, and three of those remaining had been gravely wounded in the attack. The uninjured men looked horrible. Desperate, afraid, still wet and caked with grease and grime, the men were bloody and defeated. Chattering and shivering, each man contemplated his own personal hell. All the while, with each heartbeat, they expected the firing to begin again. This tension was perhaps the worst thing of all.

No attack came. The night progressed, and the captain lost track of time as fatigue overtook him and everyone else. In another indentation in the hillside, around the corner from the main cave, the men made three makeshift beds out of life jackets and uniforms for the seriously wounded. They lay whimpering and moaning. Henry Liebe looked after them, giving them water and trying to keep bandages tight. He, like everyone else, wished they'd just die and be done with it.

As night dragged on, hypothermia threatened, and Heinz assigned to several sailors the grim task of stripping the clothes off the dead so that the living might stay warm. The sailors were grateful for their limited vision in the night. They reverently worked through the heap of bodies, removing every stitch of clothing, every belt, and every personal item and passing them down the line. Ghastly bullet wounds and torn limbs were almost hidden by the darkness, but not quite.

Werner supervised the grim task of dragging the naked, mutilated bodies around a pile of boulders out of sight of the others. Some of the men muttered words of hatred toward the enemy while some wept at the loss of a friend.

Sometime in the black early morning, they all fell asleep, even the men who were supposed to be guards. It was the first night on the island for the Germans, who had been tortured for so many days at sea and who were enduring an even worse fate on land.

The captain talked to Heinz as they fought to stay awake. Why didn't they attack? Were they toying with his crew? It must be a small force, or they would have kept up the slaughter. Where were the tanks, the mortars, the artillery? Why didn't they reinforce and attack again? Perhaps they were a remote squad or unit far from a larger operation, an expeditionary force. Perhaps they were protecting something, guarding something. Weapons? A fuel depot? An airfield? Perhaps they had a boat. Perhaps a bridge connected this tiny spit of land to something else. They both fell asleep desperately trying to think of anything that would help them understand this impossible situation.

After days of stress, the exhausted captain slept for several hours without moving. He awoke huddled with the rest under the stone outcropping. He yawned and winced as he stretched his aching frame. He was surprised to see the rocks and beach blanketed by a thin layer of soft snow. Falling snow filled his field of vision. It came down like white feathers.

He tried to remember what had happened and where he was. It came back quickly—although he didn't remember falling asleep. Maybe they should surrender. They couldn't be any worse off than they were now. The men had mostly passed out in a heap, strung out from days and nights of panic and terror. Fessenden checked his watch and shivered. Snow. Unbelievable. Snow.

The men began to stir. A few woke and furtively nibbled on items they'd had the foresight to stuff in their pockets when they abandoned ship. The captain had barely moved when shivering men crowded around him.

"Sir, the men are hungry, and we have just a few salvaged rations. How do we divide them up?"

Werner knelt down beside the captain.

"Captain, sir, I have to report—"

"Yes?" The captain dabbed at his running nose.

"Well, sir, the three injured crew men..." Werner was at a loss for words.

"Yes, how are they?" Fessenden prodded.

"They're gone, all three of them," Werner muttered.

"Well..." The captain was stunned. "When did they die?"

"No, sir, you misunderstand. They're gone, gone. They aren't here. They were here last night. We tucked them into that little crevice down by the boat. And then they were gone."

The captain rubbed his face and took a sip of water from a canteen. The water was so cold that it was beginning to crystallize.

"Why weren't they closer to us?" the captain asked.

"Well, we thought their cries might give up our position," Werner explained weakly.

"Where did they go?" the captain demanded.

"I don't know, sir. I looked around. I...I don't know, sir."

The captain had to slough this off. He could only deal with so much.

Heinz, panicked, pleaded with the captain. "Sir, we have to organize some sort of attack. We can't just sit here. We have no food. We have no supplies. We have to move. They know where we are!"

The captain studied the man. "I agree, Heinz, but we don't even know where we're going or who we're after or how many are out there."

Heinz shook his head. They had to do something. They couldn't just cower and wait to be picked off.

"It can't be many. You said yourself that if their force was anything substantial, we'd all be slaughtered by now. It makes total sense. It has to be a small force. It has to be."

The captain sat up. "Take a man. Follow the water line. Go around to the left. See if you can find anything—a road, a ship, anything. If it is a small force and they have a boat, we may have a chance."

Heinz leapt at the idea. He grabbed Hauser, an uninjured sailor, and ordered him to follow. As Heinz and Hauser waddled away, the captain, stressed beyond reason, absently marveled at how the men, wearing extra uniforms, looked like the Michelin tire man.

Caspar came forward.

"Sir, requesting permission to join Heinz on his reconnaissance mission."

"No, stay here. They'll be fine. Considering our circumstances, I'm going to pretend that you didn't hear me when I told you not to attack yesterday. But if you disobey a direct order again, you will be shot. Is that understood?"

"Yes, sir. Understood. However, I must verbally object to your order that I not kill an enemy that had, just minutes earlier, been killing us."

The captain stared at Caspar.

"Noted," he said icily. "Is your machine gun ready?"

"It is, sir." Caspar said with no emotion.

"Then you take it and two of these men. Set it up there, with a defensive angle down on us. You do not fire unless I order you to or unless we're fired upon. Is that understood?"

"Yes, sir." With that, Caspar grabbed two sailors, and they marched off.

The rest sat shivering under the outcropping.

Young Mintz, a pale kid with a bloody foot, who

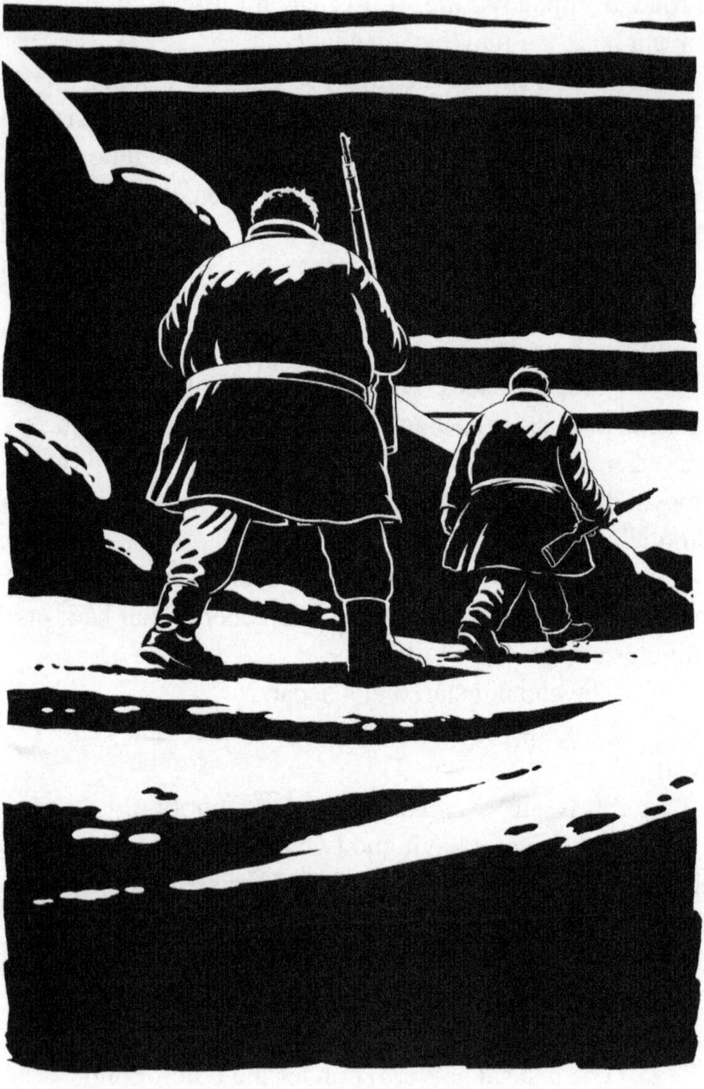

was wrapped in two scavenged uniforms, called to the captain.

"Sir, may I speak freely?" he asked wearily.

"Speak," The captain said.

"Sir, maybe we should give up. Look at us. What can we do? At least we'd get food, some shelter. Men are going to die without a real doctor."

Normally, that was treasonous talk. Surrender? The word wasn't in the German language. But in this mess, surrender sounded more and more legitimate. The captain studied the faces of the men seated around him. Each wore the same pained expression. He said nothing. He looked away.

Up on a hill, Caspar and his companions moved into position, covering the area with the big gun. Caspar waved, and the captain waved back. The captain and his men felt slightly better.

The snowflakes were dwindling, replaced by icy raindrops that made divots in the snowy layer that covered the unforgiving landscape.

4.

The day before, at the Seabee's camp, the time passed profoundly slowly once the seven-man assault team took off to attack the Germans. The three men left behind were too far apart for talk, but they occasionally looked at each other. They had nowhere else to look, as they tried to anticipate what might happen.

The minutes crawled by as they sat crouched in the wind and driving rain. Only an hour ago, the rain had been driving the men insane. Icy trickles ran down their necks no matter how they adjusted their ponchos. Water found its way up their sleeves when they lifted equipment. It ran down their chests when they hoisted lumber over their heads. Their feet were soaked and had been since the landing.

Since the discovery of Germans on the island, however, Temple hadn't noticed the water that trickled down his neck. If he had, he would have appreciated it's cooling effect because he was now soaked with sweat that poured from his underarms and soaked his uniform and winter suit. Temple looked over at Cassidy crouched among the rocks. Cassidy just looked back and shrugged his shoulders.

Through the rain came the roar of gunfire, a lot of it, bouncing off the rocks. Cassidy's mouth went dry, and he gripped his rifle more tightly. The firing died down to what sounded like one machine gun. It stopped briefly. A few more shots popped off, and all was quiet. For a few agonizing minutes, they sat in silence. Another round of gunfire shattered the quiet, and they even heard a few explosions. Explosions? The Seabees hadn't taken any grenades with them. The Germans must be putting up a fight. Cassidy now worried.

The three guards now wondered the same thing: What if our guys *do* get wiped out? What do we do? How long do we wait? Should we try to find them? Should we group together? So many questions they should have asked before Brenner and the men left.

Another excruciating half-hour ticked by until finally Temple saw movement among the boulders. He cocked his rifle, and his heart pounded. Then he saw the familiar green helmets and ponchos. He signaled the others as six men returned.

"We should have finished them off!" Preston said, breathing hard.

"I've got two shots left, pinhead. We have to save something. If we've got nothing and they come at us, we're sunk," Steele snapped.

They all panted heavily. Each man had a wild look on his contorted face. They were all now killers, no question. Each man absorbed that fact in his own way.

"I know, I'm just saying," Preston moaned.

The soaked camp was a hub of activity. The three guards joined the returning invaders. O'Connor had blood all over the side of his face and neck, where he'd caught some small fragments of shrapnel from one of the German grenades. He grabbed a bandage from his first-aid kit.

Brenner noticed.

"How you doing, Hank," the lieutenant asked.

"Just stings. I'll be fine. I caught some from the potato masher." O'Connor wiped blood off his face.

"What about Buchanan? Should we go back for his body?" Preston asked. The three guards looked at each other.

"Buchanan is dead?" Cassidy was stunned.

"Jerries shot him in the head while he was ordering them to surrender," Steele growled.

"Holy shit," Temple whispered. The gravity of the situation sunk in.

"They weren't too keen on surrendering, I guess." O'Connor dabbed his wounds and then paused, winced, and scrunched his face as he dug out a small fragment of metal from above his eyebrow.

"Not too keen," Brenner said. "Once we get the rest of them, we can go back for Buchanan, get his tags at least."

"We sure got a whole bunch, though. I got four easily. Steele, how many did you get?" Preston asked.

Steele sat away from the rest. He opened up a ration and chomped on it. "I wasn't keeping count," he said stiffly.

Brenner looked at the clip in his rifle.

"Dammit, if we'd only had more ammo, we could have finished the job. Walters, I want a tally of every round we have left. One thing is for sure, they're armed. And they know we're here. They don't, for now, show any signs of surrendering."

Murray spoke up. "Sir, from what I saw, they're in

real sorry shape. They've got no shelter, and their boat is destroyed. Sure, they've got guns, but not much else. We can hunker down. We're sitting pretty. We should starve them out. If they try and form an attack, we'll use the grenades and some of our ammo."

Brenner took a swig from his canteen.

"We can't wait. Time isn't on our side. We've got to get back to work somehow."

Steele spoke up. "Sir, we're not going to need all that dynamite for the radio hut. Hell, we're not going to need any of it. We don't need to do any blasting. The antenna will be anchored into the concrete. What if we attacked again, tonight? We could use some of the dynamite and the frag grenades and get them down to a few."

Brenner was deep in thought. He liked what he'd heard.

"That's not bad. They're all busted up. They'll be in shit shape come nightfall."

Everyone began to throw out ideas. Brenner listened—or half listened—trying to think of his own way out of this incredible situation.

"Lieutenant, you saw them," said O'Connor, "wet and pitiful, like half-drowned rats. They've got no winter gear—no tents, no sleeping bags, nothing. I say we let them ride out the night. They'll be expecting an attack. They'll shiver all night long, and they can listen to the cries of their dying buddies keeping them up all night. Then come dawn, we hit them again. No place to hide. We use dynamite, the grenades, and some key shooting. We can't see anything at night, and they're probably dug in by now."

Brenner was surprised. O'Connor's initial hesitation about killing the Krauts was gone. He wanted blood. He wanted them dead. War had a way of changing men's minds, Brenner thought.

"You're right. We can't afford to lose anyone in a blind nighttime firefight. We have to make our hits count. Let's set up that guard rotation. You two, get some rest. Get dry. And have a ration. We'll rotate in a two-hour roll."

O'Connor set it up, and the men performed like clockwork. They scurried from defense point to defense point.

Night came quickly to the island, and with the blackness came more wind and punishing rain.

Preston was frustrated and exhilarated. He wanted to be done with it, shoot them all dead. He spent his two hours in the first spot, moved to the second and the third, and then headed into the tent with Murray. Murray passed out right away, but Preston didn't sleep. He swirled in a hatred like he'd never known.

He'd gotten a taste for blood and was ready to wipe the Germans out. His baptism in battle had left him more excited and more adrenaline-fueled than he'd ever been. An hour into his bunk time, someone grabbed his foot. He nudged Murray.

"Assemble outside. We're forming up to attack."

Murray woke, grabbed a packet of rations, and chomped down some crackers as he climbed out. To his surprise, the world was powdered in fine snow. Everything was white. Snowflakes drifted around like pillow down.

Brenner explained his plan in detail. Murray would cut loose a bunch of dynamite sticks from their TNT supply and plug them with ten-second fuses. They'd push the sticks of dynamite into socks packed with pebbles and rocks for shrapnel. Each man would take a few. He and O'Connor would take three grenades each.

Walters and Murray would stay in the rear to guard the equipment. Brenner went over the plan in precise detail. The sleepless Preston felt an insane impatience. He wanted to go—now. He wanted to attack—now. Enough talk. Things had gone too far. It was time to stop talking and start shooting.

Murray worked at the equipment stash, rigging the TNT sticks under the heavy tarp.

The more Preston listened, the more agitated he became. Suddenly, without warning, his bowels churned. Aware that he might shit himself, he moved away from the group, slipped over a few rocks, and found a spot among some scattered stones. He started to squat when he caught something moving out of the corner of his eye. He turned and watched as two crouched figures moved across the horizon, silhouetted against the slate-gray sky.

Preston raised his rifle and followed the first one. He fired, hitting the first man in the shoulder. The man immediately stumbled and fell.

The whole company leapt into action behind Preston.

"Krauts! Krauts to the left!" Preston screamed.

The squad blindly opened fire toward that area, as bullets whizzed off the rocks. One of the invaders returned fire from a machine pistol as bullets zipped back over their heads.

"Krauts! We got Krauts in the base!" Walters yelled.

Brenner crouched down and peered over by the equipment. He could see nothing. A few more shots rang out. Brenner had O'Connor and Hammond next to him.

"Get over there and defend our gear. Conserve ammo! Pick your shots. Move! Walters, defend our rear in case they're trying to put us in a pocket."

Walters nodded and ran off to the right.

" I got one," Preston yelled.

The German opened fire with the machine pistol again, and the Americans ducked for cover.

"How many are there?" someone yelled.

"Don't know. I saw two, maybe three," Preston called back.

Steele had moved around the side of the camp area as soon as the firing started. Brenner watched, just peaking over a ledge. Steele jumped up just as one of the Germans fired. Steele fired on the spot, and the German dropped behind the small ridge.

"Cease fire," O'Connor yelled.

The scene went quiet for a moment. No one moved. Brenner watched the skyline. He hoped that they had killed the guy. Then he saw the rising silhouette of a man, gripping his abdomen with one hand and holding a potato masher in the other. He cocked the potato masher behind his head, aiming down the jagged slope toward Brenner's men.

Brenner leveled his rifle and fired at the figure. Several others fired, too. The German spun around. Out of sheer reflex, the dying man flung the grenade wildly. After a couple bounces, it landed beside the huge cache of supplies and materials, neatly cubed and covered by a canvas tarp. The grenade exploded with a dull thud. A second later, a drum of gasoline exploded, sending up a massive fireball. Then another drum exploded and another. Murray, who had been closest to the equipment pile, sprinted over the slick rocks as the drums continued to explode, flinging burning yellow gasoline in every direction.

"Get the hell back! There's dynamite in there!" Steele screamed.

Brenner ducked down as men hurried away from the orange fire that burned into the grey sky. Thick, black smoke blanketed the ground as more gas exploded, spraying the entire cove with burning fuel.

A patch of burning gas found Hammond's boot, sticking out from where he hid. He feverishly flung it around in the gravel until he'd extinguished the flame.

The first case of dynamite exploded, sending burning fuel even farther. Pieces of debris, tools, and equipment were shot hundreds of feet in the air by the blast. Brenner heard screams and shrieks. He looked up to see Murray, covered in burning gas, staggering across the uneven ground. Walters chased behind him, trying to knock him down. The second case of dynamite exploded, sending Walters to the ground as Murray, engulfed in flames, flopped between several rocks and continued to burn.

Brenner screamed to the men. "Fall back over here! Move!"

Preston dashed forward a few feet. He grabbed Walters and pulled him back over a small ridge. The case of flares exploded next, sending white and red flares in every direction.

The men scrambled back and gathered in a natural crater where Brenner crouched.

"Watch the horizon. Keep sharp," said Brenner.

Now it was the Americans' turn to wait. They all sat, terrified, their backs together, not talking, only watching. Each man had his weapon up and aimed, his finger on the trigger, waiting for an attack.

"We're fucked now," one of them said, as their tents burned along with their ruined equipment that was spread out over the rocks.

"Poor son-of-bitch Murray. He burned to death," Walter's mumbled. A gash crowned his head, and blood

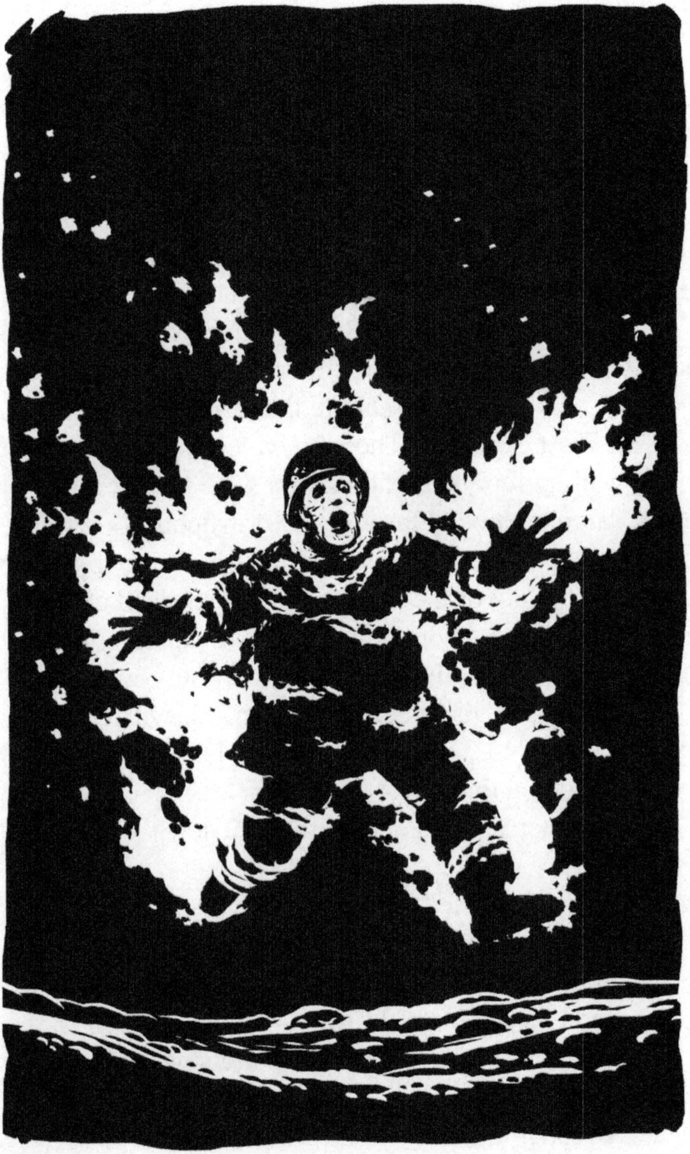

ran down his face. He was too stunned to notice.

"He may not be dead," O'Connor suggested, staring at the orange fire just a few yards away.

"God, for his sake, I hope he is," Cassidy whispered.

"Do you think they knew to do that? You know. Blow up our supplies," Hammond asked.

"No. I saw it. It was a rotten lucky shot. I think those two were just coming to have a look, and we just happened to catch them," O'Connor said.

"Damn lucky shot," Brenner grumbled. "Seems too lucky to me, but what's the difference?"

A few sticks of dynamite that had been blown away from the blast exploded. The men winced and hunkered down, waiting for and dreading more.

Brenner looked through the downpour. Low-grade panic moved through his veins. Black smoke poured from the burning pile. For the first time, the men shed clothing, as they dripped with sweat from the radiating heat. Brenner watched as men unzipped their thick coats.

"You keep that helmet on no matter what. This heat will be short lived," he said. "Let's fall back behind that little ridge down there."

Brenner stopped and sniffed the air. "God, do you smell that?"

They all sniffed the air.

"Smells like bacon, sort of," Cassidy said.

"I think it's Murray," Steele said, motioning to the burning body a dozen yards away.

They collectively winced. Walters gagged and almost vomited.

Brenner motioned to the men to fall back. They cautiously climbed to their feet and slowly walked backwards with their weapons up, waiting. Once the group had moved behind a small outcropping of barnacle-speckled rock near the ocean, they lowered their weapons. They caught their breath and regrouped while Preston climbed to the top and lay across the rocks, covering the horizon. Confused and exhausted, the men checked their weapons and their wounds.

"Whether it was a lucky shot or not, they blew up our fuel dump. And that destroyed almost everything else," O'Connor said while he checked his rifle. He had three shots left in his magazine and a few more in his pocket. "We'll have to check, but it looks like just about everything was blown to shit. No idea what the ration situation is, we'll have to scrounge around, but no drinking water."

"That doesn't seem like that big of problem," Brenner said, looking up into the continuing rain. "Someone find a poncho. Make a catch and fill all the canteens. Let's fall back to that little flat spot with our backs to the water. Scrounge what you can and we'll regroup. Get on it. Right down by the water where we landed. Just beyond the high-tide mark. Bring whatever is usable."

The men sat in the rain just staring at Brenner.

"What are you waiting for? Let's move. One man move the gear. Another help and keep cover. I want two men up on those rocks. Keep an eye out. You see any Krauts, you holler. Move."

The men cautiously went to work with their assignments.

"What do you think?" O'Connor asked, crouched beside Brenner. "Is this to be a battle of attrition?"

"Is there any other kind?" Brenner asked. "Seriously, I don't know. We're screwed, Hank. We're so damn low on ammo.

If we run completely out, then they've got us, no

matter how many of them there are. I don't know if there's anything in the manual for a situation like this. It's a damn cockfight. We've got nowhere to fall back to. If we don't attack them, sooner or later they're going to attack us."

The squad moved to their new location, keeping watch as Walters and Hammond worked to salvage what they could. On one of their trips back toward the debris at their first camp, Hammond dropped a piece of burnt tarp over Murray's smoldering corpse. He almost wretched when he caught a whiff of the body. He was horrified with himself because the body really did smell like burnt pork. The greasy odor made his stomach growl.

An hour after the blast, the team had a new ring of boulders to defend. One end of the small clearing went straight down to the waterline no more than twenty yards away. Narrow channels in the rocks created natural trenches through which the men could move if they crouched low enough.

Brenner was tired of talking, tired of trying to anticipate the thousand different things that might happen next. He wanted to just watch while the others fashioned a shelter of some sort. O'Connor, sitting beside him, sensed his fatigue and said nothing . He supervised the work, all the while paying attention to the horizon.

Brenner watched as Preston hopped around without his pants, sifting through a pile of half-burnt material, looking for another pair.

"What the hell is Preston doing?" Brenner finally asked.

"I think he shit his pants," O'Connor said flatly.

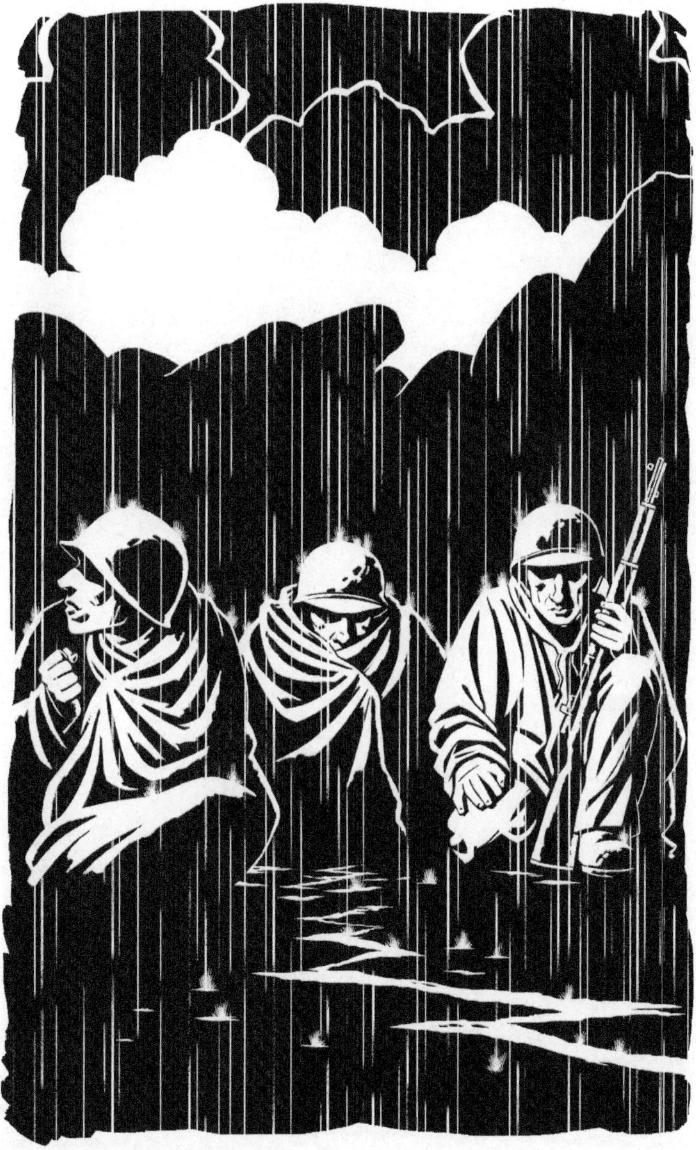

5.

The battered German crew trudged along, feeling somewhat protected under the watchful eye of the machine gun on the ridge. The Captain had also sent out other men with rifles to cover the area, and they would switch off. Heinz and Hauser had been gone for less than an hour, maybe thirty-five, forty minutes.

Someone had found a pack of waterproof matches. Someone else had fished a tiny bit of dry driftwood from between the rocks. They had started a small fire at the mouth of the cave. Fuel would be a problem as there was virtually no dry wood anywhere. Ironically, the beach was covered with diesel, but there was no oil to burn.

A hot debate had raged over a bottle of rubbing alcohol found floating in the water. Should it be used as fuel or to treat the wounded? In the end, half was poured off into a canteen for starting fires, and Liebe got the other half for the wounded. Under normal circumstances, fires were deadly. Smoke and glowing embers were a sniper's dream. But Burman begrudgingly allowed the fire; the enemy already knew exactly where they were. The captain agreed, with the condition that the fire be extinguished long before nightfall.

The surviving Germans sat staring at the flames that gave off no real heat but had a calming effect. A few tins of horsemeat, a few cans of brown bread, and a few bruised apples were fished from the sea. If each man got just a few bites, they would exhaust their provisions.

German U-boats traditionally had a complement of food that was perhaps the best in the military: fresh breads, eggs, meats, fruits, vegetables, and more were poured into the U-boats. The food came from all over Europe, and the U-boats went to sea with every nook and cranny crammed with food. The subs had two small refrigerators, but only a tiny fraction of the food would fit in them, so the fresh food was eaten first. Even after only a few days, however, thick loaves of bread, in the steamy atmosphere of the sub, were covered with a white mold that made them inedible.

Now, almost three months on, that fresh food seemed like a horrible joke, a tantalizing taste of what they would so sorely miss. No one was more aware of the food situation and its intense effect on the crew than Liebe, the cook.

Liebe was older than most—in his 30s. He was prematurely grey. His normally warm disposition was now strained by exhaustion. He was the ship's cook and now its de facto doctor because of his prewar medical experiences in Darmstadt. Generally, U-boats didn't have a medic on the crew, although there were usually a few men who knew basic first aid.

Liebe, moreover, wasn't a proper medical doctor; he was a vet who worked mostly with farm animals and some pets. Still, that was good enough for the captain and everyone else on board. How he'd become a cook on a sub and not a medic on the front lines was anyone's guess. When he first saw his assignment to sub duty in the Navy, he was relieved, but now he regretted it—even though he never had any say in the matter.

At the beginning of the voyage, Liebe was everyone's best friend. "A better cook than my dear old mother," men often exclaimed. But as the good food ran out, the comments became less favorable and then openly hostile. "What is he doing, trying to poison us?" "Is it possible that Liebe is a traitor, sent by the Russians to starve us?" Then a week or so after that, the tone from the crew switched again—to begging and bargaining.

"Come now, Liebe, be reasonable. Two packs of smokes for some of that corned beef. We know you have a secret stash for the officers." Other men took him into their confidence, as if confessing to a priest.

"I can't keep eating this stuff, I'm telling you. I'm always sick. My stomach always hurts. I need some real food. Please, Liebe, help me. Please. You must have saved some for yourself." The final insult, with the water and the food being stored so close to so much active machinery, was that no matter what the food was, everything always smelled and tasted like diesel.

Now the situation had dramatically changed, and they all needed and loved him again. A sailor with his intestines smeared all over his stomach begged Liebe for help. In the end, all he was able to do was put a wet coat over the man, who mercifully died within an hour.

Death was everywhere, but Liebe didn't care. He was so damned happy to be out of that stinking sub. That last bit—the attack, the storm, the tossing, and the turning for what seemed like eternity—was the worst thing he'd ever experienced. He had slung the dishes out from a tiny cupboard and forced himself into it to ride out the pitching and rolling. He was certain he was going to die. He swore that, if he lived, he'd never set foot on a sub again. Admiral Dönitz himself could court-martial him, line him up in front of a firing squad. He would never go into a submarine again.

Now, his nemesis, the submarine, was dead, and he was alive. The rain soaked him. He was wet and frozen, but it felt damn good. Liebe was out of the sub and drinking fresh water caught on a tarp. It was the best water he'd ever tasted, he thought, as he shivered with a secret glee. He was drinking fresh rainwater, and it was like drinking heaven.

As the war ground on into history, more and more U-boats found their way to the bottom of the sea. As the U-boats went, so did Germany's prowess. Missions were extended, and limits were exceeded as the German war machine began to falter.

The last time the 494 shipped out, the naval high command had deemed it necessary to use one of the two freshwater tanks for additional diesel fuel, extending the ship's range, and also minimizing the number of times the U-boat had to dock with a refueling ship, when both the sub and the refueling ship were at their most vulnerable. The trade-off, of course, was that the sub had only half its usual allowance of fresh drinking water. Water, therefore, was strictly rationed—no bathing and no shaving. Consequently, every man had a beard. The only men without some facial hair were the boys who could not yet grow any.

The ban on bathing was a potentially serious problem, and the German Navy responded by hastily issuing each man pungent cologne to deal with the odor. The sickly sweet cologne only made the stale air of the sub worse.

But now Liebe smelled only biting-fresh sea air, as much as he could drink in. He savored every breath. He'd do what he could do—help the captain out, help the men out. It was better than doing nothing. But for now, he was only really interested in breathing fresh air and drinking fresh water.

Maybe he was losing his mind. He had just watched men he knew gunned down. He had narrowly missed being killed himself. Yet he wasn't afraid. He wasn't hateful toward the Americans. He wasn't anything. He knew, completely and soberly, that he was going to die, that no one was going to make it. And he really didn't care. He was off the sub. That was all that mattered. He was hungry like everyone else, and that would only get worse. He too would soon curse the cold and the rain, but now he had to contain his happiness, lest someone see him.

He looked down at the waterline. It was low tide, and the waves revealed a hard line of thick razor clams peppering the rocks. Liebe thought he might be able to make some sort of mussel stew if they could get water to boil.

Liebe told the captain of his plan and Fessenden agreed. Liebe studied Captain Fessenden's face and could see the anguish. He thought he could see the last of the captain's confidence slipping away, realizing that he'd just given the OK for his men—grown men—to see if they could scavenge subsistence from the sea. Liebe realized that they all were crabs themselves now or some flightless bird lost in a storm, picking for anything that happened to be hiding among the rocks.

Liebe took two sailors and went down to the waterline. He didn't care about the rain and the cold. He almost smiled every time he caught the hulking wreck of the boat out of the corner of his eye. The sailors watched as Liebe, down among the slick rocks, pulled mussels from the rocks and dropped them into a cloth. The sailors collected a few, too.

"Liebe," one of the young sailors asked, "would we eat these cooked or raw?"

"I think cooked would be better, but we'll have to take what we can get," Liebe said as he caught a tiny crab, crushed it, and dropped it in his pile of mussels.

One of the sailors reached below a rock and pulled an object out of the icy water. It was about a foot long, with a rotten wooden handle and a corroded head covered with growth. The sailor held it up and Liebe and the other man looked at what must have been an old axe. The sailor thought for a moment, shrugged and then tried to use it to pry some of the clams from the rock. The axe simply disintegrated in his hands, and the head dropped into the waves.

"Hmmm…that sums it all up," Liebe muttered.

In the shelter, the ragged men were in the process of divvying up the last of the rations when they heard sporadic gunfire off in the distance. They grabbed their weapons and formed up at the mouth of the cave. Some found spots to hide in the rocks below. Some instinctively shoved whatever food they had in their hands into their mouths before moving for their guns.

Motionless, they waited, their weapons at the ready. Then there was an explosion, and then another. A fireball rose and lit up the sky. It mushroomed over the horizon. It was followed by another and another and another and then by several more. The men watched wide-eyed, their mouths hanging open, as two stronger explosions followed and echoed through the air. Bright white flares shot up, then a red one, then a blue one, then another white one.

They shot off in every direction.

A thick smear of black smoke filled the gray sky, and the men whispered to each other. The blasts continued sporadically for a few more minutes.

Burman sat next to the Captain.

"*That* looked like a fuel dump. My god, what in the hell is going on over there?" said Burman. "I don't know if that was good or bad."

"It couldn't get much worse," the captain said. "And as long as it's not happening to us, it's good."

"Or maybe that was artillery meant for us, and they haven't pinpointed us yet," said Müller, a junior navigator.

The captain remembered the first time the boat had attacked a convoy. Because of Müller's physicality, the captain thought he'd crack under the pressure. But Müller, simple and seemingly naïve, did just fine. He always did his job. The captain was happy to see that Müller still seemed solid and balanced.

"That was fuel for sure. And maybe flares?" Burman said. "Maybe a boat or a weapons cache exploded."

But most of their thousands of questions remained unanswered as they waited alertly for what would happen next. Excited, infuriated, mystified, they barely moved for a half hour. Smoke continued to billow into the sky.

Then suddenly they were startled by a shout of "Halt!" from one of the guards. Hauser, who had gone on the reconnaissance mission with Heinz, stepped around a corner, followed by the guard. He held one hand high. His other arm hung limp at his side.

"It's me, Seamen Hauser. Please."

Burman and Liebe ran from the shelter and rushed over to him just as he collapsed.

"He's been shot," Liebe said, putting pressure on

Hauser's bleeding shoulder.

They dragged Hauser back to the mouth of the shelter and out of the rain. Captain Fessenden and the rest gathered around him.

"Where's Heinz," the captain asked.

"Gunned down. We got close to their base. I wanted to stay back, but Heinz moved closer, and they spotted us. I got hit. They started shooting, and we shot back. They got Heinz. And then there was a huge explosion, lots of explosions. I don't know what it was. Maybe a weapons dump or something." Hauser gasped for breath.

Back when things were normal, the captain had made an effort to meet and talk with all the men on the sub, but now he didn't even recognize Hauser. He felt queasy. This sailor was no more than a scrawny boy. He looked pale and sick. Like everyone else, he was bathed in grime and grease.

"Wait. Who blew it up?" Burman asked.

"I don't know. I got hit and went down. I couldn't see anything. And then Heinz fell over on me. He'd been shot—many times. I got up and ran. And then there were the explosions. I don't know, sir. I don't know."

He was in agony, and bathed in sweat. Liebe peeled his coat open. A massive wound was all that was left of his shoulder.

"How many men did you see? What else do they have? Did you see a road or any vehicles? Anything?"

"I just saw a few men crouched down. They were all firing. Maybe a couple of tents. Some big crates. No roads or vehicles. But we didn't get very far."

"Any boats? A ship or something moored nearby?"

Hauser was losing consciousness but was trying to stay alert.

"Not that I saw, sir. Although we only got to…

one side of their camp ... The rocks ... so hard to see ..."
Hauser's eyes flittered shut as Liebe stuffed tattered rags into the shoulder wound.

"Without sutures and a way to close the wound, he'll bleed to death in a matter of hours," Liebe whispered to Burman and the captain.

"Do what you can to make him comfortable," the captain muttered helplessly as he stood up.

Caspar was there, standing squarely in front of him. "Sir, we must attack. It's a small force. That's what Hauser said."

"Yes, but he also said that he didn't get very far. Who knows what else there is?" Burman warned.

Werner joined in, pleading with the captain. "Sir, we must attack. We must! Captain, we're completely out of rations. Our men are dying. There's only a few of them over there. There's got to be. They've got food. They've got fuel."

Caspar pushed past Werner. "Sir, let me circle round with a few men and flush them out. See if we can discover if they've got a vehicle—maybe a plane or a boat—someplace. Sir, I think we can take the upper hand," Caspar pleaded.

The captain was so tired of Caspar. He wanted Caspar dead, plain and simple. In this new upside-down world, being quiet wasn't enough. Simply going away wasn't enough. Everything was done with brute force, with a sledgehammer of sorts. Captain Fessenden now wished Caspar had been killed a long time ago.

The most annoying aspect of this exchange was that Caspar was right. They had nothing left. The best they could hope for was to take the Allies' supplies and maybe find a way off the island. Other than that, they had nothing.

A sailor, still covered in grease, appeared at the mouth of the shelter. "Captain, you have to come see this at once." Another sailor, also visibly shaken, stood behind him, shivering in the rain.

Werner went to join the men, but Burman stopped him. "Stay here. Watch the line," Burman ordered. Werner stopped cold, and Burman didn't even look back. The captain, Burman, and Caspar followed the two men down toward the breakers. The two led the group down the short walk. They scaled some boulders. One of the men pointed.

A dozen feet up, on the top of a craggy protrusion, was the naked lower half of one of their men. It was hanging from a tall rock, split and wrapped around the rock just above the pelvis. Above the rock, a twisted trail of intestines led up and over the rise. A boot was on the man's left foot, and his long underwear was shredded and hanging from the ankle.

"Good God," Caspar said. The three of them and the two sailors looked at each other in utter disbelief.

"We think it's Aachen, but we can't be sure. One of the men thought he recognized the boot."

"Was he shot in the attack?" Burman was equally shocked.

"No, sir. He was drowned when we first ran aground. His body was over there last night." The sailor pointed across the gravel beach.

"And they call us barbarians. Captain, I think they're sending a message," one of the sailors offered.

"Oh, I've received the message. We go into a twenty-four-hour watch. How in the hell is it possible that they were able to sneak in here and do this?" The captain stared at the body, a torn-apart puppet, its tattered underwear blowing in the wind. Not long ago, Fessenden had seriously considered surrendering, but now he knew that could never happen. They would have to fight to the last man if need be.

"They're butchers, sir. They've no honor," Caspar said. "Sir, the message is we have no choice but to annihilate them, extinguish them, crush them like insects."

"I ... never dreamed that someone would ... " Burman was flabbergasted. "They're animals." Caspar was fidgeting.

"Captain, we must attack. We have to attack!"

The captain was transfixed by the mangled body. He raised a hand, silencing Caspar. They stood quietly for a moment with only the patter of the rain and the rolling and crashing waves behind them as they were unable to look away from the pale partial corpse. Finally, the captain whispered, "We are attacking and we'll do it my way." Walking back toward the shelter, the group saw an unusual buzz of activity. Men were standing out in the open, walking around with their noses in the air.

Burman and the captain ran up to them. "What the hell are you doing?" the captain barked. "Get down, goddamn it! Find cover. This is a goddamn battle!"

Men tried to comply, but they were transfixed by a smell that wafted on the air. Werner tried to corral them.

"Those bastards, those ruthless bastards! They're doing it just to drive us crazy." Burman and Fessenden were baffled until they stepped into the invisible cloud the carried the odor. Instantly they were hit by a faint but delicious smell. Their mouths began to water.

"Those rotten sons of bitches. We're over here dying, and they're roasting pork! Oh my god, I can almost taste it!"

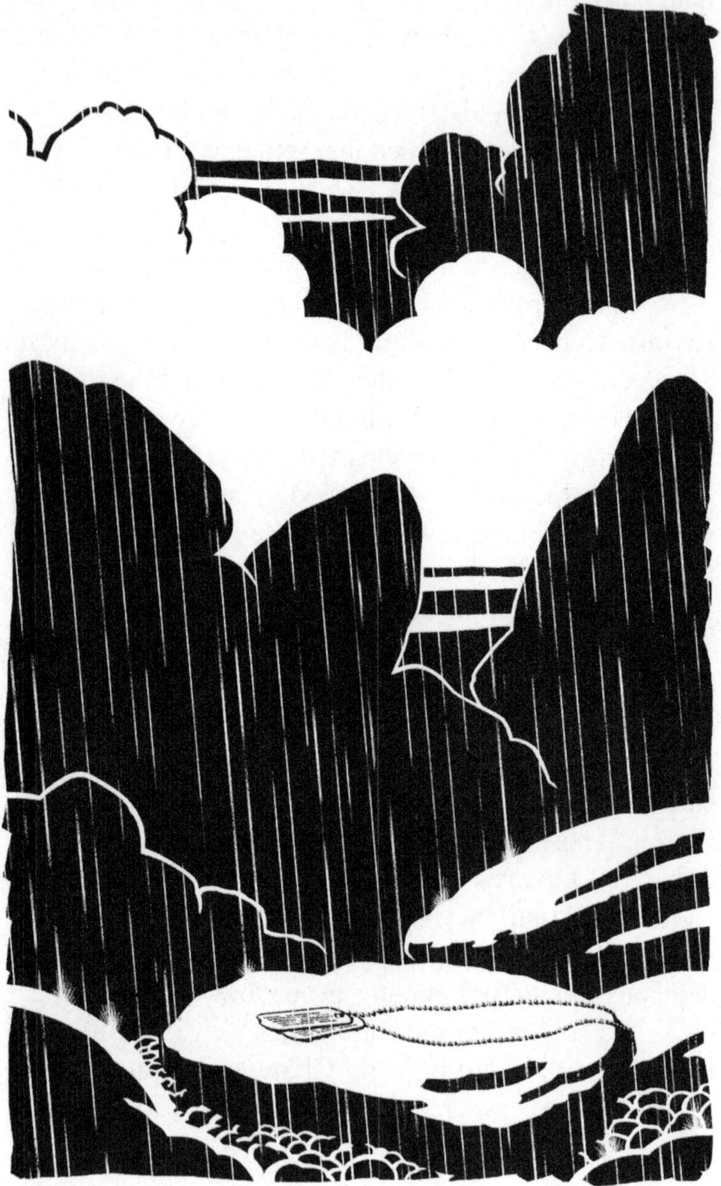

6.

The squad of US Seabees spent the entire day and night waiting for a German attack that never came. By morning, the men were so stiff that their fear had almost been displaced by boredom and fatigue. They had to move around.

Brenner pulled together the last of the ammo. He gave extra clips to Steele and Preston and sent them up onto higher ground to watch for the approaching enemy.

O'Connor and Hammond, closer in, were also keeping watch, backing up Steele and Preston. Brenner and the rest moved what they could down to their new camp, closer to the water.

The men used hunks of the burnt tent platforms to construct a makeshift lean-to against a short rise of stone between two mounds of granite. They scavenged what they could from their first camp, snapping up tent pieces, parts of a rubber boat, and burned sleeping bags to make an uneven floor. They piled rocks and maneuvered boulders strategically to create a crude fort.

Once the shelter was built, Brenner again had the

men go into a defensive rotation. Once their camp was established and each man had found his position, there was a fragile air of calm.

As night fell, Brenner and O'Connor conferred. Completing their mission was out of the question. All they could do was wait to be rescued.

O'Connor slid down a wall and took off his helmet. From his eyebrows up, his skin was pink, and matted brown hair crowned his head. Below, he was caked with dust and soot.

"We've got food, we've got water, and we've got grenades and bare-bones ammo," he told Brenner. "And we've got one flare, but the flare gun is nowhere to be found."

"We wait, they aren't going anywhere. They come, we defend. We don't stick our necks out anymore. We're no good dead, and these Kriegsmarine assholes aren't going anywhere. They're trapped just like us. We wait until the ship arrives. We get aboard, circle around on their side, and blow them to kingdom come with the deck guns while eating pork chop sandwiches."

Brenner nodded. It sounded right. Dig in and defend.

"But, sir, what if they radioed for help before they cracked up?" Walters asked.

"Who are they going to radio? The German Navy was chased out of the Atlantic last year. Now they're fighting the Russians in the Baltic. I don't think anyone is coming for 'em, and they sure as shit ain't going anywhere," O'Connor said.

Brenner was in command, and it was his choice. But that warrior in him had to make an excuse, had to say something that indicated that he wanted to keep fighting and destroy them. No one was questioning his allegiance or his courage—except himself.

"I'd love to attack the bastards again, but we've lost too many, and we haven't enough ammo. You're right. Let's just dig in. There can't be that many left. Let's starve them out. If they come looking for a fight, we'll give them hell. But I'm not losing any more men. There's nothing to build, so let's just stay dry and alive until the ship arrives," Brenner said.

O'Connor was relieved. They could wait this out. Let the Navy big guns come in and destroy the bastards. The Krauts weren't going anywhere. It was stupid to risk lives to extract vengeance, as delicious as that sounded.

They spent the next day hunkered down, rotating the watch and trying to stay vigilant.

In the late afternoon, when no attack had come, Brenner pulled out his map of the island and plotted the most likely routes the attacking Germans might take. He put a man at each point. No two men were ever out of shouting distance, and they followed the rotation to stay sharp. Somewhere above the thick wall of clouds, the sun was beginning to set.

Temple wanted off the rock. Of course everyone did. Temple, like everyone else, felt that he was different, that his situation was truly unique and his predicament far more dire than anyone else's. Now he was guarding one of the narrow passages that the Krauts might come through, and it only made his situation that more desperate.

He hoped to god they didn't come his way. He manned his post, but he was so tired that it hurt his head and eyes. He kept his mind on the rotation. In two hours, at 20.00, he'd move to the position above the beach. Then at 22.00, he'd move to the right. After that, he'd get his turn in the bunk. He relished the idea. Just four grueling hours. The rain ceaselessly beat on his helmet and poncho. Just four hours.

He sat square in the middle of a little ravine that was just slightly wider than he was. If he sat too close to either wall, a fine spray of water from the splashing rain would find its way onto his face and neck. So he sat directly in the middle.

In his haze, through the endless drizzle, he watched as some of his men up ahead started to build something, getting back to work in the heavy rain. In all honesty, the other men annoyed him. Working in the pouring rain, that seemed like something those guys would do. They all took it so seriously. God and country and all that.

He never felt that way. He did his part, of course, but he wasn't doing it to please President Roosevelt. He was doing it because he had to, plain and simple. He was forced to. Otherwise he'd wind up in the brig or be called a coward. Gung ho. That's what everyone was saying these days. He hadn't heard the word before joining the navy, but that was the buzzword for the commanders trying to rally troops. It was the greeting of the overly eager, enthusiastic solider. Gung ho! It sounded like something stupid the Marines dreamed up. Regardless of its origin, he knew the meaning, and he was not in any way gung ho.

He and his wife of just one year corresponded with each other often, and both repeatedly wrote how grateful they were that Temple wound up with the Seabees instead of on the frontlines of battle. Now he scoffed at himself. Apparently, he and his young wife, Emily, had jinxed it because he *was* on the frontlines, in an impossible situation. Yes, he was a trained sailor, but he knew he wasn't a very good one. He was a builder first and foremost. He wasn't a great builder, but he at least knew what he was doing. He was good at taking orders, he figured, but he wasn't rabid about it. He wasn't gung ho.

Look at those guys, he thought. All get up and go. Through the rain, he watched the three of them. One of them had a tripod, and the other had ... He couldn't tell through the rain and the mist. Maybe it was the transit level. Why were they even out doing that? No one had gone back to work. They couldn't work. It was all blown to hell because the island was crawling with Germans.

Germans. From Germany. Germanic people. He knew so little about them. Germans. Germ mans. Germany mans. His thoughts flittered about in his head as he fought to stay conscious. Four hours, just four hours and he was going to get his rotation in the bunk. He couldn't wait.

And yet something was amiss as he muttered the word over and over in his mind. Germans. The Island was crawling with Germans. The island was crawling with Germans. He studied the figures through the rain, and his foggy thoughts slowly peeled away. He was delirious, he realized. He hadn't really slept well in days. As his body figured it out before his mind did, adrenaline poured into his veins, and his heart began to race.

Over the wet terrain, through the curtain of water, he now realized that he wasn't watching his guys building anything; he was watching the Germans quietly setting up a large machine gun.

Temple didn't move. He held perfectly still. But inside his skull his brain had kicked into overdrive.

He continued to watch. They hadn't seen him. He was just another rock. They set up their gun very quietly but precisely. They loaded it and pointed it to the left, where the rest of Temple's squad was. One of them unfolded a tarp and draped it over the gun so that only the gunner and the barrel could peek out. And then they waited.

Temple swallowed hard and stood as still as the rocks around him. What were they doing? They couldn't see anyone. Who were they going to shoot at? Suddenly he realized. Other Germans must be coming around to the back of the cove, down by the water. They're going to attack, he thought. They'll try to push our men into the waiting gun. Temple needed to warn Brenner. He needed to move slowly back and find Brenner. The lieutenant would know what to do.

As he contemplated moving, Temple began to quake with fear. He felt as if his shaking was so obvious that the Germans would see it and swing their gun toward him. But they didn't. They just sat, hidden, waiting to spring their trap.

Temple lowered his head as slowly as he could and turned to crawl backwards. Suddenly, he heard shouts and the telltale sound of gunfire behind him. Too late. They were already attacking. Temple heard the cacophony of the all-too-familiar small-arms gun battle not far over the next rise. The shots were growing louder, and a few rounds even whizzed above Temple's head.

"Temple!"

He heard someone yelling for him from behind, down the narrow passage between the rocks.

"Temple, we're taking fire. Get the hell over here!"

Then, at the top of his lungs, Brenner yelled, "Fall back."

Temple heard him loud and clear. The Jerries were close, really close, and their plan was working. Temple's men were just on the other side of the ridge. They were falling back, right into the sights of the machine gun. Temple's racing thoughts still didn't seem to be going fast enough, for just as he realized the gravity of the situation, it happened. It played out, and he was helpless to do anything.

O'Connor, fleeing from the attack, scrambled over the top of the rocks, exactly what the Germans were waiting for. Temple screamed with all his might, but the roar of the German machine gun drowned out his cries. O'Connor leapt into a hail of bullets and caught a dozen rounds in stomach, chest, and neck. The massive bullets easily passed threw him, taking bones, tissue, and anything else in their path. He dropped to the rocks face first, a limp heap.

Temple shrieked. And before he could even think about it, he felt himself standing up and firing his rifle into the machine-gun nest. He couldn't see the men, but he knew they were under the tarp, and he fired off rounds as quickly as he could pull the trigger. He was horrified when he missed and saw the bullets ricocheting in every direction.

Now they would kill *him*. He had no doubt that they would kill *him*. He had tried, and he had failed. And now he was going to be killed. He was certain. But then the last three rounds from his rifle found their mark. Temple heard a loud, guttural grunt, and the roaring gun went silent, with only the sound of shell casings bouncing around.

The wet tarp fell away. He saw two lifeless silhouettes heaped over the gun. A third, still moving, put his hand on the gun and waved the smoking barrel toward Temple.

Temple, with a massive burst of energy, instinctively flung himself up and over a wall of rocks. He scrambled as fast as he could, and the gunner tried to follow him with a spray of bullets. It was vindictive. He could feel it. This guy was going to kill him for shooting at him and killing his friends.

Temple slid on his stomach across a flat rock. He felt a hot sting as a bullet fragment from the machine gun ricocheted off a rock and cut through the side of his shin. He dropped down, ignoring the pain, fumbling to reload his rifle. It was quiet for a second, and Temple's heart raced so fast that he could feel his head throbbing with pressure.

"I'm alive!" his brain screamed. "I'm still alive. I haven't been killed!"

The machine gun fired again in his direction, and he ducked back down as the bullets ricocheted above him.

Now the German position was compromised. Preston and Hammond pinpointed it. They screamed and yelled as they fired at the gun.

"Machine gun. We've got a machine gun!"

Beyond the ridge, the others were fighting the Germans who'd come around to outflank them.

After some commotion and a flurry of activity, the firing stopped again. It was strangely silent until Temple heard the telltale twang as the spoon popped off a hand grenade. Against the sky, Temple caught sight of the fragmentation grenade flying through the air, leaving a thin trail of smoke as the fuse burned. It dropped down near the machine gun. Temple guessed the throw was too short. But there was a sharp blast followed by an unmistakable guttural cry as the remaining German was hit.

More small-arms fire erupted behind Temple.

"I got one!" someone yelled. There was more shooting and then silence.

Relieved, Temple stood up. They'd done it. He'd done it. He'd taken out a German machine-gun nest. He had barely pulled himself to his full height when a bullet, followed by a loud report, ricocheted off a rock inches from his shoulder. He dove again, and then ran up and over a mound of rocks as someone continued to fire at him. Either a German had found him, or one of his own guys was mistakenly shooting at him.

He scrambled up over a large boulder and hopped to the safe side. He slipped on the slimy surface, and his feet shot out from under him. He landed hard on his back, his rifle flying out of his hands as his helmet smacked against the rock. He slid down the smooth boulder for a dozen feet until the slope leveled out. His ankle screamed in pain where he'd been hit, and he could hardly use it to stop his sliding as he headed toward a small overhang.

The drop off didn't look particularly high, but it didn't matter. Even if it were just five feet, if he flew off it, he was sure to land on more jagged rocks. With his good leg, he dug his heel in and wildly grasped at anything on either side. He was able to grab into a shallow crevice just at the lip of the drop off. His feet swung out over the edge, but he stopped and was able to pull himself back.

He lay back, gasping for breath. He glanced around to see if his rifle was visible. It was gone, somewhere above him, presumably wedged in the rocks. Off in the distance, the sound of small-arms fire continued sporadically, punctuated by an occasional shout or the sickening bang of a grenade. But through all of it, he was strangely calm as he lay still and panted.

He wasn't afraid anymore; he wasn't sure how he felt. He had just killed two—maybe three—men and escaped a firefight. It wasn't like before, when they were shooting the Germans on the beach. This was a battle. And he had prevailed. His shin ached, and he could feel the warm blood on the back of his calf, but at the moment, he didn't care. He was alive, and for that instant, that was enough. The gunfire died out, leaving the ever-present patter of rain and the crashing of waves against the rocky coast.

Slowly, he slid up, pulling himself away from the sharp edge. He sat up and looked at his leg. It was a clean wound, right through his left shin and calf, missing the bone. The neat hole oozed a steady stream of thick blood. He slid up further, well away from the edge, and leaned against a boulder. His rifle was lost, but he checked his holster, and his pistol was still there. He dug in his pockets and found his emergency first-aid pack. He tore into a packet of sulfa powder and dumped the contents on either side of his leg. He wrapped his leg in a damp bandage, covering the wounds tightly, circling around and around his leg until he was out of bandage. A red dot immediately appeared on the cloth as the blood soaked through the dressing.

He had to get back to camp. He knew it was to his right, and he'd follow the coastal rocks until he came upon it. He took out his pistol, righted his helmet, and started to crawl away.

As he moved quietly, he passed through a stinking cloud that smelled of rotten fish and worse. He looked behind him and was startled to see what he could have fallen into. The ledge he'd almost gone over wasn't just a lip; it was the edge of a gaping hole in the rock. He stepped back and peered down into the deep pit. The jagged hole was round, probably twenty feet across. The roof of a cave appeared to have collapsed long ago.

Temple shuddered. Falling into that pit would have been far worse than just landing on rocks. It was at least thirty feet to the bottom. He could barely make out a floor of sticks and driftwood down in the dark, stinking pit. The stench suggested a whole school of fish rotting in there somewhere. Temple moved away, stunned by how yet again he'd cheated death.

7.

In the dark German shelter, the men sat motionless. Those who had weapons kept them in hand. The captain had placed several sentries to stare out into the night. Down by the water, in the small, protected indentation in the rock, a wounded man cried out. The men in the main shelter tried to shut their minds to it. Some pulled themselves tightly together and jammed their fingers into their ears. But the pitiful wailing was impossible to ignore.

The wounded man screamed in agony and then went silent. The quiet was a relief, but the men felt guilty because the poor bastard was now probably dead.

Liebe wound his way from the shelter out into the weather to see if he could do anything for the wounded and the dying.

From out of the darkness, the men heard the results of the captain's attack plan. Off in the distance, they heard machine-gun fire, small arms barking back and forth, and two small explosions. Sound bounced around on the stony island so that it was hard to pinpoint exactly where a sound had come from. They all strained, watching the skyline, waiting for fireballs and flashes of light. This time, they saw nothing. Silence quickly filled in the night. The agonizing waiting began again.

Only Liebe moved. Coming in out of the rain, he ducked down and approached the captain.

"How are the wounded?" the captain asked without taking his eyes off the horizon.

"Captain, they're gone. Like before. They're not there anymore. All three of them are gone."

The captain turned to Liebe.

"What? How is that possible? We heard one of them screaming his goddamn lungs out not five minutes ago."

"I don't know. Maybe the enemy is coming in boats. The medicinal alcohol bottle is gone as well."

"Why would the enemy even want wounded men? They must have walked away." The captain vainly searched for answers.

"Sir, Kastell was shot in both legs. He couldn't have walked anywhere. None of them could have."

Burman was listening to the exchange. "They didn't walk anywhere," he said. "There's nothing out there between this pile of rocks and the North Atlantic. They were swept out by a large wave—obviously. They never should have been down by the water in the first place."

"Their bedrolls are still there," Liebe countered.

Burman impatiently dismissed the comments and turned back toward the enemy.

The captain couldn't deal with any more problems. He stood up and walked alone out into the rain.

All he could do was wait to learn the outcome when the hunters returned.

After an agonizing forty minutes, two men came back. Fessenden stared as they walked into the camp. He was crestfallen to see only two. They stepped into the dark cave.

"Where are the others?" the captain asked, already knowing the answer.

One of the men shook his hanging head.

The captain had sent out seven men, and two returned. His mouth trembled, and his empty stomach lurched and jerked with pain.

"Sir, there's at least a dozen of them. They're dug in, sir, well camouflaged. They were waiting for us, sir."

The men huddled in the shelter groaned and moaned with the news. Burman rubbed his head in defeat. Werner was angry. He picked up a rock and slammed it against a wall. He jumped to his feet and yelled at the captain.

"Captain, you can't keep sending a small force against them! These tentative steps are killing us. Can you not see that? We have to blitz while there are still enough of us left to do it."

Burman stood up and shoved Werner to the ground.

"Sailor! You watch your tone with the captain!"

Fessenden ignored the outburst.

"What about Caspar? What about the machine-gun crew?" The captain's thoughts and emotions were a jumble, but in the darkest recesses of his mind, he still secretly hoped that Caspar was dead.

"I don't know, sir. We went around to the left. They went in the opposite direction."

It was obvious. They hadn't come back. They were captured or killed.

The captain dropped his head in defeat. The men in the cave were silent. It was a pathetic scene. This infernal island was consuming the starving men one by one.

Then in the dim light, through the clouds, someone moved along their rocky perimeter. Whispers zipped through the air. "It's Caspar!" And moments later, Caspar and another sailor stood soaked at the mouth of the cave, shouldering the machine gun and tripod.

"Sir, the gun crew was killed, but I was able to rescue the weapon."

"How many of the enemy remain?" the captain asked.

"It's difficult to say. They've figured out a series of trenches and have their area well covered. I'd say no more than ten, maybe as few as six or seven."

"How many enemy killed?"

"Four, five, maybe," Caspar said. "I believe I got two," Caspar lied.

He'd wanted to fight. Truly he did. But in the hastily planned raid, amidst all the commotion, he never saw a target to shoot at. He'd hoped to be on the machine gun when the battle started, but as they waited, he got bored and circled back to see where the attacking group was. He was between the two spots when the fighting started.

When the machine gun went silent, he pulled back and went to the gun, hoping to get on it and hammer the enemy. But by the time he arrived, the shooting was over, and the gun sat amid three dead men. He'd waited a few minutes, hoping to shoot in a counterattack. But he gave up and instead carried the gun back, worried that enemy would recover it. He ran into his companion as he worked his way back to the camp.

"Sir, I believe there is a weakness in their defense. I think that we can work around to the right, further than where the gun was, and then come up behind them. They think they've repelled us. This is the time, Captain."

The men watched the captain closely. Fessenden

was nothing more than doubts and second-guessing now. He wondered why horrific events made him think he was having a bad dream, a nightmare. He'd heard each man say it at one time or another: It was a nightmare from which no one could wake up. Was it some sort of mental cushion, some defense mechanism, so that in your final moments of life, instead of being faced with the ultimate fear, the brain just switched over and said, "You're just having a nightmare. This horrible death you're about to go through? It's just a harmless bad dream. You're actually in bed—at home, between clean sheets, under a thick warm blanket. A cup of cool milk sits next to the ticking clock on the bed stand, where your favorite book lies, as you sleep, dreaming the most horrific dream that you've ever dreamed. It seems so real, and you can't wake up."

The captain knew the truth. He wasn't dreaming. He was coldly and brilliantly awake—on a tiny island that was now little more than a meat grinder. His instinct was to stop the attacks, to hunker down. So they had to eat clam stew? At least they weren't being gunned down. Maybe they could fish, catch more food.

Then the captain's mind flashed to the image of the lower half of the body that the Americans had stretched over the rock. How could he stomach that? How could he not fight against that? He'd never been a Nazi. He was embarrassed when almost everyone in his country fell for that bullshit. But how could he stand by idly in the face of such barbarianism?

His instinct was to hunker down and defend, but his instincts so far had brought him and his men only unspeakable pain and grief. And if they did hunker down, then what? No one was coming for them. There would be no rescue. Their long-shot chance was to find out how the Allies had come to be there. It wasn't possible that two ships from opposing sides had both run aground, stranding their men on the same tiny rock. Even war and fate couldn't be that cruel. Attack was the only possible way out.

"Agreed." the captain muttered. "Caspar, you take four men. Switch off with the others so that you all have automatic weapons. Circle wide to their right, and strike during the darkness. Kill as many as you can. Bring back any supplies you find."

Caspar was dumbfounded. He had expected an argument.

"Er … Yes, sir … Of course, sir! We will turn this around for our beloved Führer and the fatherland." He snapped to with an energetic Nazi salute.

The action was comical to everyone but him. The soaked and freezing men, clinging to life and sanity, could easily follow the trail of bad ideas that had put them all there. They all were keenly aware of what the Führer had now done for them.

The ragged and weary men seated in the cave, dropped their heads and tried to go invisible as Caspar selected his men for the next assault.

"You and you and you. Mintz, how's your foot?"

Young Mintz opened his mouth to speak.

"Looks OK to me. You go with us," Caspar said before the boy could even react.

They all begrudgingly stood up and exchanged weapons so that the attack force all had machine gun pistols.

The captain was expecting some "glory to the country" speech before Caspar set out, but Caspar gave a silent wave as the five marched out of the shelter. Fessenden was horrified to see how few were left once those five had gone.

Outside, in the rain, the four men followed Caspar single file. The four figures trudged along behind Caspar as they moved deep behind their camp to follow a wide circle around what had become the battlefield.

They walked and climbed in silence, each man in his own misery. Only Caspar truly felt that they had any chance. The others were resigned to death. Death, in fact, was sounding better and better with every uneven step they took. The five trudged through the rain for an hour until Caspar waved them to a shelter under a large outcropping. "Let's take a break," Caspar said, gasping for breath.

They all dropped to the ground. One of the only benefits of walking and being on edge and ready to fight was that for a brief time they weren't cold or aware of their soggy clothes and their waterlogged skin that had started to slough off where their ragged uniforms rubbed. Once they stopped, once they relaxed, they were immediately shivering and hungry.

Young Mintz should not have come. He'd found a boot, and Liebe had dressed his wound, but now it ached and was probably bleeding.

"Listen to me," Caspar said. "You watch me. You keep on me. We approach silently. We get into their trench system from the back." Caspar could see the weariness and distress on the men's faces.

"We can win this back. We just need to get into their trenches."

Richter was the sailor nearest to Caspar. Desperately afraid and fatigued, he'd been with the ship since its christening. He had been through so much, had seen so many die, and yet he hadn't so much as a scratch. But he wished he were dead, and he knew he was going to be dead soon. When Caspar gave the order to attack, he was fairly sure he was going to swim out into the ocean and simply drown or just put his machine pistol in his mouth and pull the trigger.

This was screaming insanity. What trenches? What was this Nazi idiot talking about? They knew nothing. They had no maps, no idea what they were facing. It was all just pandemonium now, blind stabs into the darkness. But like the rest, Richter said nothing when Caspar got to his feet and motioned for them to move out.

Caspar led the men down into a valley, maybe thirty yards across, full of large, ankle-twisting stones. As they meandered through the rock-strewn field, they were very near the shore. They could see the white breakers below to their right. They worked their way across this field, surrounded by tall spires of wind-worn stone.

The small squad approached a large, round rock in the middle of the field. Caspar blinked. Perhaps he was dizzy from hunger because, for a split second, he thought the rock in front of him had twitched. This massive boulder, bigger than a car, had twitched. As Caspar thought this, he was suddenly aware of the men behind him. He turned to see that they had all stopped walking.

Their faces glowed like lanterns, white and stretched in horrific expressions as they looked past him.

Caspar turned back and saw that the rock had somehow unrolled and was now a thing, some enormous creature. It was dark in color, and the details were hard to make out, but it's huge head moved snakelike on a thick neck. At the other end of this mass was a tapered tail easily ten feet long that slid around the beast.

It was slimy and wet, with deep gouges, thick scars, and a bony protrusion poking out of its back. Its skin was riddled with scratches and scrapes, fissures and growths. Clumps of stringy seaweed hung from the protrusions. When it was still, it did look like a massive boulder; but when it moved and showed its teeth, there was no mistaking this living thing. The beast was the only thing moving as it drew itself up to a towering height. The men stood motionless, frozen, watching.

Their minds couldn't process such a horrific creature. There was no instant leap to run away because their brains couldn't comprehend the true danger until the creature lowered its head and roared at them.

The sound of the beast was primal. It shocked every man to his core. They leapt from the spot, blindly running away from this thing. Caspar dove into a narrow ravine behind a line of rocks, scrambling behind another boulder and continuing on all fours down toward the water. Richter was behind Caspar. He ran a few steps before stepping into a deep crevice and breaking his leg.

The beast moved quickly for its size. It didn't lumber. Instead, it used huge muscles to fling its weight around. It was instantly on Richter. It snapped down on the man, taking off his head and upper torso in one bite. His lower half stood upright for a few seconds as his hands and forearms dropped to the ground next to him.

With a swoosh of its tail, the creature spun around to face the other three sailors. Two of them instinctively fired at the monster. It shrieked and lunged at the first man, slapping him against the rocks, killing him instantly. It turned and grabbed the next scrambling sailor in its huge mouth, catching the man's mid-section, snatching him off his feet. It hissed and screeched madly even while it ate.

The beast slammed its powerful jaws shut, and the man's body folded under the incredible force of the bite. The sailor's spine was snapped in twenty odd places, and his head, a twisted expression on his dead face, was entangled with his feet as his boots kicked and flopped. The dead man hung briefly from the side of the creature's mouth and then was swallowed completely in two more powerful bites.

The last sailor, young Mintz, backed away, firing his machine pistol until he ran out of ammo. He dropped the gun and sprinted off blindly into the night in sheer terror. But he only ran a few yards before he stumbled and fell, cracking his head open on a jagged boulder. The beast was already behind him. It pounced like a predatory bird, stepping on the young Mintz with its massive claws. Mintz was unconscious and transitioned mercifully from unconsciousness to death. His pelvis was shattered under the crushing weight of the monster. The beast held the small body down and bit into Mintz's back, pulling and chewing on his spine and head. After a few bites, it stepped back and finished off the rest of Mintz's legs.

Caspar was wild with fear. He scrambled blindly down the incline until the cold ocean water stopped him. His mind reeled with what he'd seen. This beast, meanwhile, chewed on the remnants of Caspar's men. It shook its massive head like a dog, and a bent pistol dropped from its mouth.

Caspar was becoming unhinged as he searched for ways to save himself. As the insanity set in, a thought occurred to him. He was a Nazi, a member of the perfect race, a race that originated from super beings, the supernatural, supernatural creatures like this one. Perhaps this was the ultimate test for the perfect Nazi.

The men who had come into contact with this thing so far were cowards. They acted like little girls and scattered like rodents. Half insane, Caspar took up the challenge. This creature fed on fear, and Caspar would have none—or at least he would appear to have none. Caspar jumped to his feet and held his ground.

"Stop!" he screamed.

The creature did stop. It obviously could hear well, and it stood very still. It inhaled a massive breath, its tail slowly sliding around behind it. Caspar felt himself propelled by his ideals, driven by his valor.

This was the ultimate test, and no matter the outcome, if he was true to the Führer and his Nazi principles, then he had nothing to fear. He walked toward the creature with confident strides.

"I am not your enemy. I am your friend," he yelled.

The creature stood, and Caspar was unable to grasp the size of the thing. The thing was now quiet. It cocked its huge head, and Caspar could hear its leathery skin crinkle and crunch as it moved. It studied Caspar with some sense of curiosity. Caspar couldn't believe it. He was weak in the knees, but this thing was now subdued.

Being fearless was the key. It always was, he thought. This was his destiny, Caspar figured. This was the single most important moment of his life. Perhaps he was meant to land here. The sub, the Americans, maybe even the whole war were somehow cosmically aligned so that he—and he alone at this moment—tamed this incredible beast.

He shouted through the night at this massive thing that stood not a dozen feet from him. "I'm German, one the greatest people ever to live on earth, descendants of gods, as you are. And I understand you. I want to help you. I salute you." Caspar stood at attention in his rags, soaking wet. He saluted a stiff, sharp Nazi salute.

The beast slowly lowered its head and stepped gently forward. Caspar stood his ground. He could hear the crunch of gravel under its enormous claws.

It inched closer to Caspar, who saluted with one arm while gripping his pistol with the other. Caspar wasn't suicidal, and he had a backup plan. It was the golden rule of battle. If you have enough backup plans, you never have to admit defeat. So he remained prepared. If it made a fast move, Caspar would aim for the eyes or the brain.

The beast lowered its huge head even closer and looked at Caspar. It was so close that Caspar could smell the stench of its hot breath. He held his salute as the head passed above him, eyeing him. The creature moved back. Caspar remained at attention.

"It is our destiny to meet this day, and I—"

And then Caspar's detached head and arm where in the creature's mouth. Caspar's last confused thought was the feeling of the rough texture and the odor of the beasts leathery tongue on the side of his face. His other hand seized up, and the machine gun fired into the ground as his limp body twitched and flopped to the rocks. The body had barely landed when the creature scooped it up into its hungry mouth. The creature didn't even break stride as it finished off Caspar and slid into ocean, disappearing below the waves.

8.

Temple awoke from fitful dreams to a screech like he'd never before heard. The sound was followed by small machine-gun fire and yelling off in the distance. He sat completely still, listening, until the faint sounds stopped. Suddenly, more shots rang out and then abruptly stopped.

Temple was beaten and sore. He had found a little pocket to hide in under a stone ledge, and in his utter desperation and complete exhaustion, he'd fallen asleep. Now he unfolded his body and felt the painful throb of the shrapnel wound in his leg as he stumbled off into the darkness. He staggered across the rocky surface for almost an hour with his pistol at the ready.

Eventually he came across the twisted body of O'Connor. The corpse was a mess. The ghastly exit wounds looked like someone had torn the stuffing out of a doll.

In the faint light, Temple avoided looking at O'Connor's face, but he patted down the body for ammo or a weapon. O'Connor's rifle was nowhere to be found.

It had probably dropped to the other side of the ridge. Temple did find two clips of rifle ammo in O'Connor's bloody pocket as well as his Navy-issued flashlight. He felt ghoulish pawing over the corpse, but they were going to need everything. He also took one of O'Connor's dog tags and stuffed it in his pocket.

Temple rose from the body, rounded a corner, slipped into a narrow ravine, and approached their pitiful camp. He held is hands up so that his buddies wouldn't shoot him, but Hammond saw him and waved him in.

"Where you been?" Hammond asked as Temple slipped past him.

"Got chased by those German bastards and wound up out there someplace. What the hell are they shooting at?" Temple asked.

Hammond shrugged. Hammond was lost in thought and stared off into the drizzly night.

Temple wound his way back to the makeshift shelter. The two men sitting by the lean-to vaguely acknowledged him, maybe not even realizing he'd been gone.

But Brenner noticed. "Temple," he said.

"Got into it with those Krauts on the machine gun. Wound up out there someplace. And O'Connor is dead," he added, fishing out O'Connor's dog tags.

"We know," Brenner said.

Out in the rain, a dozen feet from where they squatted, a German body lay flat out on the rock as if he were asleep. A watery puddle of blood encircled him.

"I took out a couple of those bastards on that machine gun," Temple offered flatly, somehow trying to justify his absence.

"Preston tossed a grenade in there and finished it off. They tried to outflank us, but we pushed them back," Hammond said, handing Temple a ration and a cup of cold coffee, both of which Temple eagerly accepted.

"We went back for their big gun, but someone grabbed it, so there's still more of them out there," Brenner muttered.

"Who got this guy?" Temple asked, pointing to the body.

"I think me and Brenner got him at the same time," Preston said. "Stinky bastard. Smells like shit. He's filthy and had nothing on him. He's like a tramp in a uniform. I think we ought to filet the bastard just like they did to Buchanan. He was, however, nice enough to let me borrow his snappy machine-gun pistol." Preston held the weapon up.

Walters trotted back from the rear. He was out of breath.

"I went to the left and I found this." He held up a long cloth German ammo belt.

The group perked up. They pawed over the ammunition. Hopes quickly faded, however, when the ammo fit neither the American weapons nor the German pistol.

"Probably for their rifles. Damn rotten luck," Walter's said.

Brenner was visibly dazed. He looked bad. His face was sallow, and his eyes darted wildly about.

"Sir, what's the plan?" Temple asked.

Brenner appeared to be deep in thought, mumbling to himself.

"So we got maybe five or six of them. They've got to be down to less than us now. They've got to be." Brenner's brain was stuck in scheming mode, strategizing over and over, unable to come out of this blind loop of survival and strategy.

"Sir, what's the plan?" Temple asked again.

Brenner studied Temple and slowly pulled his

gaze back in.

"Er ... Oh, well, we ... we ... dig in—same as before. There's nothing else. We've moved the perimeter in, shrunk the area. We've got outposts there and there."

He pointed through the rain, and Temple could make out the shadowy figure of Cassidy hunched between two granite spires on the other side of the cove. Steele was out there somewhere, too.

Preston was behind them, inside the lean-to. "You know, this place should be called Candy Apple Island," he said.

"Why's that?" Temple asked.

"Well, look around you. We're sitting crouched in the rain like drowned rats, waiting to be picked off by some crazy cannibal Germans. Doesn't that just sound so-o-o-o-o sweet?"

"What do you mean 'cannibal Germans'?" Temple asked.

No one was listening to Temple. Brenner looked at his watch and pointed. "Hammond, you go into that position on the next rotation," he said.

"This is insanity," Hammond blurted out. "We're not combat. We're builders. And we're too few, and they're too many. They're going to kill us all. They've got some vicious squad out there. You saw what they did to Buchanan."

Temple was confused.

"Wait! What did they do to Buchanan?" he asked.

Buchanan was the real reason they had changed the lookout posts. No one wanted to go back to the right forward point where Buchanan's body was. Walters had seen it, and it was the worst thing he'd ever seen. After the German attack, he had moved up to the right forward point, and there was Buchanan. Skinny Buchanan, who owed him sixteen dollars and with whom he was huddled in a tent just a few days before talking about who makes the best pizza in Queens, was torn apart and stuffed between jagged rocks.

The last anyone had seen him previously was when he was shot in the head by the Jerries while reading the surrender terms. He dropped there. They assumed he was still there until Walters discovered this new monstrosity up by the lookout post.

Walters had seen Buchanan's almost comically contorted face hanging below a twisted blob of skin and limbs. At first glance, it looked as if someone had tried to pull Buchanan through a narrow crevice between two boulders. His left arm was stretched between the rocks, and the other was torn off at the elbow. Below his chest, his skin was torn. It looked as if it had been savagely ripped or even bitten. Below the navel, there was nothing.

Walters had called to the men. Each man saw it and swore vengeance on the horrific Germans. They were obviously savages, and they were sending a message. They'd shot Buchanan, and that was fair. It was war. But this, this was different.

All of them, after seeing Buchanan, worried that perhaps the Germans, if they could sneak in and commit such an act not fifty yards from the American camp, weren't completely starved and exhausted after all.

How was it possible? Hammond played it over in his head: Sometime after the battle, the Jerries took Buchanan's body, tore it up, and then stretched it between rocks. It was horrifying. It filled him with terror and rage. How were these men capable of this?

Hammond closed his eyes, trying to expel the image of Buchanan's partial body, now no more than a blob of rotting tissue that hadn't yet washed into the ocean.

"They're goddamn barbarians. How … how did

it ever come to this? How could they do something like that?" Hammond rubbed his tired eyes.

Brenner was almost unable to process this new horror, but he tried to factor the new information into his fragile plan. They were savages, they were barbarians, and they would all consequently have to be killed.

As time wore on, they sat in silence again, waiting. Hours passed, and finally Brenner noted the time and signaled the rotation. Hammond grudgingly trotted off. He would send Cassidy back to camp.

Walters left to switch places with Steele. Fifteen minutes later, Steele cautiously emerged, wet and tired, from the ravine. He said nothing as he sat down against a rock under a ratty poncho that someone had secured on a little ledge.

Cassidy came back as well, but he had a peculiar look on his pale face. He dropped down, set down his rifle, and grabbed a ration can. He peeled it open with shaking hands.

Brenner could tell that Cassidy wasn't doing well. He was probably suffering from shock. "Cassidy, how you hanging in there?"

Cassidy was frazzled, his eyes bloodshot, his mouth taut. He twitched and squirmed as if insects were biting him. His voice was weak, and his speech was punctuated by long pauses.

"Uh ... Lieutenant ... um ... There's a bear or a ... bear thing ... I mean there's something on this island, sir," Cassidy muttered.

"A bear?" Preston asked, not sure what he heard.

"Sir, I know what I saw. This huge ... bear thing moved out on the horizon. I aimed at it, but it went behind the rocks..."

"It's the damn Germans. They're jerking our

chains," Steele said.

"It wasn't a man. It was big, and it was moving. I swear. I saw its tail," Cassidy insisted.

"Well, there you go," Temple said. "Bears don't have tails. Maybe a piece of tarp flew by in the wind. It's dark out there, rainy. You haven't slept in forever. Maybe it's your eyes playing tricks on you."

"Maybe a walrus was taking a break on this lovely spot," Preston suggested.

Cassidy wanted to believe anything rather than what he saw. Maybe it was something else, a trick of the light, he told himself, but he knew immediately that wasn't true. He knew what he had seen.

Preston sat up against the wall of the shelter. It was his turn to rest. It had been days since he'd slept any more than an hour here and a few minutes there, and yet he fought with his thoughts as he tried to sleep. He sat quietly, ready to explode, ready to kill, ready to die. But mostly he sat waiting for the inevitable catastrophic event to happen. In light of their recent experiences, all the men knew that something else was going to happen, something horrific. That knowledge, that certainty had everyone in a state of quiet but gripping panic.

Preston hadn't known he was capable of this sustained level of anxiety and discomfort. He'd heard the military jargon about getting men "off the line," meaning out of the line of fire where the actual killing happened. He now knew why it was so important. There were so many thoughts, so many soul-crushing fears and worries, so many wild emotions to process, so many extreme feelings, so much anguish and pain. Anyone who felt it recognized immediately that the feeling of constant fear and rage, given enough time, would kill just as surely as a bullet. He drifted in and out of sleep, his hands gripping his rifle, as these broken thoughts churned in his head.

Preston awoke in a slight panic to the tapping of Steele's revolver on his helmet.

"Let's go, sailor. You relieve your buddy Hammond up there. Get up there. Your watch. And keep any eye out for any damn bears."

"Screw you, Steele. I know what I saw," Cassidy said to Steele.

The sun was rising far beyond the clouds, and a dense, fast-moving fog filled their gray world. Preston stood up slowly and stretched weakly, hoping to untie some of the muscles that had been in knots for days.

Like everyone else, he was groggy, disoriented, and achy. Sleep, the only escape, was so fleeting. And he felt as if he had never really slept. Now it was his turn at the most forward point. Preston walked forward out of the encampment to the outpost where Hammond was.

The lookout spot was just a few hundred feet away, but as Preston made his way up to it, he felt that something was different. It took him a moment to realize that it wasn't raining. The world was instead shrouded in dense fog. He climbed up a line or stones and slowly crept between the rocks to where Hammond sat.

"Hey, Mark, you awake? Better not let Steele catch you napping up here. Mark?"

Something wasn't right. Hammond wasn't in the spot. Pale orange sunlight diffused through the thick fog as Preston moved into the alcove. Preston began to panic. Where had he gone?

"Mark, where the hell are you? Hey! You OK, pal?" Preston whispered into the mist.

He switched on his flashlight and checked the bottom of the crevice to see if Hammond had left any equipment. Preston jumped back when he saw that Hammond was still in the small hiding spot but was now little more than a twisted mass at the bottom of the crevice. Preston's eyes snapped shut. He stumbled back, the image of his friend, Mark Hammond, twisted and contorted, burned into his eyes. He was revolted to see how much of Hammond was missing.

Preston was horrified. Hammond's head was there, with his helmet still strapped under the chin. His legs were there, but the rest was just a smear of deep red, coating the floor of the small hole. Preston staggered, as if hit by a prizefighter, the scene burning like acid. He became aware of a sound and realized he himself was screaming, yelling. He fired the rifle blindly out into the night.

"Goddamn savages!" he screamed as his rage exploded. He flung himself over the rocks and fired into the fog at the distant Germans. He leapt into a clearing, firing from the hip, screaming and yelling. The Germans were nowhere to be found, and only the occasional zip of a ricochet responded to his firing.

"Preston! Preston! Get the hell back here," someone yelled from behind him. "Goddammit, that's an order! Get the hell back here!" Brenner dashed up to the forward position. The early morning was silent, and Preston stood in the open, his head slumped and his rifle hanging limply from his hand. Brenner could hear his pitiful cries as Preston stood sobbing.

"Goddamn German sons of bitches," he blubbered.

Brenner ran forward and wrestled Preston back behind their perimeter.

At the camp, the men sat against the slimy wall with their weapons ready. Brenner marched Preston in and threw him to the ground. He ordered Steele to take

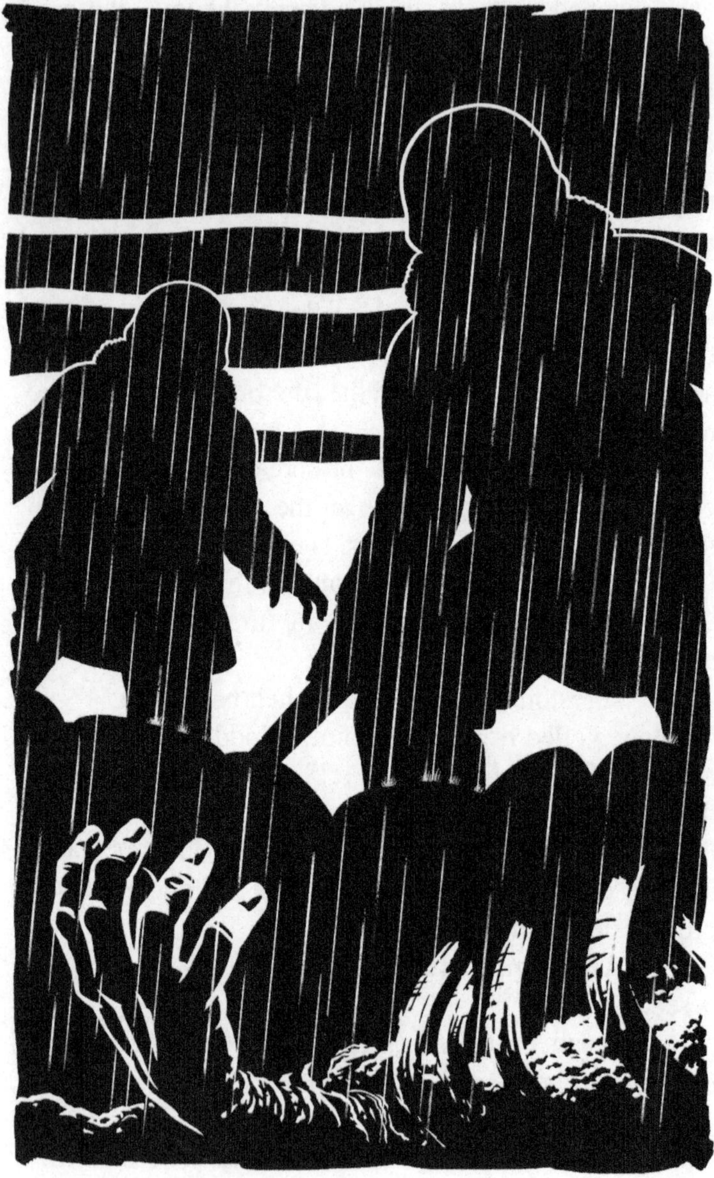

Preston's place. "Get up there. I don't know what happened, but they might attack."

Preston dropped down, sobbing openly. "They tore his goddamn guts out! Those Nazi sons of bitches tore out his goddamn guts!" Preston was on all fours. The other men watched him, emotionless, as he took his turn, sobbing into the ground. "I swear to God I will kill every one of those German pieces of shit, so help me. They tore his guts out," Preston cried. He just had to hear it again and again. He blubbered it over and over. Someone offered him a cup of cold coffee. He brushed it away and slid up against the rock wall, his eyes fixed on the dense fog.

9.

At the German camp, there were thin hopes that Caspar would prevail, and when there was a brief blast of machine guns far off in the distance, men perked up. Then the shooting died out. Minutes passed, and there were a few single shots. Then those died out as well. Not knowing was unnerving. When Caspar hadn't returned after two hours and the sun had come up somewhere behind a bank of fog, it was obvious that Caspar and his men weren't coming back.

The Germans were so low on men that the captain took his turn as sentry at one of their lookout points. He was miserable, soaked and freezing, but he was alone. He relished the solitude.

They had been completely out of food for two days. Liebe had made a clam soup on a tiny fire. It was horrible, and each man could have only a sip or two. They had plenty of clams, and a few desperate men had eaten them raw, only to vomit them up a few minutes later.

The stewed clams weren't vomit inducing and, disgusting as they were, they were all there was to eat.

But the tiny fire and the lack of any real wood allowed for only small batches.

It was pitiful, horrifying, and pathetic. Fessenden couldn't shake his gloom and his "if only" thoughts: if only he hadn't joined the Navy, if only he hadn't obeyed orders, if only he had gone AWOL and taken off to Switzerland with Elsa. If only.

If he had to die, so be it. But he wanted to be alone. He didn't want to be with these men anymore. Maybe it was his fault that they were there, or maybe it wasn't. Perhaps all the best decisions and luck in the world couldn't have prevented this. Fessenden began to feel that way. It was probably self-preservation at its simplest form, but the captain was no longer blaming himself. He just wanted to be left to die alone.

He sat in a small cradle of wet stone looking out toward the enemy. He was soaked to the bone, and his teeth chattered so much they hurt. When his shift was over, he would go back to the shelter and lie on the life jackets and uniforms and sleep. If anyone disturbed him, he would shoot the man dead on the spot. He peered out into the grayness of the day, and his head wobbled on his neck as he fought to stay conscious.

"Ps-s-s-st, Otto. Ps-s-s-s-s-s-s-st! Otto!"

Fessenden almost didn't recognize his name. Then it took him. Who was calling him by his first name? Off to his left on a short ridge was Burman, waving him over. Fessenden stood up and climbed the short path to where Burman manned his post.

"What is it, Hans? I should be at my post," the captain said.

Burman had changed dramatically in the last couple of days. He had become frantic and seemed like an old rummy, the way he shook and trembled and the way he seemed to get lost in inebriated thoughts. Everyone reacts differently to this extended incredible pressure, Fessenden thought.

Burman spoke as if he were telling a scandalous secret. "I have to tell you something, Otto. It's not the Americans. It's something else. It's a … I don't know what." Burman was anxious. He seemed in shock. His eyelids flittered.

The captain called down to the shelter. "Get Liebe over here," he ordered.

The sleeping Liebe was roused. He trudged through the fog and joined the captain at Burman's post.

"What is it, Captain," Liebe asked, puffing for breath.

"Something is wrong with Burman. He's not well."

"I'm OK, I'm OK. But it's out there. I don't know what it is, but it's out there. I saw it carrying one of them in its mouth. It's out there, and it's gobbling them up."

Liebe looked at Burman. He had Burman follow his finger with his eyes. He took Burman's pulse. "I'm not sure. Some kind of shock, I think." Liebe leaned closer and caught a whiff of alcohol. Burman just stood there, his eyes half closed, his mouth half open, swaying back and forth. Liebe patted Burman down and found the empty bottle of rubbing alcohol in his coat pocket.

"Here we go. He's been drinking this. I'd guess he most likely has alcohol poisoning." Liebe slapped Burman to get his attention.

"Hey, Burman, can you hear me? Were you trying to kill yourself?"

It was now obvious that Burman was very drunk.

"No-o-o-o, I just wanted to get warm." He grew serious and pointed off in the distance. "But then I saw it last night. It was big, and it was eating—what's his name?—the dead man."

Fessenden's head was pounding, who was he talking about? There were so many dead men now.

"Goddammit, Hans. What the hell are you doing? We needed that. Liebe, take him back to the shelter. And send someone up here to watch his spot."

Liebe helped Burman up and walked him back toward the shelter.

"Look, Otto. Look over there. You'll see. You'll see who the real enemy is."

With that, Liebe dragged Burman back down the short hill and back up into the shelter.

Fessenden was baffled. He looked around Burman's post. It was like the rest of area. Spent shells and garbage littered the site. Stepping over a few rocks and looking behind a boulder, he was jolted once more. He saw another partial corpse of a man. It looked as if it had been shredded, and he could only recognize part of an arm, a shoulder, part of the head. The captain swallowed hard. His mouth went dry.

The rocks around the body were covered in blood and flesh, despite the ongoing downpour. The captain's skin crawled, and he felt his face flush. He began to rethink the events of the past days—the bodies, the missing wounded.

Another weary sailor climbed up to the spot.

"Never mind this spot. Come back to the shelter with me," Fessenden ordered.

The two returned to the cave, where Liebe had seated Burman. Burman was sipping water from a canteen. The others sat, nervously watching. Werner paced back and forth.

The captain took off his rain-soaked coat and

pulled on a slightly less damp coat. He noticed Werner's agitation. "Sit down, Werner. Conserve your energy. We might have a bigger problem," the captain said. He couldn't believe the ideas he was now entertaining. Was he losing his mind? Was he already insane? Did he even know what was real anymore?

"Sir, begging your pardon, but how in the hell could we have a bigger problem? We have to attack. We have no food. We're dying. We've nothing to lose. You've heard it yourself. They're low on ammo. They never fire more than one or two shots. Sir, we must attack. It's all we have. They cannot be reasoned with. They turn our men inside out. They're savages. Burman told us about another torn-apart body he found over there."

"No," Burman insisted. "There's something else out there. That's the real enemy. That's what we should be frightened of."

"You're delirious, Burman," said Werner. "Look at you. If you don't eat soon—and I don't mean some stinking clam water—you're going to die, just like me, just like the rest of us."

The men in the cave watched as Werner paced back and forth. The captain tried to calm Werner.

"I agree with you, Werner. I do. But men are dying too quickly. We can't continue these blind expeditions. We have to send out a man, see what their position is, perhaps infiltrate—"

"No!" Werner shrieked. "What does it take? Your plans, they *do not* work. You systematically and logically dissect everything, all the while the floor is falling out from under you."

Burman tried to stand up but dropped back down, still very drunk and sick. "You check that talk, sailor. That's-s-s-s an order," Burman was able to slur out.

"No, sir," Werner said. His face was gaunt. His eyes burned with an intensity that frightened the captain. Werner clumsily pulled out his machine-gun pistol and aimed it at Fessenden.

"No. With all *un*due respect, you forfeit. Nothing you do works. We're attacking. We're going after their food and whatever we can grab. We have to go all at once—a blitz. You can't keep whittling us down. I'd rather die fighting than starve or be torn apart by these savages."

The shelter was awkwardly silent.

Werner dropped his tone and continued. "And I'm sorry to report that the men all feel the same."

The captain scanned the faces of the remaining men. They wouldn't meet his gaze, but a couple brandished their weapons in a pathetic display. Müller sat up and moved away from the group.

"Sir, I had no part in this," Müller said defiantly and stood next to Fessenden.

Werner scoffed at Müller. "Suit yourself, you idiot. Die together. It doesn't matter."

Werner turned to the captain. "We're attacking, and when we have food and shelter, you're welcome to join us. No hard feelings. But you're not cut out for this."

The men loaded their weapons and formed up behind Werner outside the shelter. Müller and the captain remained in the shelter. Liebe pulled another coat around Burman's shoulders and then stood, took up a rifle, and joined the men outside.

Fessenden locked eyes with Liebe.

"I'm sorry captain, "Liebe explained. "I just want to get this over with one way or another. I'm sorry, sir, but I've had enough."

Werner gave two of the men a nod and motioned toward the large MG 42 machine gun. The two men moved to pick up the gun and tripod.

Fessenden raised his luger and aimed it at Werner's face. "Under these circumstances, I can see why you'd mutiny. And you're right. I am not cut out for this. No one is. But you're not taking that gun. If any of you mutineers steps back into this shelter, Werner is a dead man, so help me."

The two weary men raised their hands in surrender and stepped back. Without saying another word, Werner and the sailors shuffled off and faded into the foggy morning.

The captain relaxed, exhaled, and sat in silence. After a few minutes, he turned and looked at Müller. Müller sat shaking, wrapped in two ratty coats. His eyes darted about feverishly. He was confused, hungry, and frightened. Müller needed something. The captain realized that he must say something to the one man who had stood by him.

"Thank you for your bravery and for not following the others. Why don't you go and see if Burman is feeling any better?" the captain said softly. Müller nodded and turned around to find that Burman wasn't passed out on the filthy pile of uniforms and life jackets. Somehow, he'd crawled out and away as they both sat immersed in their own terrifying thoughts.

"He's gone, sir," Müller said, glancing around the shelter. "He must have--" Müller was cut short by loud singing echoing from outside.

The captain and Müller crawled to the edge of the shelter and looked down to the debris-strewn beach. Burman stood out in the open, singing at the top of his lungs. He pumped his fist as if he were in a German beer hall, and the captain recognized the song, a dirty bar tune about a promiscuous woman who loved sailors.

"We've got to get him and shut him up," Müller said.

Fessenden and Hans Burman had been friends for years. The captain patted Müller on the shoulder. "I know Hans. He'll come in for me. You stay here."

Fessenden stood up and moved to the mouth of the cave, but he jumped back and flattened himself against the wall. Müller leaned out, saw what the captain had seen, and lay down. He kept his eyes glued on the cove below, unable to look away from the gravel beach.

The creature had emerged from the breakers and was just a few yards behind Burman. It was inching up behind him. It dwarfed the staggering man.

The captain thought of turning the big machine gun down to the water, but he knew it was no use. It was too heavy. It would take him too long. Now just a few feet behind Burman, the creature inched closer as Burman sang, conducting an invisible brass band. The beast was slow and careful. It knew how to sneak up on its prey. It turned its massive head sideways, eased up, and opened its mouth wide.

Fessenden had to do something. He jumped up and found a rifle, but it was too late. The captain moved to shoulder the weapon as the festive singing turned into violent screaming and high-pitched shrieking. Fessenden looked back and saw the creature biting down on the lower half of his friend. Burman let out a pitiful wail that was quickly silenced as the monster pulled him back into the pitching surf.

10.

Steele sat crouched in a ball, his submachine gun wrapped in his arms. He was slumped over, and his head was hidden under his wet, battered helmet. He was supposed to be on watch, but, like everyone else on the island, he was navigating a harrowing course, from adrenaline rush to fear to crushing exhaustion and back again. As soon as all was quiet and as soon as he was no longer active, no matter how he tried, he would slump into a deep, motionless sleep.

Since the fighting had started, Steele had been overtaken by a dream he had whenever he slept. In the dream, he was back at his parents' farm in Pennsylvania helping his mother and grandmother as they loaded their season's haul of canned fruits and vegetables into their cellar.

The recurring dream started up anytime he was able to sleep, even for just a few minutes. It was almost always the same. He was perplexed.

He wasn't one to reminisce or discuss the meanings of dreams and all that mystical mumbo jumbo. That

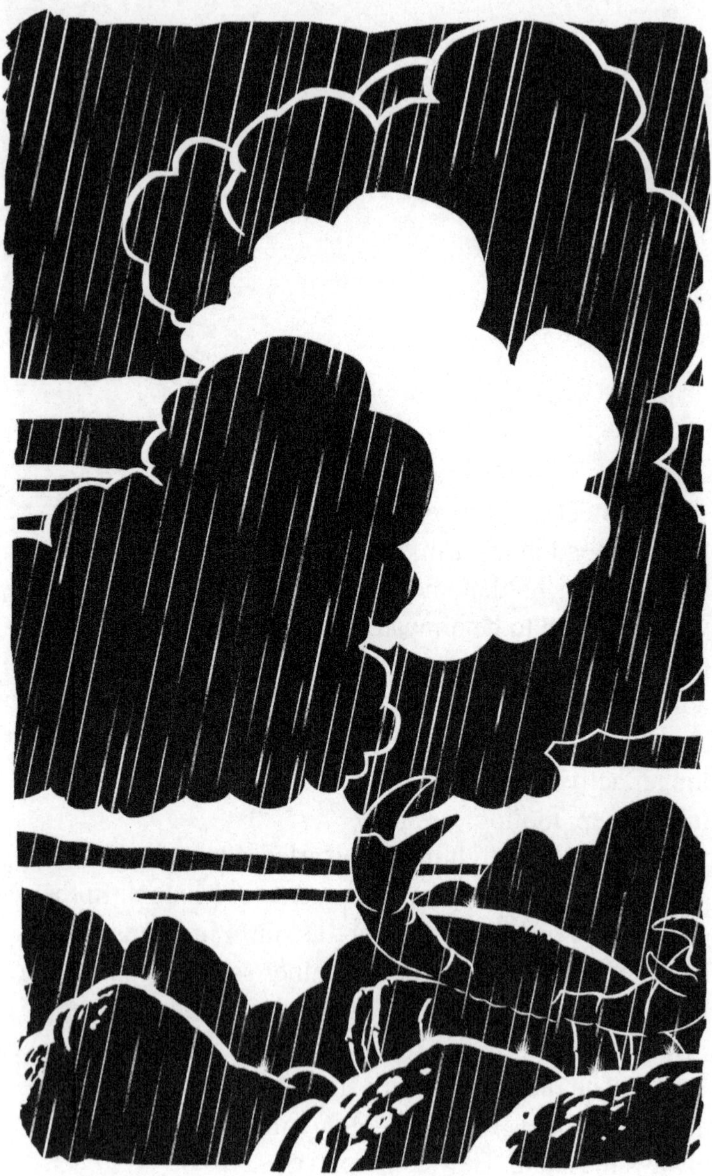

was all just sideshow antics as far as he was concerned. But now, on this miserable island so far from home, he was plagued by this dream, this mundane dream of him simply helping his mother and grandmother load their fruit cellar with jars and jars of freshly canned fruit and vegetables.

Steele didn't know the first thing about psychology. He found the experience awkward when, upon joining the Navy, he briefly talked to a doctor about his mind. But now this recurring dream frightened him, It never left his thoughts.

He couldn't know that his dream wasn't a metaphor for anything; it was just a face-value dream, it was his subconscious expressing a deep need be out of this horrific mess, to be in a place opposite from where he was now. Steele didn't know what to make of it, He was almost relieved to be awake and thinking about something else.

Steele awoke from the dream again to a noise, but it was gone before he could identify it. He sat in silence, straining to hear, as he shouldered his gun. All at once, bullets whizzed out of the morning mist, zipping off rocks with brilliant flashes.

Still crouched in his hole, Steele saw silhouettes moving through the fog. The Germans, he figured, were attacking, hoping to overrun all the American positions with a big, final push. The Jerries were undoubtedly starving. They had little choice.

The faint outlines of two German sailors emerged, as they hobbled over the rocks, sporadically firing their rifles. Steele's hiding spot was right in front of them, and he easily gunned down the first man, with a short burst from his machine gun. The man dropped against the rocks and slumped over. The second German turned and fired on Steele, charging directly at him out of the mist. In an instant, the man was so close that Steele could see a flash of gold from his teeth as he screamed unintelligible German.

Steele pulled the trigger, one shot rang out, grazing the man's arm. He stopped in his tracks and looked at the wound. Steele pulled the trigger again. Nothing happened. He was out of ammunition. He savagely ripped the empty clip from his gun. He reached to his belt for another clip, but it wasn't there, it must have fallen out. He was sure he had pocketed a second clip, but now it was nowhere to be found.

The German raised his rifle and fired two shots, narrowly missing Steele. Steele fumbled with the pistol in his holster as the German ran toward him, firing two more shots. And then Steele heard the unmistakable "click, click, click." The German, too, was out of ammunition.

The German's rifle, however, was fitted with a long and lethal bayonet. Steele could see that the Kraut was crazy with fear, rage, and revenge. He charged as Steele continued to fumble for his pistol. Steele was too cramped in his hiding place to stand up as the German closed it. He knew that he would not be able to get a shot off, Then suddenly something huge and slick, moved behind the German, and yanked him so hard to the left, that Steele saw his neck and arms snap back as if a car had hit him.

Steele's first thought was that a huge boulder had somehow broken loose and rolled down the mound, taking out the German. But then he caught a glimpse of a wall of muscle and a long, thick tail. It was over in an instant,

Steele continued to grope for his pistol, and he finally pulled it out, even though there was nothing to shoot at. He sat, dumbfounded, until another random shot zipped over his head. He jumped up, dazed and terrified, and sprinted back in retreat as the firing continued.

At the Seabee camp, the men had jumped into action at the first sound of gunfire. They had so little ammo that they had to resist the urge to fire indiscriminately into the fog. Brenner studied the landscape, but nothing could be seen through the morning mist. They waited, their adrenaline-infused hearts pounding.

"Spread out, fan out," Brenner barked. "keep each other in sight, anyone comes between you, kill them." Brenner passed two of the last grenades to the men. "Use these if you need to"

Preston, crouched by the line, took one of the Grenades. He looked at the weapon in his filthy hand, and something snapped. He stood straight up.

"You stay here and be sitting ducks, I don't give a rat's ass, I've had it with these bastards!" Preston jumped up, pulled the pin, and threw the grenade wildly into the air. Wielding the German machine-gun pistol, he changed into the fog. The other men yelled at him and grabbed for him, but he jerked free and disappeared into the veil of gray. Somewhere up ahead, the grenade exploded.

They waited, their eyes straining to see anything in the mist. Off to the left, they saw someone running, Brenner aimed but recognized the silhouette of Steele running back toward camp.

"Steele!" he yelled hoarsely, but Steele disappeared behind them.

Without warning, directly ahead of them, a loud volley of gunfire erupted. The Americans ducked down, expecting bullets to fly in their direction, but none did. Instead, they heard screams and shout, and more of the screeching sounds that Temple had heard before.

The strange noises echoed through the rock, and were followed by more shooting, and then the whole world went quiet again, that unnerving silence was once again all they were left with. There was no patter of rain this time, only the waves crashing off in the distance. But then strange noises echoed through the mist, followed by thuds against the rock and then quiet.

"Goddammit" Cassidy cried."What the hell is going on out there"

No one moved for a full hour. Finally, Brenner signaled for the rest to stay put and indicated that he would take a quick look. Keeping low, he climbed up over the rocks and slipped into the fog. The rest of the men looked back and forth at each other, wondering what to do. In fewer than five minutes, a guttural scream pierced the gloom.

"That was Brenner! I think that was Brenner, we've got to find out." Walters said as he jumped up,

Temple felt himself moving to help Walters, although he didn't know why; moving, for some reason, seemed more tolerable than just sitting and waiting.

Fifty yards beyond their perimeter line, Walters and Temple stopped. They found the remnants of Preston's uniform, torn and twisted across the rocks. It trailed across the landscape mixed with a long ribbon of flesh and shredded organs. Walters picked Preston's dog tags out of a large lump of tissue and skin.

Twenty yards further, enveloped in the dank fog, Brenner lay out in the open, flat on his back, his legs badly smashed, broken, and bleeding. Lying there, staring up into nothing, Lieutenant Brenner knew he would never move from that spot. Whatever had struck him would eventually get them all and finish him off as well. It was a painful truth, but it was strangely calming as well.

Brenner knew he was going to die, he was sure of it. Finally, he could stop worrying about the others, the Navy, and his duty, that was all over now. He wouldn't be saved, Very shortly, he would be off this miserable rock no more fear, no more pain, no more cold, nothing. Knowing that this was the inescapable truth put him at ease for the first time in a long time. The smell of gunpowder filled the air, and the mist now felt good on his face.

Close by, the creature hissed. Brenner craned his neck to look up. He saw the upside down bodies of two Germans torn up and draped among the boulders. He could hear and feel the deep vibration of the creature's feet stomping on the ground as it approached.

"Brenner! Lieutenant Brenner, are you OK? Hang on, I'm coming to get you."

From off to his left came the voice of Walters. Walters and Temple were crouched between the rocks, Brenner could see the two wide-eyed men looking at him laid out and ruined.

"Get out of here," he yelled. "It's coming, it's coming…" With that, Brenner pulled the last grenade from his belt and pushed it into his mouth. He looped his finger through the pin. Walters and Temple saw what he was doing and dove behind the boulders.

The creature stomped forward over the rocks, hissing and roaring.

Brenner pulled the pin. His last thought was of how much the detonator burned his lips. In five seconds, there was a blast. Brenner's head and upper body were simply gone.

The creature was at Brenner's feet when the grenade exploded. It was blasted back, peppered with searing shrapnel. It shrieked and danced in pain. Temple and Walters heard the strange noises, but by the time they looked, they could see only the huge shape fading into the fog as it galloped off across the rocks. It disappeared over the hill, and they heard the sound of something enormous splashing into the sea.

Back at camp, Cassidy held the perimeter and almost shot Steele as he scrambled in. "What the hell is going on out there," Cassidy yelled.

"They tried to attack," Steele said in a shaky voice, "but something else - I - I saw ... I think I saw your bear. But it ain't no bear, it's a ...—lizard or something. It's huge, the goddamn thing is as big as a house" Steele's hands were shaking as he dumped the few remaining rounds out of a box of ammo and stuffed them into an empty clip.

Walters and Temple returned to camp, horrified at how Brenner had killed himself and even more terrified by the huge thing they'd seen moving through the fog.

All The men were a nervous, quaking mess as this new information began to sink in. Obviously, *that* thing had smeared Preston all over the rocks, probably Buchanan, too. Silently, they sat and looked at each other, amazed to be rising to a new level of fear. Steele, who'd been unflappable, was now shaking so violently that he couldn't even load the clips for his Thompson. The four Cassidy, Temple, Walters, and Steele—were, as a result of sheer luck, the only ones left.

"It's a goddamn monster. It's a monster. All your life, everyone tells you monsters are not real, there's no monster in the closet, no demon under the bed, but they were wrong." Steele muttered.

"Do you think the Germans brought it with them?" Cassidy asked.

"You can't bring a thing like that. No, they were just like us, in the wrong place at the wrong time. It got a taste for us, and when we weren't killing each other off fast enough, it got tired of waiting." Walters guessed.

"What is it, do you think" Cassidy asked.

"Beats the hell out of me, some sort of sea serpent or lizard or something. It was hard to make out its shape" Temple said. "We only saw it for a second, but it's giant, bigger than a goddamn elephant"

"What does it matter what the fuck it is, you can't shoot it. You heard all that gunfire, a grenade blew up six feet from it, and it just ran away. It's going to get us, we'll all be like Buchanan and Preston, just leftovers, picked over chicken bones," Walters whined.

The remaining men sat in a tight formation watching for movement beyond their camp. Everyone was deep in his own thoughts and fear, until Walters muttered to no one, and everyone.

"I ain't ... I ain't getting eaten by that thing. I saw what it did to those guys. " He held up a grenade and swung it gently by the pin. "Not me, no goddamn way, Brenner had it right, this will be my last damn meal."

"Put it away." Steele grumbled.

"Maybe we should try to contact the Germans, now that we know that there's that...thing," Cassidy suggested.

"Screw that, it's their fault we're doing all this, there's a war on, and if I'm going to die here, so are they," Steele hissed.

"We don't even know how many of them there are, it might have gotten all of them," Temple offered.

Steele sat, motionless and taut, looking out into the thick fog. "Well, that's fine, but if I see a Kraut, I fire," Steele said as he sat back, and wiped the grime and sweat from his brow.

"Steele, you're the ranking officer now" Cassidy said. "What do we do"

"Fuck if I know," Steele said.

"Maybe we should save our ammo for that —

thing" Temple suggested.

Steele wasn't listening and Walters was still thinking about the reality of eating a grenade like Brenner had.

"How is it possible," continued Temple, "that a giant thing was able to get past our lines and get at the dead? The damn thing is huge; you can hear it a mile away."

"It's a hunter, obviously" Steele said, "It can be as quiet as it needs to be when it's stalking prey." He took out a pack of cigarettes from inside his coat and lit one. He didn't offer anyone a smoke. "And now it's stalking us."

11.

Müller and Captain Fessenden were slumped up against each other's backs. Müller was supposed to be on guard either for the Americans, or for that creature, but he was too tired, He had fallen deeply asleep leaning on the captain.

The captain slept fitfully through nightmares that were fresh replays of what he'd experienced. He slept for only a few hours, but the nightmares seemed endless. The scenes played over and over: that thing, the killing, the screams, the helplessness, the cold, but as his endless night wore on, something slowly changed.

In his dream, the captain felt a warmth that he hadn't felt in as long as he could remember, it eased in and was taking over, wrapping him in a calming, pleasant tingle. This delicious, radiating heat slowly burned away the hellish scenes he'd been forced to watch over and over. This feeling, this calming warmth, slowly washed away the terror in a tranquil wrap of golden yellow and

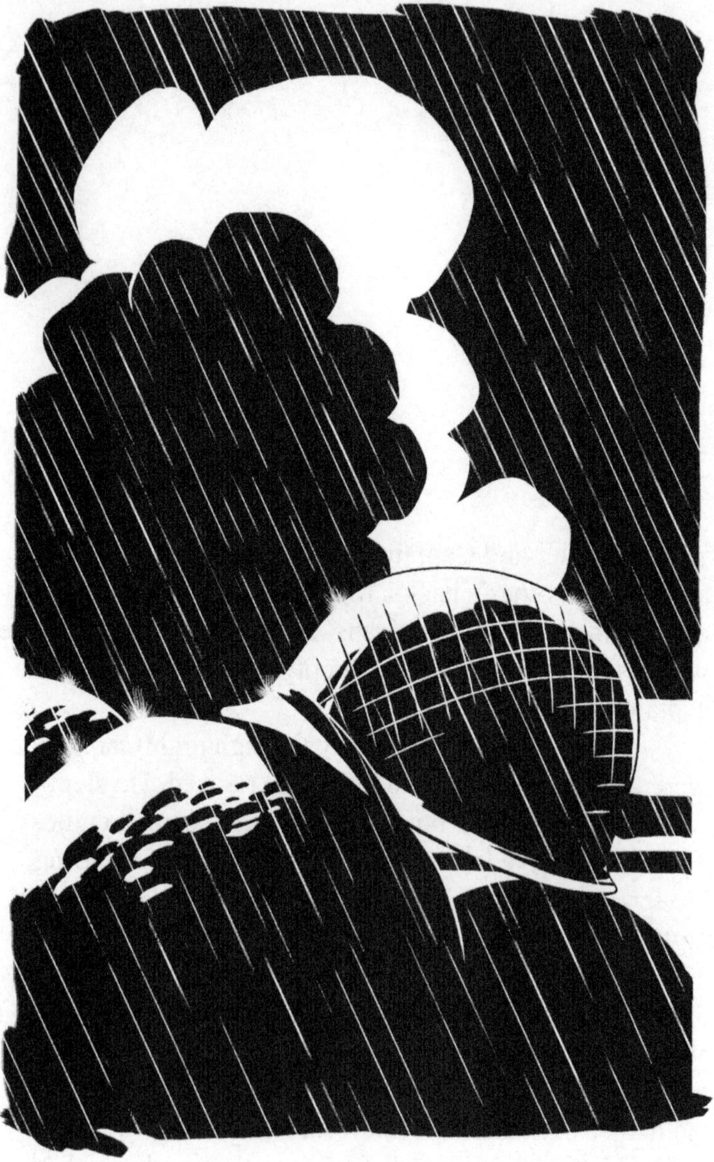

orange.

Fessenden's eyes fluttered open, and he immediately closed them. He lifted his arm and shielded his eyes. If was sunny, for the first time in over a month, the unfiltered sun shone on him, nothing, it seemed, was between him and the wonderful burning star. He sat crumpled, as the unmistakable feeling of warmth gently enveloped him.

Fessenden stood up, his aching body resisted, but he, overcame the resistance so that he could stand in reverence to this thing, this thing that was the opposite of everything he'd recently been such a part of. The war, the killing, the creature, the weapons, the sea all, paled in comparison to the sun.

The sun was oblivious to such insignificant pettiness. It was pure good, it was so good that it burned with that unmistakable brilliance that only the sun can attain. It brought all to life, and it was so good, so pure, so perfect that it sustained life as well.

"Cook me," the captain thought. "Just bombard me with heat and sweep me back up into the sky."

He stood there and let the sun warm him. Müller had sensed the movement. He slowly awoke, amazed as well. He painfully climbed to his feet next to the captain. Off to their right, the blue sky met the blue sea, but they could both plainly recognize they were in a small break in the never ending North Sea system of storms. Off on the horizon, thick, gray clouds, fat with moisture and moving briskly, pushed toward the island. But between the gray clouds and the two men was a vast, brilliantly blue sky from which the radiant sun blasted them with its heat and light.

Fessenden had always been an eager student of science. He knew all about astronomy and the known universe. But now, like never before, he truly felt himself clinging to a giant ball in space; and that star, that massive, burning, exploding star, was beaming its energy straight to him. In a moment of confused dazzle, the delirious captain briefly glimpsed his place in the universe.

"I've never been so happy to see the sun," the captain whispered.

Müller stood next to him, squinting and using his hand to shade the sun from his eyes. "It's so clear," Müller said.

They stood silently for a long time. Finally, Müller rubbed his head and opened his coat a bit. "Captain, sir, do you think we'll ever get home?"

The captain turned to Müller. "First off, it's not *sir* or *captain*. I have no boat. I lost it. I have no crew—besides you. They're all dead. I long ago lost the right to be called by either of those titles. My name is Otto."

"Sir … er … I mean, Otto, you did the best you —"

"Please, don't say anything. And, sadly, no, I do not think you or I will ever get out of here. For that, I'm truly sorry."

Müller stiffened and glanced around. A thought had struck him. Their camp was in a shallow depression of a rocky field. To their left, where the sun had risen, their view was clear to the horizon. Around them, the rocks obscured their view of the rest of the horizon that they assumed wrapped around them.

"Sir … I mean captain. We should use this opportunity to see if this is an island for sure." He motioned to the tallest point on the island. "If we get up there, we can see the whole island, see if there's a bridge or a small chain of islands or a boat or who knows what."

The captain wasn't as optimistic. "It has to be an island. Otherwise, the enemy would have retreated or overrun us. They must have crashed here as well. No sea birds…" He mumbled.

Müller stood up and moved toward the tall mound. "But we can't be sure. Maybe they have a boat. Maybe … maybe they have food and—"

The captain pulled him back. "No, Müller, it's an island. There's nothing to see. And you know that thing is out there as well, waiting."

Müller pulled free from the captain with surprising strength. "We have to look. We have to at least look."

"Ok, wait. You're right. But let's climb up slowly."

Müller was already up and scrambling over the uneven terrain. "No, the storm is coming back. We've got to make the most of this." Müller moved quickly. The captain tried to follow, but Müller moved even faster.

"Müller, goddammit, slow down! Müller! There's enemy around. Slow down! Müller, slow down. That's an order!"

Müller looked back and almost smiled. "You're not the captain anymore. Remember? You quit. Come, Otto, this might be our way out of here." Müller moved even faster, hopping up the hill. Cracks riddled the mound of stone, and Müller used the deep gouges to plant his feet and climb to the top.

The captain joined Müller at the top. Both were out of breath and weak. Fessenden collapsed with the pain of stabbing hunger and nausea. Müller spun around, taking in a three hundred sixty degree view of the horizon. Tears rolled down his face as he saw the empty horizon that wrapped their world. Down near the waterline to the north were two tiny islands a hundred yards offshore, dots in the white-capped ocean. Each of the two islands was slightly bigger than a house. They were smaller versions of the conglomeration of volcanic boulders that Fessenden and Müller stood on. There was nothing else, nothing but the vast sea stretching off to the horizon. Müller slumped and wept openly.

"Not one tree, not one bird, not one shrub," the captain whispered.

To their right, they could see that their day in the sun would soon be cut short. Their weather window was closing quickly. Silently they watched a wall of gray clouds charging toward them. Its shadow moved over the surface of the water, turning the blue sea a dull grey.

It would be just a matter of minutes until the clouds moved in, the captain guessed. They watched anyway, drinking in that last few rays of the sun. As the sun moved behind the wall of clouds, their thin wisp of hope was carried off by the wind.

The captain sat down on the rock and put his head in his hands. Raindrops speckled the back of his neck. A minute later, the drops became fat and numerous as the rain poured onto the island once more.

Müller stood motionless as the wind began to whip at his ragged coats and other wraps. Müller coughed deeply and fell over onto the captain as the crack of a gunshot split the air. The captain was pushed off the boulder and slammed facedown against the stony ground. He lay there as a second shot ricocheted off the rocks near him. Another shot hit Müller in the back, but he was already dead. The shooting stopped.

Müller was tangled on top of Fessenden, who wriggled and squirmed to get free. Fessenden was able to squeeze his upper body out from under Müller. Above Fessenden's head was Müller's face, hanging upside down and wedged against a smooth rock. His dead eyes were pointing in different directions, and his mouth, saliva pouring freely from it, was pulled into a strange sneer.

An apple-sized hole, where the bullet had exited, was all that was left of Müller's right ear. Steam rose from the warm blood and was whipped around by the wind. The captain, once again, could do nothing but close his eyes to the horror.

Fessenden lay there until it was dark. He knew the enemy had nothing to do but wait. It was ludicrous. They must know about the creature by now. They must have figured out that the beast was far worse than any man with a gun.

Once it was dark, Fessenden stripped Müller of his coat and weapons and crawled back down to his base. He was alone now. He thought there might be two or three Americans, but he couldn't be sure. It was a guess based on nothing.

He imagined himself going steadily insane. He was alone and starving. Why not just march toward the Americans firing wildly and end this? They'd happily gun him down. But he knew he could not.

The pressure and the stress was so gnawing and so deep that he was sure that if he endured it for one more day, he would certainly go barking mad. The rain was steady all day, and night came on quickly and seemed dark and endless.

As night fell, fears tag teamed each other as a new level of panic set in. The lone captain sat in the dark, listening to the storm and hearing phantom sounds. The tension and the fear proved too much. The panic became muddy and then confused. Try as he might to stay awake, the captain drifted off to sleep sitting up, manning the machine gun.

He slept for five hours straight. By early morning, the rain had come back with a vengeance. It was bit-

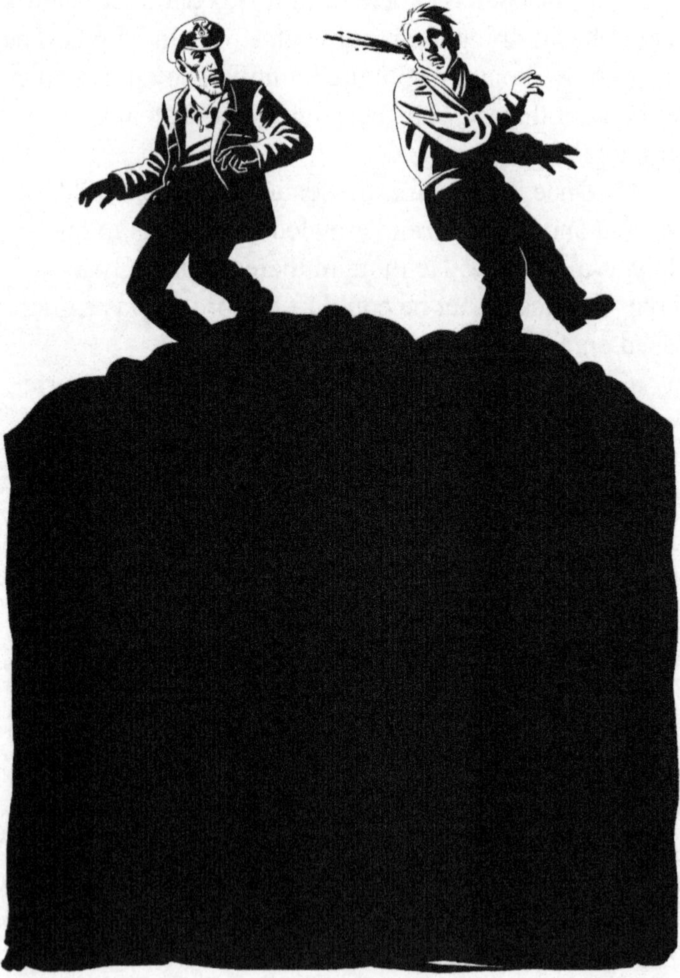

terly cold now, and Fessenden bundled himself into more uniforms. He waited and watched the horizon, but he saw nothing. The gnawing in his stomach made him less cautious, and he finally abandoned the machine gun at the mouth of the cave and went in search of something to eat.

He searched the clothes of the first bodies they had stripped and found nothing. On his orders, three of his men had brought a few more bodies of the recently killed down to a spot around a rock corner. There had been no time to strip them. The captain climbed down to them, his small machine-gun pistol in hand. As he stepped into the protected area, he could see that the creature had been at the bodies. The captain had seen a lot, but this scene made his head wobble and his throat close. The bodies were smeared across the boulders. They'd been viciously shredded, and only ribbons of uniforms and strips of flesh hung among the stones. A clump of hair and part of a scalp flapped in the wind and made a faceless wet rock look as if it were wearing a toupee.

Turning back, away from the scene, he wondered how many of these ghastly images his mind could hold and for how many years. If he managed to live, would he ever be able to shake what he'd seen? He almost laughed at himself. It was so blatantly obvious that he wasn't going to survive.

He returned to the cave and looked through the pile of weapons, boots, equipment, and raincoats. He pushed the pile of battered life jackets away and spotted a canteen, battered but sealed.

It must have been Liebe, saving some of that awful clam soup for the dying men. He grabbed it and was delighted when it turned out to be heavy and nearly full. He opened it, and the fishy clam smell wafted from the canteen to his nose. He chugged the cold liquid and greedily swallowed as the tiny, cold clams slid down his throat.

He could have downed the whole container, but he knew he'd be sick if he did. He forced himself to stop. He felt dizzy for a second, and his ears buzzed as his stomach finally got what it had been demanding for so long. He carefully put the cap back on the canteen and leaned back. A strip of canvas channeled rainwater from the rocks above into a broken container at the cave's entrance. Fessenden took a big drink and splashed his face with cold water. He repositioned the gun so that he could sit behind it and still lean back on the life jackets.

He sat all day, drifting in and out of consciousness as his dreams mixed with reality. More than once he almost fired because he had dreamed that the Americans were sneaking into his camp or, worse yet, that the creature was coming for him. When he was lucid, he simply watched the weather move over the island. At what he guessed was midday, he took a short walk to relieve himself and vigorously moved his arms and hands to keep his blood circulating. He didn't know what he was going to do, and he couldn't think of anything at all. He was out of ideas, and he was terrified of meeting the creature. But for the moment, he'd slept a little, and that awful clam soup had briefly staved off his hunger. He had no options, but he wasn't going to think about it now. Something might come to him, and it might not. For now, he would just sit and wait. And he would shoot anything that moved in front of him.

Night came right on time. A storm howled across the rock, whipping the winds and driving the rain. The captain was used to the weather by now. He had no memory of falling asleep. But then a noise woke him. Of this he was certain.

He listened. It was painfully dark. The moon was blotted out by the thick clouds. He listened and listened. He had begun to imagine things when, unmistakably, shots rang out. He tucked up onto the gun and rode another jolt of adrenaline. But the shots were far off, probably in the American camp. There was a blast—an explosion, perhaps a grenade. He was awake now, and his hunger returned as soon as the adrenaline wore off. Once again, the world was achingly quiet.

Fessenden muttered to himself, "If the Americans weren't aware of the creature before, they are now."

12.

Only horrible things, it seemed, happened on this island, and when nothing was happening, the silence was horrible in it's own way. The sun had shone unexpectedly, and the men all squinted and blinked in confusion. They hadn't budged since they were all but wiped out. The four of them sat in their camp, waiting.

For some reason, the Germans—two, maybe three of them—with the bright sun shining, climbed up on the highest rock and just stood there.

Walters, Cassidy, and Temple watched. Cassidy suggested that they were surrendering, that they thought the Americans were down below them someplace. Walters guessed that they were looking for a boat. Cassidy wanted to call out and get them to surrender.

Steele said nothing. He listened to the discussion. He casually set down his machine gun and gently took Cassidy's rifle from his hands. Cassidy handed it over without protest. Steele stood up, sighted down the barrel at the two men standing atop the distant mound staring at the sun. He fired a shot, and one man fell. He quickly fired two more.

"Well, I think that solves our Kraut problem," Steele said, handing the rifle back to Cassidy.

A fragile sense of relief found the four when no shots echoed back. Had they won? Perhaps they'd really won. Perhaps they had eliminated the last rotten Kraut. Perhaps they would now be rescued and decorated as heroes for destroying the entire crew of a damn German submarine.

Still, lest they be wrong, they dared not stand up or do anything rash. They sat the whole day, crouched, sure that they'd won but unwilling to gamble. In their subdued excitement and relief, they collectively dismissed the idea of the thing, whatever it was. They irrationally decided that, whatever it was, it went away with the Germans. Only Steele was dubious.

Night came, and the men got a fire going in the shelter. No one was jubilant; it had been too rough, too grueling, too brutal for anyone to recover quickly. They were exhausted, shocked, and beaten. They sat in silence for a while, staring at this new, wonderful thing—a fire. Darkness fell on the island, and the rain turned to a soft sprinkle. For now, with this small fire, they weren't in that darkness. Shadows danced on their gaunt faces and on the wet stone walls.

They still had rations that they heated near the embers. They tasted delicious no matter what was inside—pudding, soup, pears—and all of it was profoundly better when hot.

"I can't wait to get off this shit pile," Walters said. "First thing I'm going to do when I get on that boat is order the mess cook to make me the thickest steak they have, and I swear to God I will do it at gunpoint."

They almost smiled at the idea—except Steele.

"Are you assholes kidding me?" Steele snapped. He sat away from the rest, his hands on his gun. "You saw what I saw. You know what's still out there. Now put that fire out."

Steele stood up. He kicked through the fire and stomped the embers.

"Pick up those weapons. We've still got problems, and I'll be damned if we're going to relax now. We're going to hunker down and wait until the Navy shows. Now keep those weapons ready. You can tell your damn stories about what you're going to do when you're off this rock, but let me remind you, we're *not* off this rock pile yet."

The men were tired of orders. They groaned but begrudgingly pulled their guns closer. They had no more fight. Steele was right, of course, but what could they do? If this thing was as powerful as it seemed, they couldn't do one single thing if it came back.

Temple set his rifle across his lap to placate Steele. A wrapped ration sat by some still-glowing embers. Temple picked it up and ate the warm raisin cake inside. He leaned back on the wall and fell instantly asleep. He slept soundly—until he was knocked awake into absolute chaos.

The lean-to had collapsed, and the men were flailing and yelling and slamming into him. Not six feet in front of him, the creature's massive head arched down into their tiny fortress. The top half of Walters was inside its mouth. The creature jerked Walters back and forth so ferociously that his boots flew off.

The beast wasted no time. It ate Walters with huge, gulping bites. Walters screamed from inside the monster's mouth as Steele fired point blank from the Thompson and tried to scramble away.

Cassidy crawled on all fours in the opposite direc-

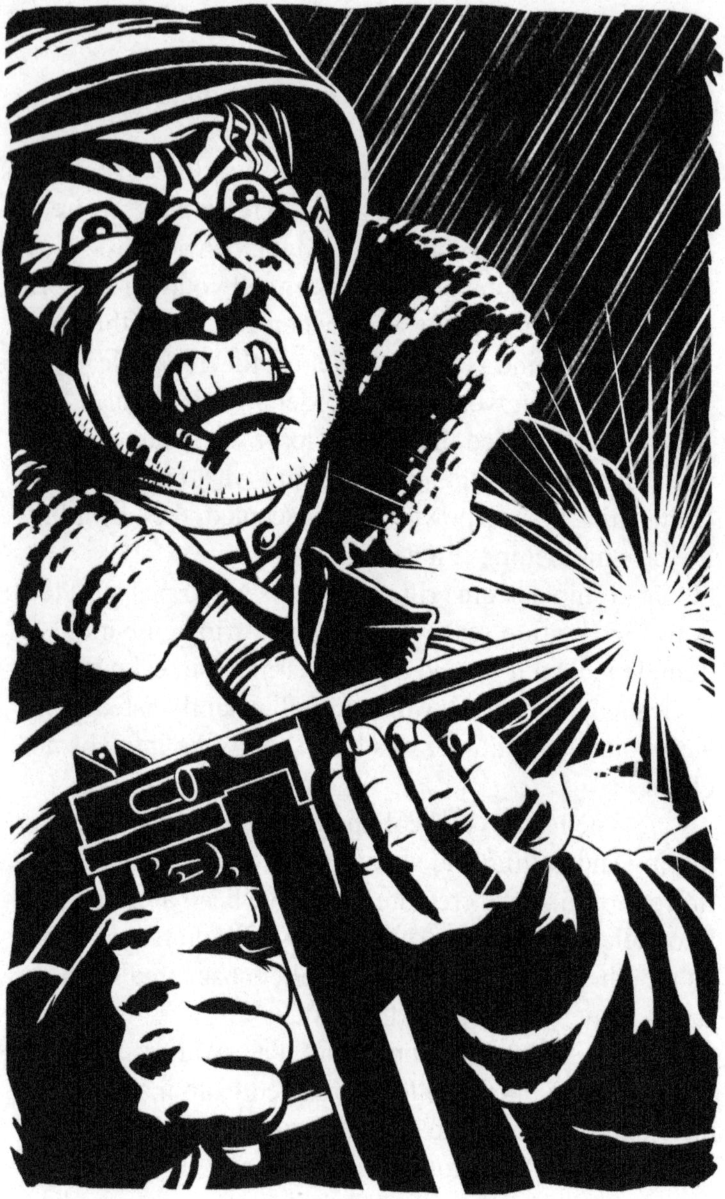

tion, and Temple leapt up over a small rise and blindly ran off.

Temple had never been so terrified, shocked to his core. The primordial fear in any living thing that has ever been hunted had been released. It was primal. It was pure. Temple ran, stumbling blindly, thinking of nothing but escape.

With his last glance back, Temple saw Steele standing defiantly, shooting his machine gun as the creature charged him and then swatted him down to the ground before pouncing on him. Unlike all the other men who had been attacked by the giant creature, Steele didn't scream or shriek. He died without uttering a sound.

Temple heard screams from Cassidy. Shots rang out. But Temple didn't care. He just had to get away. Fueled by pure adrenaline, he sprinted for the rocky shore. He climbed madly down the rocks and only stopped when his next step would have taken him into the rolling sea.

Temple clung to a rock with the sea just below him, the waves breaking at his feet. It wasn't really much of a fall into the water, except the jagged rocks below were covered by sharp barnacles and mussels. The water wasn't particularly deep, but it could still knock a man down, and it wouldn't let him up. It would pull him out into deeper water, water that was as cold as ice.

Temple was on the verge of mental collapse. For days he'd been tested. He had experienced levels of stress and anguish that only come with killing and knowing that someone is trying to kill you. He'd seen things that no one should have to see, and he'd done things that no one should have to do.

Above him—up there somewhere—there was more desperate screaming, and another shot rang out. Temple just closed his eyes and gripped the rock. He was a rat in a cage. The endless, torturing nightmare cut at him more and more deeply. Like a starfish, he clung to the rock, at the mercy of everything around him.

Temple's hands and feet ached, burning and freezing at the same time. He adjusted himself and found a footing. He slid down a few inches and was able to relax a little. He found a crook that he slid into, and he was able to pull his body into a tiny ball on a narrow ledge as the rain and the sea continued, as always, to surge and swirl.

Temple clung to his indentation in the rocks for hours, playing the same thoughts over and over. How did it come to this? How could this be? What could he have done to avoid this?

The questions were rhetorical. There were no answers. The longer it was quiet, the more he was able to think. Above the clouds, the moon was out. Occasionally, a thin spot in the clouds would allow a feeble beam of light to dance across the vast, moving ocean. Only the sounds of the ocean somehow soothed Temple and allowed him to think. Try to get to a weapon, get some warm clothes, see if Cassidy survived, he thought. He instinctively knew that Cassidy had not survived.

Temple almost began to move. Then he heard an unfamiliar sound and was struck again with fear and panic. The night was dark, but he could peek around the corner of his little alcove and make out a beach off to his left. The beach was perhaps thirty yards across and ten yards deep, covered with rocky pebbles and larger rocks that jutted out into the water and dropped beneath the waves.

Patches of moonlight pushed through the rolling clouds, and Temple froze at what he saw. There, sliding over the rocks, was the creature. Was it looking for him? Sniffing him out?

He held his breath and watched as it rooted around

on the beach. It opened its huge mouth, and the body of one of the men—maybe Cassidy—dropped out, mangled and torn. Thankfully, because of the darkness and the distance, Temple couldn't see who it actually was. He should have been revolted, but his mind was consumed with the idea of the creature spotting him and devouring him next. In the dim light, he could see the arms and legs of the dead man flopping around as the hulking thing consumed the man's torso.

Whatever it was, it was huge, bigger than anything he'd ever seen, even bigger than an elephant. But it was thick and round with a flipping tail that made determining its exact shape almost impossible. As it ate, the lifeless human body was little more than a rag doll in its thick claws and gaping mouth. Temple quaked with fear, unable to take his eyes off the nightmarish scene in the dim moonlight. Its tail slapped around in the surf as it devoured its meal. Temple could hear its teeth crunching through bone and tissue.

It hissed, growled, and angrily clawed at its food as it ate. Occasionally, it would stop and turn and scan the area, sending new shock waves of fear through Temple. To Temple, it sometimes seemed to move almost like a gorilla, and yet its neck was always low, its flat, square head close to the ground.

Temple was frozen to the rock, afraid to do little more than breathe and strain his eyes. Once again, his fear had a discovered a new level. He felt as if sharks were snapping at his heels. Only the forty or so yards between him and the creature helped him in any way. Of all the scenarios that ripped through his mind, the idea of just waiting until high tide and then slipping into the icy water and drowning seemed the most logical. His fingers were numb with cold, and he shivered uncontrollably. He had to do something, but he was paralyzed with fear.

When he thought he really could hang on no longer, he heard a rushing sound, not from the island he clung to but from behind of him, from the ocean, beyond the waves. He craned his neck around, trying to see. Mountains of clouds muscled in again, blocking the moon. The night went black, and he could see only streaks of bioluminescent algae glowing from the waves. He strained to see anything at all off in the distance when something much closer caught his eye.

A huge waterspout startled him, and he grappled to steady himself to avoid sliding into the pitching sea. Not twenty yards from the rocky edge, the telltale body slid by like a slow-moving freight train, some humongous species of whale was behind him. Temple closed his eyes hard and opened them wide as the giant tail gracefully rose up out of the water. The mammal lazily swam by. Further out was another whale, and Temple could just make out the spout of a third.

Temple watched, unsure how to react to something that wasn't terrifying, something that was actually extraordinary. As he pondered this new wonder, he noticed that the disgusting sound of the creature eating the body had stopped. Turning back, he was stunned to see that the creature was now standing on the beach. It hadn't missed the offshore spectacle.

The creature stopped eating, and chunks of flesh fell from its mouth as it rose up on its hind legs to get a better view. The creature gave a hissing roar and galloped full speed into the waves. Its tail gave a loud slap as it disappeared beneath the churning surface. Temple, for what seemed the millionth time, questioned whether this was some profoundly strange dream, some horrible nightmare from which he could never wake.

His feet, however, knew better. The beast was gone for the moment, and his legs pumped as he shimmied up the slippery rocks. His legs and arms were numb from being so cold and so still for so long, and he flailed and slipped around on the ground. Finding another small reserve of energy, he flung himself up over a small rise and hide in another angled nook. As soon as he stopped, he felt a tingling burn as the feeling returned to his limbs.

From offshore, the sound of a huge commotion reached the beach and quickly died out. Temple moved for cover. He swung himself around and dropped behind the rocks, just peeking over the edge. He reached up to adjust his helmet and touched his wet, matted hair. His helmet was gone. When the hell had he lost his helmet? How could he have missed that? He shuddered. It was now very apparent how bad off he really was.

The clouds thinned, and the moon illuminated the water and the cove. At first, Temple could see nothing. But he heard churning and splashing offshore. Above the breakers, the unmistakable growl of the creature mixed with the other sounds. A rush of foaming water sprayed thirty feet into the air. Temple watched wide-eyed, as the whale, a shiny, black behemoth, charged the beach with the creature firmly attached to its massive snout.

With a spray of foam and green water, the whale, moving at full speed, rammed the beast's back directly into a flat overhang just above the water. The howling of the monster was almost inaudible compared to the roar of the bellowing whale.

Temple slid down and lay flat on his stomach, watching the incredible battle, his hand firmly clasped over his mouth lest he gasp or utter some other stupid, uncontrollable sound.

The scene boggled his mind. The whale, with

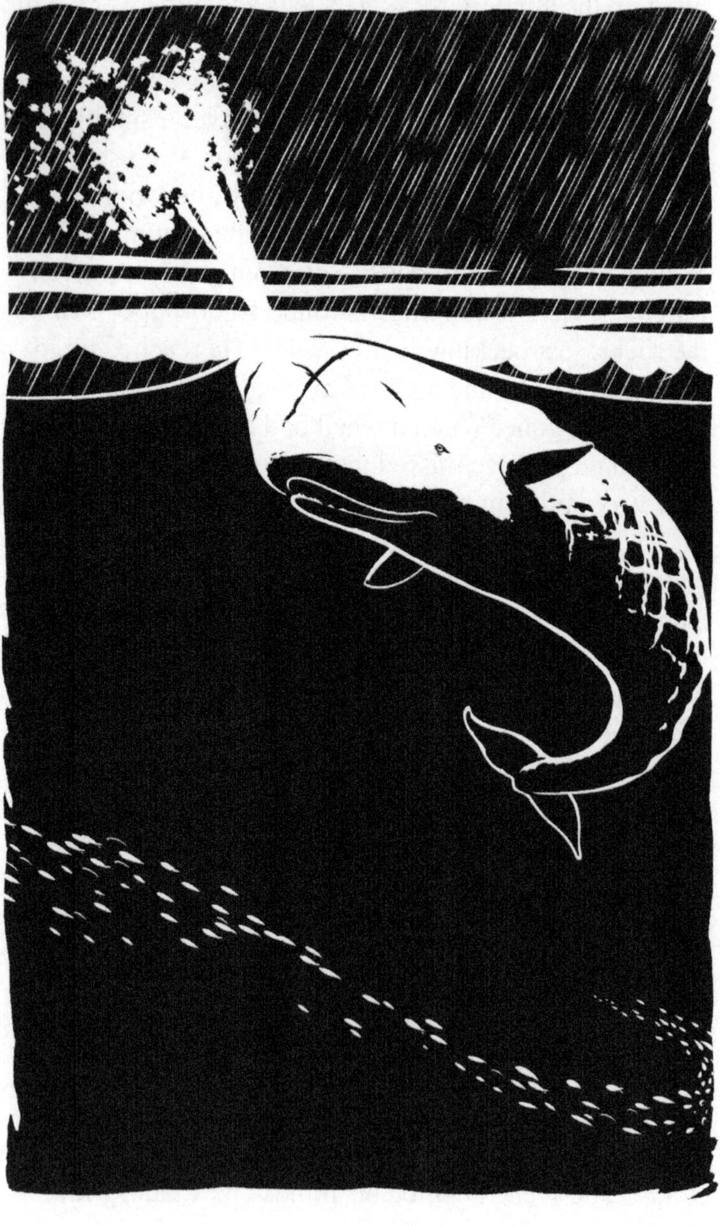

considerable effort, used its tail, which must have been a dozen feet wide, to pull itself back off the beach with a thrashing that produced an exploding spray of water. The creature seemed stunned. Still firmly attached to the whale, it moaned and hissed as its thick head flopped around on its neck. One of its arms was stuck in the barnacles and growths on the whale's head a few feet above the giant's eye.

The whale pulled back into the water, dragging the creature with it. Rocks crumbled and fell into the ocean as the whale dragged the monster off the wall. The creature had carved streaks of red into the whale's massive snout, but the whale was all but unaffected.

In that astonishing moment, the whale backed out to sea. The beast finally pulled free, just as the whale dropped down below the choppy surface. Temple could see that the beast was stunned. It floundered in the churning waves and didn't seem to know where it was or what it was doing.

The creature started for the shore, but one of the whale's companions, an even larger whale, probably the male, shot back up from below the creature. The surface of the water bulged like a giant bubble before the gigantic whale punched through with an explosion of water that blew into the sky. It was a direct hit. The creature shot out of the water and flew fifty feet into the air before slamming back down into a sloping rock wall that crumbled from the impact.

After a moment of quiet, the creature screamed and roared with agony. Temple was stunned. He had been certain that the fall from such a height would kill it.

Lying among the rocks, it moaned, hissed, and finally screeched. Temple hoped that its back was broken, and that all he'd have to do was put a steel pipe through its head. Yet, after just a few seconds, it rolled over, got up, and hissed. Amazingly, it seemed barely injured as it ambled up over the rocks and disappeared into the night.

Temple quaked with fear. He was in bad shape. He tried his best to look at his predicament rationally. It was some sort of beast, hearty as hell. There was no way he could kill it, but it wasn't magical or invincible. He had seen that it at least could be hurt. And it didn't seem to know he was there. Temple instantly had a plan: hide and stay hidden. There might be Krauts. There might be other men, his men. But to hell with them. He'll stay hidden and wait for the rescue. It was the only thing to do.

By his count, he had to stay alive for only five days. Then some Navy ship would arrive. When he and the rest of the men weren't at the rendezvous site, they would send a search boat. He'd hail it and get off this godforsaken rock, leaving the horrific memories and that thing behind. Perhaps the Navy could use a destroyer on the island and just wipe it off the map.

Temple waited and listened. He moved a few yards and then found another spot to hide. He moved from spot to spot and hid at each—sometimes for an hour or more—waiting, alert. He felt naked and helpless without a weapon of some sort, so he moved with the utmost care and fear.

It took him a full day to move back fewer than a hundred yards. He wasn't sure what kept him going, but continued. He drank water directly off the rocks or found little puddles and slurped them up. He found a shallow ravine. He dropped into it and slept for a couple of hours—maybe days, he had no way of knowing.

When he awoke, stiff and starving, the world looked the same, gray and wet, with puddles of watery blood becoming more and more diluted. He slowly made his way back toward their camp, winding around wet chunks of flesh that he knew were the remains of his comrades. In one smear of red, he discovered two more dog tags, picked them out, and shook off the hanging pieces of flesh and hair.

At what he guessed was midday, he slipped down the rocks by the little gravel beach. Their camp was a shambles. Their pathetic shelter had been torn down in the battle with the creature, and what little they had was strewn around on the ground.

Temple crept forward, scanning the horizon, trying to sense any movement, looking behind each boulder, expecting something awful, something deadly, ready to attack. Moving through the wreckage, he spotted a pistol wedged between two rocks. He picked it up. Then he jumped back and dropped it. Cassidy's hand still had a firm grip on the gun.

Temple gingerly lifted the gun by the barrel and jiggled it until the hand dropped off and flopped to the ground. Glancing nervously around, he wiped the handle of the gun on his pant leg. He pulled back the lever on the pistol and saw that there was still at least one round in the chamber. He dropped the clip out. It seemed to have a few rounds as well.

He holstered the pistol and felt a tiny bit better now that he was armed. It wouldn't be much use, but he didn't care. He did it anyway.

He scouted through the wreckage and the carnage. He saw Steele's tattered helmet and a trail of blood that went off over the hill.

He knew it had gotten Steele and regrettably put on the dead man's helmet. He looked for more guns but could find nothing. Somehow, Steele's cigarettes, with his lighter inside the cellophane, sat out in the open, almost undamaged. Temple didn't smoke, but he pocketed them

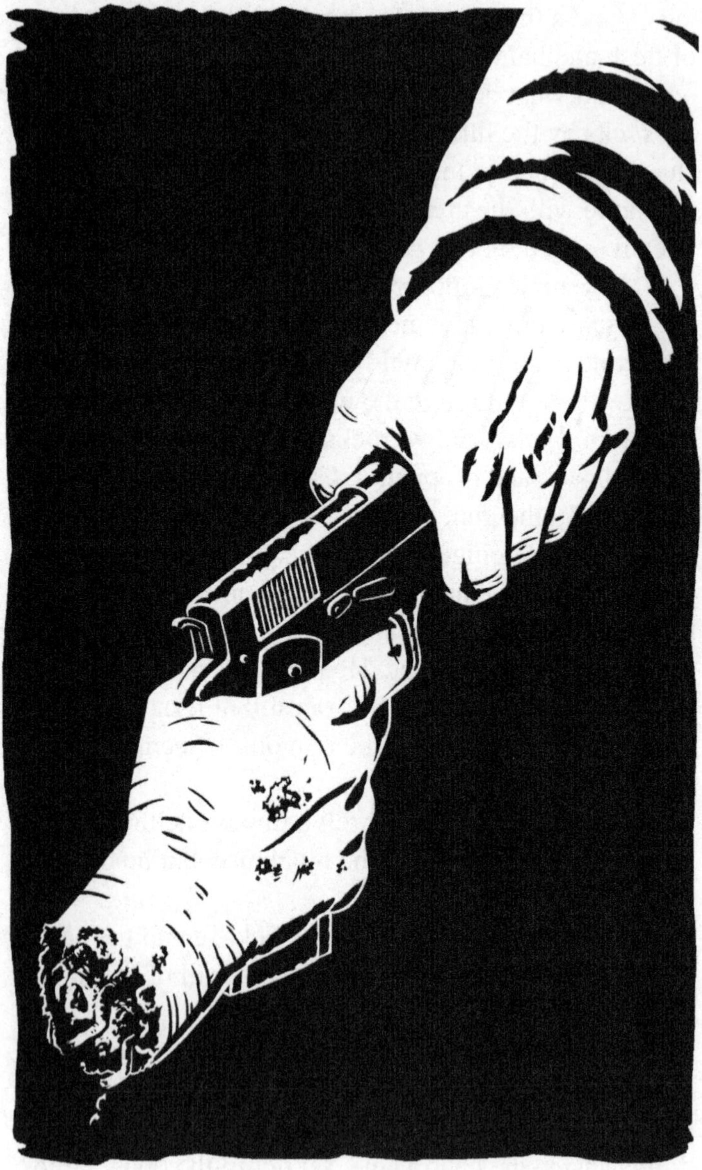

anyway, mostly for the lighter.

Temple's stomach ached from hunger. At the lean-to, now little more than a pile of splintered debris, he spotted a can of rations. He picked it up and moved away from the camp. The spot wasn't safe, and he wanted nothing to do with it. He wandered back into the valley of tall boulders until he found a small indentation up and out of the rain. It was about five feet off the ground and looked like a good place to hide for a while.

The rain picked up again, and the wind howled. He climbed up the rocks and perched in the little alcove. He felt hidden by the rain, but he also felt fearful because the creature seemed to come out when the weather was at its worst. He felt like a primitive creature himself now, huddled in this dry gouge in the rocks that wasn't much bigger than a phone booth. He was like a worm or a salamander, sliding around the rocks, terrified of what could drop down and pick him off at any time.

He crouched down and felt in his pockets. He still had O'Connor's flashlight. He'd lost his can opener but had his knife. He cut into the can. He didn't really know what starving meant. The German sailors had a better idea. But he was still so hungry that he felt stabbing pains in his gut; and when he swallowed, he could taste stomach bile.

He went to work on the can. He didn't care what was in it. He poked a first hole and poured a clear liquid onto his tongue. Canned peaches. Government issue, and they tasted great. He sucked the peach juice out of the can in one go.

It tasted so sweet as he slurped out every last drop. He eagerly cut the thin lid off with the knife and slurped out the soft peaches. They tasted like pure heaven.

He set the can down and took a sip from his

canteen. With a tiny bit of food in his gut, fatigue overtook him once more. He closed his eyes briefly, just to rest them. He fell deeply asleep. He slept, curled tightly, for a few hours.

He awoke with a start. He had heard something. Around him, the world was still the same shades of gray and black, and he could make out the rocks and a dim glow from the moon somewhere above the ever-pissing clouds. What had he heard? He tried to clear his thoughts. Was it a gunshot? Did he hear a shot? Did someone call to him? Was it that thing? What was it?

A flash of lightning scared him, but he relaxed slightly when he heard the distant rumble of thunder. It must have been thunder that had awoken him. Instinctively, he reached for his pistol and found it secure in his holster. He relaxed a little more when he felt the butt of the gun against his hand. His body was taut and sore from being cramped in the tiny space. He turned and moved his legs out. He swung his feet around, bumping the empty peach can, now filled with rain. It teetered and then rolled loudly down the rocks, bouncing and clanging.

Temple held his breath, but it was too late. He suddenly had a sinking feeling that it wasn't thunder that had awoken him. He poked his head out at the exact wrong moment, for the creature was just beyond the mound. It spotted his head moving.

It saw Temple, reared up, and screeched at him. Temple felt his legs kick into gear as his animal instincts took over. He burst from his hiding spot and dashed over the rocks, fumbling with his holster for his pistol. He could hear the heavy pounding of the creature's claws on the rocks behind him as it closed in.

Running for his life, Temple dove, slid, and turned over the rocks, as sure-footed as he'd ever been. But the creature was too fast, and Temple could hear the growl and its breathing as it closed in on him. It ran on all fours, galloping and grabbing at the terrain, flinging itself along at a staggering speed.

Temple rounded another corner through a deep ravine, running like he'd never run before. With the creature closing in on him, he glanced down and fumbled for the holstered gun. He looked up again and, slipping and sliding, stopped abruptly. The barrel of a machine gun was aimed directly at his chest.

In the shadows behind the mounted gun, Temple could see the outline of whoever was manning the weapon. Instinctively, he dropped to the ground, and the machine gun opened up.

The MG 42 machine gun fires a thousand rounds per minute and sounds more like a roar than rapidly fired shots. The gunner had perfect aim, and the creature leapt directly into the line of fire. Temple rolled over and covered his ears, as the gun, deafeningly loud, belched out a white hot fire of searing metal just three feet above Temple's head.

The concussion blast was so jarring that it made him think he might have been hit by a ricochet or something. Small pieces of still-burning gunpowder rained down on him as he watched. More than a dozen bullets found their mark on the creature.

The giant beast writhed and jerked at the onslaught. It let out a screech louder than the roaring machine gun. With a violent twist and a jerk, it leapt upward and beyond the tilt of the mounted gun.

With a deafening scream, it was gone.

Temple lay on the ground in the wet gravel, a large stone uncomfortably jabbing at his back. He held still until he felt a burning. He wiped at his neck. An

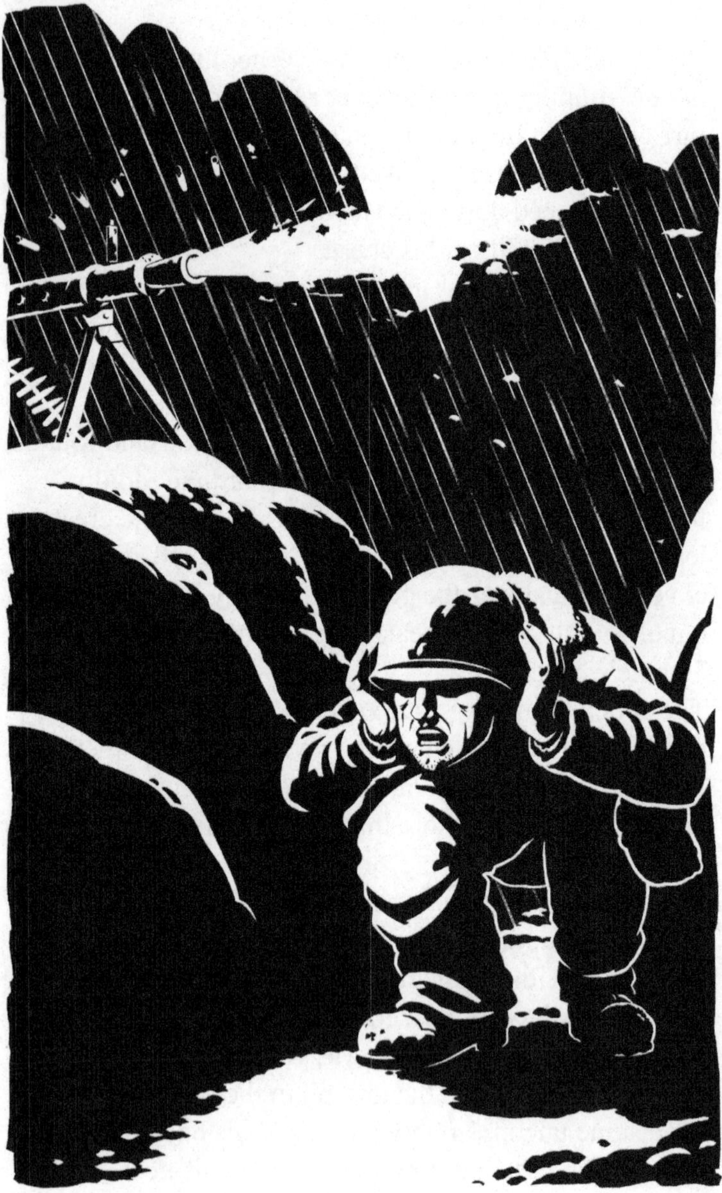

ejected shell from the machine gun had dropped into his coat collar.

He gasped for breath and moved to get up, when an outstretched hand from above reached down. He clasped the black-gloved hand that pulled him to his feet. He stepped around the machine gun and stood between the towering rocks.

Temple stood face to face with Captain Fessenden, the U-boat commander. Fessenden wore a tattered leather coat and a ratty captain's hat. A small machine-gun pistol hung from a strap under his arm. The captain looked ragged and worn. His face was smeared with grease, soot, and dried blood. His eyes were bloodshot and floated in deep, dark sockets. He, too, was a man on the edge.

Temple looked at the captain blankly, but he put his right hand on his holster and found the butt of his pistol.

The captain noticed it. "Yes, you have a pistol or a knife. I've got one too. But I think, considering the other indigenous inhabitant of this island, we should postpone our cultural hatred and mistrust for the time being."

The captain picked up a rifle and studied the tall, jagged cliffs around them. "Regrettably, I don't think I've killed it but maybe I hurt it this time. At least it's run off for the moment."

Temple was surprised that this weary man spoke perfect English.

The captain continued, speaking more to himself than to Temple. "How is that possible? What kind of armor must this thing have? I've seen a machine gun like this destroy a vehicle. It's just not possible," he muttered.

"You speak perfect English," Temple said. It was all Temple could think of to say.

Captain Fessenden studied Temple. "When I was

a boy, I spent summers in Connecticut with my relatives. Do you know Connecticut?"

"Never been," Temple said. "I'm from California." Temple stopped short and tensed up. He realized that he was having a friendly chat with the enemy.

Fessenden sensed Temple's reserve. He closed his eyes and rubbed his head. He pulled himself up straight. He stuck out his hand and formally introduced himself. "I'm Otto Fessenden. I was the captain until my sub ran aground —over there." He pointed off into the distance.

"Well…" Temple returned the handshake with awkward courtesy. "I'm Lawrence Temple, United States Navy, Second Seabees Division."

Fessenden gave him a questioning look. He didn't know the term.

"We're engineers. We build stuff—bridges, airfields, whatever is needed. Seabee, like *C-B*." He drew in midair with his finger. "Construction battalion. That explosion—when your men attacked—that was the gas for the generator for the installation we were going to build. It destroyed almost everything."

"Let's go back to my camp. It's not safe in this narrow canyon. The creature could easily trap us in here."

Temple looked up at the surrounding walls and realized that the captain was right. Temple eyed the huge machine gun behind them.

"Wait. Shouldn't we take that?" He motioned to the machine gun sitting on its tripod. Wisps of smoke still drifted from the barrel.

"No point," Fessenden said. "I just used the last of the ammunition saving you." He turned and headed away with Temple following.

Winds picked up, and the rain continued as they slid over rocks, working their way back to the German outpost.

An hour later, Temple and Fessenden came out of the rain and into the German shelter. Temple was impressed. Fessenden had an orderly, dry little base, surrounded by the usable remnants from the sub—life jackets, uniforms, weapons, all organized into a tight bunker, a dry bunker. A tidy, flat bed could hold perhaps five or six, Temple guessed. One spot looked as if it had once held a wounded sailor, for a dark red stain covered the cloth. But the makeshift bunk was now empty.

Using uniforms and dead men's shirts and underwear, he and Fessenden dried off. Then they put on dry coveralls and pulled on thick wool coats. They used all manner of uniforms to bundle up. Temple couldn't remember how long it had been since he'd been dry.

"I'm sorry, but I don't have much in the way of food to offer you—just this clam stew Liebe made." He offered a cold cup to Temple. "Honestly, it's revolting, but we are starving."

"We've got … I mean … I've got a rations back at my spot. We just have to go … out there to get them."

They sat in silence. It was awkward. Staring off into the rain, Fessenden broke the quiet. "Listen to me. I know we were sworn enemies. It's hard to get past that. But I don't want to be killed by that thing. I want to live, and I'm guessing you do, too. We're all that's left. Do you get that? And I want to get off this rock—alive. I don't know how or when, but I want to try. I've endured too much not to try." He studied Temple, and his gaze was unflinching.

"A ship is coming for me—in four days, maybe. I lost count. I don't know what day it is. We were supposed to have built a radio installation and antenna and then gone off shore to meet the ship. Our rubber boats were destroyed when our fuel exploded. When we don't show, they'll send a search party to look for us."

The captain leapt at the news. He leaned into Temple. "A ship? A ship is coming here?" He closed his eyes and exhaled. Temple could see the exhaustion in his face, the weariness of so much catastrophe and disaster. Fessenden rubbed his face, and Temple saw the tears of relief forming in the corners of his weary eyes. The captain actually smiled and whispered to Temple. "OK, OK, OK. Four days. Four damned days. That is possible. We can stay alive. I believe we can do it. I formally surrender and am your willing prisoner."

He clapped Temple on the shoulder, and Temple was startled by the gesture. Temple was simply happy to be dry.

"We have to try, right?" the Captain said as enthusiastically as he could. "Maybe we can keep it occupied, somehow, long enough for us to get out of here.

"I think I know where it lives," Temple offered.

The captain looked at Temple, and Temple saw something he hadn't seen in a man's face for a long time. He saw it just behind the captain's bloodshot eyes. It was unmistakable. He saw hope.

The captain rubbed his hands together and looked off into the distance. "Then, perhaps we have a chance."

13.

Together, each man looking out for the other, they made their way back to the American camp. With its broken equipment and chunks of bodies strewn about, it was pitiful. The captain stood guard as Temple rooted through the soggy items, and Fessenden was happy to see him retrieve several stacks of unopened rations.

They scooped up the food and grabbed a few more useful items—the last two grenades, the smoke grenades, and a good length of a slightly burned but sound rope. Temple grabbed the dozen or so rounds of ammunition that he had left and stuck them into his pocket.

Together the two men made their way back through what had been no-man's-land, where they had all fought so brutally. Blood stained the rocks here and there, and Temple found Steele's submachine gun. He picked it up and pulled back the clip. It had a few rounds in it.

The captain watched as Temple checked the weapon. The weary captain didn't move. He held his breath. If Temple had a change of heart, he could easily just aim that gun at Fessenden right now and finish him.

But the captain was certain that Temple had no such ideas; he wasn't that kind of person. They needed each other now, and Temple didn't seem to be the resourceful type.

Together they scouted around the ground for anything useful. The captain found Steele's mangled dog tags and handed them to Temple. Then carefully and quietly they worked their way back to the German shelter.

When they had tallied the few bent cans of this and several packs of that, they determined that they had plenty of food. For the first time in countless days, the captain had real food. Each man ate a filling meal of cold but welcome rations. From the abandoned uniforms and equipment, they were both able to find gloves, hats, and thicker boots. The clothes were still damp with the salty sea air, and Temple was not convinced that they would ever be dry again. But now, at least, they weren't soaked and cold; they were just damp and warm. Who'd have thought that would be preferable, he wondered.

They ate food. The captain's belly was full. At first, the shock nauseated him, and he ordered himself not to vomit. He would choke it back. He wasn't going to waste this wonderful full feeling. He drank liberally from a canteen, and that seemed to ease his nausea. As the food sank in, he became very sleepy. They both did.

With half-closed eyes, they discussed everything they'd learned about the creature. They agreed that it prowled the island when the weather was at its worst and that, despite its thousands of pounds, it could be stealthy and almost silent when it wanted to be, a truly formidable killer. They knew it could be hurt, but it wasn't likely they could ever kill it. It didn't seem to have a great sense of smell but was perhaps driven by sound.

"I think it's more of a sea creature, an amphibious thing," the captain reasoned.

"It can swim like the dickens," Temple said. "It's as comfortable in the water as it is out of the water, maybe even more so. It attacked a damn whale, for Chrissake."

Temple offered Fessenden a cigarette, and Fessenden gladly accepted. The captain noticed there were only three more in the pack.

"Are you sure you want to give up one of your last cigarettes?" he asked.

"I don't smoke. I found them back there. They were Steele's. He's done with them." Temple handed the captain his Zippo lighter.

The captain took the pack, lit up the cigarette, and inhaled deeply. He exhaled warm jets of smoke out of his nostrils. "Hitler and his insane cronies were foolish to think they could ever go up against a country that could grow tobacco as fine as this," the captain murmured.

The captain opened a ration of dry crackers and offered the first one to Temple. Temple accepted it and handed the Captain a small can of cold vegetable soup he'd been sipping from. Fessenden took a sip, closing his eyes and savoring the flavor. They sat in silence for a long time, each man deep in his own thoughts, and fears. Finally the captain spoke up, while looking out at the driving wind and rain.

"Temple, that sounds Jewish," He said.

"It is, but I'm not, my father was, but my mother wasn't. Your mother has to be Jewish for you to be officially Jewish. We didn't have a very religious family, anyway.

"You know, my neighbor in Heidelberg he was a Jew, Abe Eisenhändler, he came from a family that had their own mountain in the east, actual old world royalty. He was an advertising illustrator, and worked in

Frankfurt, but came home to Heidelberg on the weekends. He was a lovely man, and such a talent, their whole family was so nice, they were our good friends, we even had dinner a few times a year. One day, I came out to go to work, it was a cold morning, and I remember it so clearly. It was a few weeks before the notorious Crystal Night. I came out, expecting to see him on his way to the bus stop, but instead his house was empty, completely empty, not a scrap of paper, nothing. It shocked me. It was as if they'd vanished, almost as if they'd never been, but I guess that was the point, one way or another. I have no idea what happened to him, or the family. I hope he had the good sense to leave." He stared blankly into the rain. "Ah, he was a very smart fellow, I'm sure he and his family slipped away, I hope so anyway. "

"You weren't a career sailor?" Temple asked.

"Me? God, no. I wanted nothing to do with the Military. I was a public accountant. I used to spend my summers with a Swiss cousin sailing and boating on Lake Geneva, and in Connecticut as well, I always loved the water. You see, I came from money, so I thought I was immune to all of this. At first it was easy to avoid the whole craze, but you could see it getting more and more fevered every single day. After the war really started, you didn't have a choice, you were either with them or against them. I joined up, hoping to get a quiet job someplace to hide out the war. My father was going to help me, he had friends in high places, but somewhere I made the mistake of mentioning my boating experiences. As you can see, it didn't turn out the way I had planned."

They continued to talk. They wondered what they could do to last just a few more days on this isolated chunk of land. The captain thought they should check out the creature's lair to see if there was a way to trap it or ambush it. But as he spoke, he grew more and more tired. The two men finally passed out sitting across from each other, warm and fed.

The captain did not dream. He was unconscious for what seemed like a blissful eternity. Only a painful jab in his ribs finally awakened him. He woke to the all-too-familiar sound of driving wind and rain as a new storm battered the island. As his eyes focused, he was startled to see Temple's face just inches from his own. In the dim, predawn light, Fessenden could barely see Temple's wide and terrified eyes. Without making a sound, Temple pointed up with a shaking finger. The captain knew exactly what he meant. The creature was near, hunting around up above them, just beyond the next rise of rock.

The captain went for the machine-gun pistol hanging at his side. He gripped it and held it close. The gun provided little real comfort. An MG 42 machine gun, with its huge slugs, hadn't killed the creature There was no way the tiny pistol could do anything worse. But he reasoned, as Caspar had, that if it got close, he would shoot for the eyes or into the mouth. If it got closer, he'd use the final round on himself. There was no way he was going to be eaten alive. He'd heard the screams of Burman. If he lived, he would never be able to shake those horrific screams.

Temple had Steele's Thompson. He held it close. Fessenden could see that Temple's tight grip had turned the tips of his fingers white. They listened. They could hear the beast slapping around on the rocks just a few yards away. It's weight sent deep vibrations through the rock pile with each thundering step. They couldn't see the creature, but they could hear it. They could even smell it. The tension was maddening.

Now, up close and not on the attack, the creature

sounded different. Instead of roaring and screeching, it made strange guttural gurgling sounds. Its roar was now more of a cry. It was so close to their shelter that each sound it made was more unnerving that the previous one.

The captain whispered so softly that Temple could barely hear him. "How's your arm?"

Temple, trembling with fear, didn't understand what the captain meant.

The captain reached behind them into their combined store of weapons and fished out a grenade. They could hear the strange howling and growling just above them and to their left. The captain silently stepped out of the cave, pulled the pin, and, with all his might, hurled the grenade as far as he could, up and over to the right. It was good throw. The grenade sailed into the air and exploded before hitting the ground. The crack echoed across the island, and they heard the distinct angry growl of the creature as it stormed off to investigate the noise.

"Do you think it's looking for us?" Temple whispered.

"I do," the captain answered. "I don't think it can smell us, but, somehow, I think it knows we're here. OK, let's go now. Show me where it came from while it's distracted."

Temple was horrified by the idea, but Fessenden was right. It was now or never. They could be sure it wasn't at home. The captain yanked Temple to his feet, and they stumbled off across the island.

Temple led the captain over rock fields and through a narrow pass. He got turned around twice, but eventually they emerged on the other side of the island on the smooth face of rock where Temple had slid down, dodging the machine gun. Ahead of them, the pit was visible. As Temple and Fessenden stepped slowly to the edge, the stench from the pit was also unmistakable.

"It's deep, deeper than I expected," the captain said.

Temple shone his flashlight down into the pit, but the light did no good. It was too deep. It did have a bottom of driftwood and debris. They could faintly see it. But it was too deep for them to jump down into. The captain lay down on his stomach and slid up to the edge, peeking in. He grabbed a handful of pebbles and dropped them in.

"I wish we had a flare," he said.

"Me too. Ours went up with the gas and the dynamite and everything else."

"Ours are at the bottom of the sea," Fessenden said as he climbed to his feet. "The creature must have an entrance from the sea. Despite its size, I don't think it can come out this way. It's just too high."

"What good does that—"

"Shhhh. Listen," the captain whispered.

From the cavern came the distinct sound of waves and lapping water.

"You're right. I can hear it. The creature must have a tunnel out to the water."

The rain picked up as Fessenden peered into the stinking black cavern.

"I've got a really stupid idea that probably won't work—but it might. Let's get out of here before it comes back."

The two men cautiously worked their way back to the German camp. It was daylight now, but the turbulent weather blocked any sun, while winds whipped and lashed at them mercilessly. They climbed over the rocks and followed the path through the narrow ravines back to the German base.

Temple stooped into the cave, immediately dropping on a pile of uniforms and life jackets. Fessenden sifted through the materials that his crew had salvaged before the sea swallowed what was left of the U-boat. As he rummaged, he gathered up rope and wire.

"What are you looking for? " Temple asked.

"Perhaps we can make an explosive device," the captain said, as he wound a coil of wire.

"A bomb? All our TNT was destroyed. I don't think we have enough ammo to make one. We're out of any real ammo."

The captain found a bayonet. He rubbed the tip vigorously on a rock. "We're not entirely out of ammunition," he said.

"What do you mean?"

Fessenden set down the bayonet, stepped out of the shelter, and cautiously led Temple down to the water's edge. Temple followed, gun in hand. On the rocks at the waterline lay the destroyed sub. The beach and the shallow water were still littered with debris that rolled back and forth in the waves. The captain climbed over rocks and pulled a wad of seaweed from between two barnacle-covered boulders.

"We've got this," he said.

Fessenden peeled back the seaweed to reveal the shiny brass nose of a German Mark IV torpedo. The weapon's eighteen-foot body was bent and twisted, but the front end was completely intact. Its polished surface dazzled Temple.

"That's a torpedo," Temple murmured.

"Yes, it is. It's packed with explosives, a battery, and a detonator. Perhaps we can use it on our friend in his pit. Or at least we can trap him there long enough for us to be rescued by your ship."

Temple felt a smile spreading over his face. "Holy shit. Why not? What do we have to lose?"

The captain nodded his head, and he formulated a plan. They made another trip to the ruined American camp. They found usable lumber, cord, wire, metal rebar, and a burned but usable tent piece. Together they moved all of the usable materials from the beach to the other side of the island. Work was slow because every few minutes they were forced to stop and listen and wait, always terrified that the creature had found them.

On the last trip, Temple looked around the remains of the shelter once more. He spotted the dog tags that had been collected, hanging on a splinter of broken wood. He stuffed them in his pocket. He was happy to be leaving this spot on earth. He hoped never to return to it.

Back at the German camp with their supplies, Fessenden was quiet, obviously working out the details of his plan. He smoked another of his last two cigarettes. Temple didn't mind the silence. He was full and neither freezing cold nor dripping wet. He felt better than he had in a long time, despite what was out there just beyond the rocks.

Temple drifted off to sleep, realizing that this was the first night in a long time that he hadn't fallen asleep terrified. He was wedged into the cave on what had been a German bunk, lying on his side in a bed of old uniforms. Fessenden was seated in front of him, his machine-gun pistol at the ready.

As crazy as it seemed, Temple actually felt safe when Fessenden was on guard. He slept heavily until Fessenden gently woke him and they switched shifts. There was no sign of the creature, and Temple wondered if the big machine gun had done more damage than they'd realized.

Maybe the American ship would arrive, and they'd never see the creature again. They'd get the hell off this godforsaken rock forever. But it just didn't seem likely. Temple worried that it was keenly aware of them—out there just beneath the waves or behind a slope of rock. Maybe it was toying with them, knowing that they were stranded on the island and that it had nothing but time. Temple had thought it wasn't capable of such complex thought—it seemed like a wild animal—but there was no way of being sure.

As the new day began, Fessenden and Temple worked as a team, one man as a general guard, keeping a weary eye out for the creature, while the other ate, worked, and slept. When Temple was guarding, he watched Fessenden. He was astounded by the precision with which the U-boat captain worked.

Using rebar and rope gathered at the American camp, Fessenden improvised a litter for moving the torpedo warhead. The captain was formulating a plan. He drew rough plans on the back of a life jacket with a burnt stick. Temple understood immediately. Together, using the burned lumber from the American supplies, they assembled a pair of tall sawhorses with a metal bar across the top. Temple wasn't sure this idea would work, but the project gave them something to do, something to keep their minds off what had happened and what could happen.

They had no nails or screws, but if they had, they would have been too worried about the hammering noise to use them. Fessenden was clever. He showed Temple how to notch the long planks so that they could be tied together with wire originally meant for the antenna. Temple knew how to build, and he felt helpful as he and this German captain put together the contraption.

When the frame was complete, Fessenden set about

taking the torpedo apart. He draped the torn tent piece over the torpedo as he prepared to do mechanical surgery.

"We must keep it dry once I open the case. Don't worry. There's no danger." He realized what he had said as Temple glanced around the barren landscape. "I mean of it exploding," he added.

Using the bayonet, he pried off the outer casing pieces of the torpedo. Inside, bundles of wires and fittings wrapped the warhead housing.

Temple held the machine gun tight against his hip, always vigilant. The creature would be back. Soon enough. When it was dark. When the creature was ready, it would be back. He was never so sure of anything in his life. It was a horrible feeling, but he knew it was true.

As the captain worked on the torpedo, he talked to Temple. "Here's what I'm thinking. It takes a very solid hit on the tip of this to set it off once it's armed. We set the frame at the mouth of the pit. Then we hang the warhead down from it so that it's hanging over the edge attached to this rope. Once it's in place, we cut the rope, and gravity does the rest. It falls, nose down, hitting the detonator on the rocks below. Should be enough to set it off. It blows and collapses the cave. Maybe the blast will kill the thing. Maybe not. Depends on where it is. We'll hope it at least does enough damage to keep the creature at bay until your ship arrives," the captain said dryly, knowing the chance of success was profoundly small.

Using the bayonet, Fessenden worked on one of the dozens of screws on the warhead. He fumbled with it, trying again and again.

"What's wrong?" Temple asked, dismayed to see the captain, who worked like a surgeon, fumbling.

"I thought I'd be able to improvise a screwdriver with this bayonet, but it's not working. If I keep it up, I'm going to strip out this screw, and I'll never get it out."

Fessenden got up and rubbed the bayonet on a rock again, trying to create a more screwdriver-like shape. Temple sifted through the pile things taken from the dead men. Digging through the pockets of the torn trousers and coats looking for a tool they could use was ghastly work. Most of the clothing was caked with rotting blood that was sticky and smelled foul. The only things he came up with were a can opener and a pocketknife. He handed them to Fessenden, who studied them, tried them, and then gave up. Nothing worked.

Temple's hopes began to fade as Fessenden worked relentlessly, trying to file and shape tools. In the end, nothing worked. Out of frustration, Fessenden twisted the can opener too hard and scraped the skin off his knuckles. He bolted upright, shouting a curse in German, and threw the can opener to the ground.

"It's no goddamn use. I need a screwdriver—and a big one at that."

Temple walked back and forth, watching the horizon as he talked. "Damn! We had a whole tool set, but that stuff was lost when our supplies exploded. I mean, we could poke around the rocks to see if any of the tools are still around. There's no telling, with that explosion, how far things got thrown. It's anyone's guess where all that stuff wound up."

Fessenden stood up over the torpedo and stretched. The rain had become just a slight drizzle. Fessenden looked thoughtfully at his scraped knuckles. He peeled off a little piece of skin and looked down the short slope to the water's edge.

"I know where there are more tools, a whole tool set, in fact." He turned and pointed to what was left of the submarine wedged between the rocks. The churning sea had been rough on the massive boat. The front was torn off, but the body was mostly intact until about midship. Obviously, the fire that had gutted the engine room had compromised the metal structure, and the sub beyond its midsection was, after just a few days in the savage North Atlantic, a twisted, crumpled wreck, crowned with two large brass propellers that poked up from the waves at low tide.

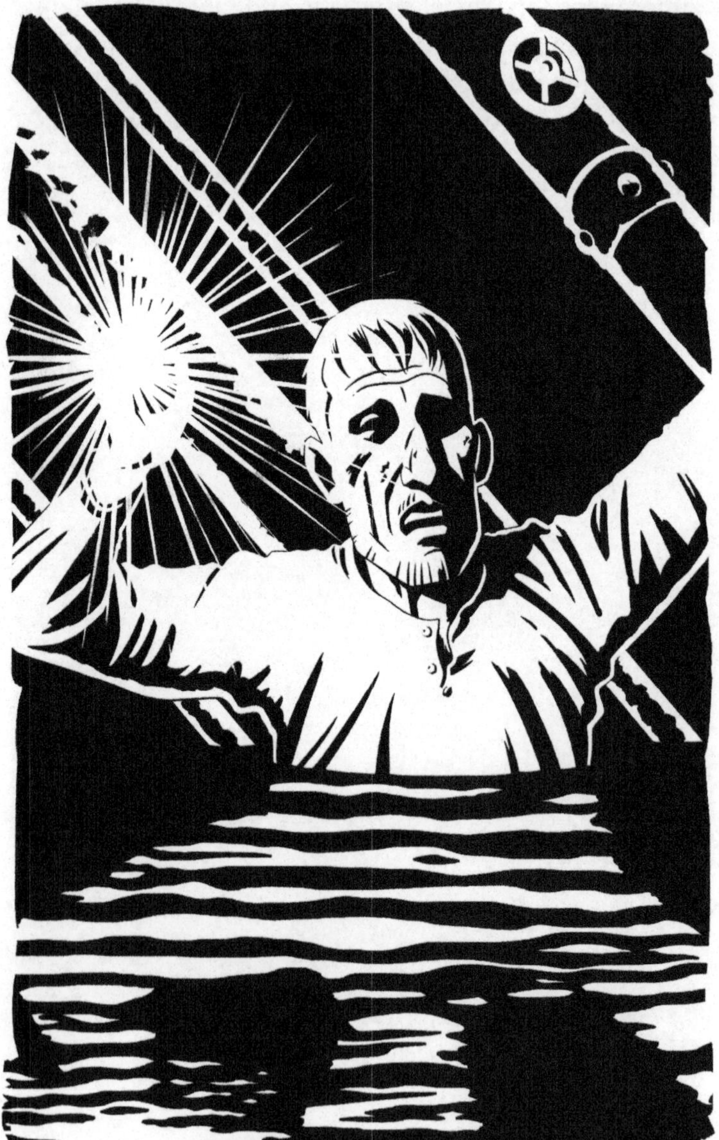

14.

Fessenden, wearing just his long underwear and a scavenged pair of boots, stepped down into the choppy waves as they broke on the boulder-strewn shoreline.

The waves were comparatively calm. Fessenden cinched the rope around his middle. Temple stood on the beach, bracing against a rock as he let out a steady stream of rope. They looked at each other silently—no need for words. They had to try. They had to try to do something, even as insane as this seemed. Under the circumstances, it was all they had. Fessenden moved across the side of the sub. He'd been cold since landing on the island, but he'd somehow forgotten how cold the ocean was. His feet and legs began to ache immediately.

Fessenden knew the sub, knew that the tools were in a storage compartment immediately outside the engine room. With the sub on its side and the top almost sheared off, he thought he should be able to climb through and up and get at the tools—that is, if they were properly secured when the ship ran into trouble.

He estimated that the swimming would simply be

a dunking. The waterproof flashlight was tucked under his arm. He pulled it out and clicked it on. He dipped into the icy water and felt the edge of a ragged hole just a few feet away. Fessenden took a huge breath and then ducked his head below the water. He dipped below the jagged metal and cautiously surfaced on the other side, the flashlight shining ahead. He shivered uncontrollably as he shone the light around the derelict ship.

Fessenden thought he'd have no problem orienting himself in the twisted chunk of the sub. He knew every inch of the thing by heart. But as soon as he surfaced inside the hulk, climbing onto a metal beam to be free of the icy water, he realized how damaged the boat truly was. The hull was already so broken that here and there little slivers of light shone through. The captain had hoped he'd not surface right next to a dead body, of one of his men. He'd already prepared himself to see the now-bloated remains of crewmen who never made it out. Yet as he shone the feeble light around, he was relieved to see no corpses. He briefly wondered if they'd already been swept out to sea.

The sub, apparently, wasn't as solidly grounded as it had appeared to be from the outside. It shifted and pitched slightly in the current. The waves outside the ship slapped against the hull, and the sounds of dripping, creaking, and the bending of metal were amplified inside the hull, creating a cacophony of painful noises in the now-dead ship.

Fessenden had hoped he'd go right to his target. But his idea of establishing his location and finding the tool cabinet now seemed perhaps impossible. He moved along, baffled by the twisted mess of wires, pipes, metal, and other debris. The dank tomb was all but unrecognizable. He had to squirm and duck and even dip back into the water briefly to pass through another tangled section. The ceiling was now the floor and was a maze of broken pipes, valves, and other dislodged equipment.

He recognized the upside-down stove and the white floor of the galley above his head, and he continued, guided by the feeble flashlight. The ship groaned and creaked in a hundred different places as the sea worked to dismantle this metal folly of man.

The North Atlantic was slow but relentless, and the process of taking the hulking metal craft apart was already well underway. Fessenden knew that the sea wouldn't give up. As the ship sat there, it would eventually dissolve. It might take fifty years, maybe a hundred, but eventually the sea would eat the vessel until it was nothing more than hunks of rusted metal. Even those would eventually wind up as oxidized particles of debris in the vast, empty sea.

Randomly, Fessenden called up a memory of his college chemistry professor. "Water: the universal solvent!" the old man always proclaimed. And it was true. Fessenden could attest to that from his steel boat in the middle of a salty ocean. The whole thing was slowly and continuously dissolving.

Fessenden's brief dip into the water had sent frigid chills through his body, and his legs and feet were still throbbing and numb. He maneuvered slowly and carefully through the upside-down craft, careful not to snag or cut himself on the countless broken and splintered objects that turned the interior of the sub into a dangerous labyrinth. He passed over the gaping hole where the conning tower had been, the upper bridge deck crushed and below the water. What a waste, Fessenden thought. Just like everything else about this war—the lives, the materials, the effort, all of it. Wasted.

Outside, Temple hung on as the rope moved out in a steady flow. He was standing near the shore where the sub was wedged. He could see the tail of the boat—upside down with its massive brass propeller occasionally appearing above the waves. Even as a wreck, the sub was big. Temple marveled at its size. It was two hundred and twenty feet long and thirty-five feet tall from top to bottom. Even tilted on its side, it was taller than any buildings in Temple's small hometown.

He found a slight protrusion to stand under to shield himself from the rain and wind as the rope slowly crept out. With one hand on the machine gun, Temple kept a watchful eye around him. He knew what the captain knew. The thing was practically invincible. Hell, a god damned whale had launched it fifty feet into the air, and it had survived.

The pitiful gun wasn't much consolation, but he had to be ready. If the creature came, he would tug on the rope hard, three times, to signal Fessenden. Two tugs would be just to check in. He also told himself, just as the Captain and Caspar had told themselves, that if the creature appeared either from the rocks our out of the sea, he wasn't going to be trigger happy. He had little ammo, and he would have to wait until it was on top of him. He would aim toward the head or the face.

Inside the sub, Fessenden again dipped into the icy water to swim below a collapsed wall and reemerge on the other side. He figured he was close to the bulkhead that was in front of the engine room. He shone the light around and up, and behind a mass of wires and pipes was the tool stowage. He was relieved to see that it was still sealed. He climbed up on a pile of debris but discovered that a girder had dropped and was blocking the bottom of the metal door to the cabinet. The girder was solid steel. He pushed and pulled, but it was simply too heavy to move. He looked around for some other odd piece of metal to perhaps use as a lever but found nothing. Running out of ideas, Fessenden even swung himself into a position where he could try and free it by pushing with both his numb feet, but it was no use. It was too heavy, and he was too weak.

Outside, Temple noticed the rope go slack. He felt a wave of panic. He reeled it in until it was slightly taut, but it went slack again. He gathered up the slack. He gave two short tugs to signal Fessenden. Two short tugs responded, and Temple began to reel the rope in. He continued to gather the rope until, finally, Fessenden's head popped up from beside the tall steel wall that was the side of the sub. Fessenden hung on to the rope, and Temple helped him ashore. Fessenden's teeth were chattering. Temple grabbed a tattered and burned sleeping bag and tossed it around Fessenden. Fessenden sat down.

"Did you find one? Did you find a screwdriver?" Temple asked.

Fessenden nodded slowly as he dried his head. "I found the tool cabinet, but a piece a steel beam is blocking it. I need a lever or something, and then I don't know if even that will be enough to pry it loose."

"Well, we've got to try. We've got nothing else. I'll come with you. Maybe we both can free it."

Fessenden thought for a moment and reluctantly agreed. "I guess we have to."

Temple wasted no time. He glanced around once more and handed the machine gun to Fessenden as he stripped off his thick coat, boots, and hat.

"Nice day for a swim. I never thought I'd be joining a polar-bear club."

"Polar-bear club?" Fessenden asked as they waded

in.

The water took Temple's breath away. "Je-e-e-e-sus Christ! A p-p-p-polar-bear club was all these old men who used to swim across the Little Chico Creek on New Year's Day. Crazy old bastards! Of course their wives were on the other side with hot coffee and blankets. And it was only twenty yards or so."

"That sounds like what they do up in Sweden. Never sounded like a good idea to me either," Fessenden said. "Let's go before we die of hypothermia."

And with that, they dove below, ducked under the torn side of the ship, and resurfaced inside the destroyed boat.

Fessenden shone the flashlight around again. "Here, follow me. Watch out. There are all kinds of projectiles."

They climbed up and out of the water. Fessenden stopped for a moment and shone the light on Temple. He spoke very seriously through his chattering teeth. "Listen, Temple, I know we *were* enemies before all of this, but I'm asking you, man to man, if that thing comes again and the situation goes badly and you're in a position and there's no alternative …"

He stopped and they stood in a strange silence in the ruined sub. Temple knew what Fessenden was getting at, but he let him finish.

"Burman was one of my friends, and I saw what that thing did to him. I do not want to be eaten alive. If it comes down to that …"

Temple nodded in agreement. "I know what you're saying. Don't worry. And if the same thing happens and you've got the upper hand, just put one of those bullets right here." He tapped his forehead with his shaking finger. "Right in my coconut."

Fessenden was able to smile briefly. "Coconut. I thought my English was pretty good, but I've never heard one's head called a coconut."

They stood shivering for another awkward moment and then abruptly shook on the agreement.

"First, we're trying to kill each other. Then we're trying to protect each other. And now I'm asking you to kill me again," the captain mused.

"We really ought to make up our minds. We could have killed each other earlier and saved a lot of trouble," Temple said.

As they inched through the boat, Temple spotted a solid piece of railing. It was about six feet long and heavy. The slapping of the waves on the hull and the creaking and moaning of the ship was loud enough that Temple had to call to Fessenden. "Captain! Captain, what about this? Could we use this as a lever?"

Fessenden looked it over. "Yes, that might help. Bring it, and we'll see. And, I'm sorry to say, we're going to have to go below the water twice to get back to the cabinet. There's too much debris in the way."

"Sounds swell," Temple grumbled.

They worked their way back to the tool cabinet. Using the lever that Temple had found and pulling with all their combined strength, they were able to move the bent piece of metal far enough out of the way. Temple shone the light on the cabinet. He held his breath while Fessenden slowly opened the cabinet door. Seawater poured out. But inside the light illuminated the shiny tools, still in the cabinet, neatly stowed with secured fittings. Fessenden grabbed screwdrivers, pliers, cutters, and whatever else he thought they might need. He dropped them into a cloth bag that Temple wore. Fessenden studied the tool cabinet, wondering what else they could use.

Suddenly, from deeper in the sub, the howl of the creature reverberated through the metal. It was inside the sub. Terrified, they froze. Both men could now recognize the creature's voice, but this time it sounded different. This sound was weaker, almost a cry.

Fessenden motioned toward the hatch that led to the engine room. It had been sealed when the fire broke out during the initial attack on the sub. The fire and the explosion had made it inoperable, but the grounding, the crash, and the rolling of the sub had jarred the hatch loose. It was now slightly open.

They heard the howl again, followed by gurgling and retching. They were ankle deep in the frigid seawater, and Temple's feet were screaming in pain. He tapped Fessenden, frantically motioning for them to leave. But Fessenden waved calmly to Temple. He stepped silently forward and gently eased the hatch slightly open.

Both men were instantly struck by a horrific stench that smelled like a disgusting mix of death and sewage. Fessenden suppressed a cough while Temple covered his mouth and gagged until his eyes were so full of tears that he had to wipe them away.

At the base of the hatch, water and what looked like fecal liquid flowed out. Temple dared not shine the light into the burnt engine room because the creature was surely in there. He held the flashlight at his side, but something flowing through the liquid caught his eye. When he recognized it, he jolted in disgust. At his feet, a partial human foot, sheared off at the ankle, floated and twirled in the brown, stinking flow. Temple tapped Fessenden on the shoulder and pointed to it. Fessenden saw it and swallowed hard. A tattered brown sock, wrapped around bloated toes, was still attached. Mercifully, the foot disappeared into the mix of sewage and seawater.

Temple closed his eyes. It was time to go. He yanked on Fessenden's wet shirt.

Fessenden eased out of Temple's grip and made another calming gesture with his hand. He whispered above the noise of the water and the creaking of the boat, "Wait. Just wait. It doesn't know we're here."

Gingerly, he eased the hatch open, just wide enough for them both to poke their heads in. The stench was unbearable, and only a few shafts of weak light shone through. In the tangle of the engine room, they could just make out the creature as it slithered among a mass of bodies and body parts.

It was too much for Temple. He backed out. But Fessenden lingered. Though he quaked with fear and near hypothermia, he wanted desperately to know what the creature was. As he strained to see, he had to wonder why it was in the sub. Perhaps it found the cache of drowned bodies and decided to feast there. Food seemed to be its only motivation. The driveshaft of the sub and the housing that held the two enormous engines hung from the ceiling, obscuring Fessenden's view. But he could partially see it, through a tangle of pipes and wires, beyond the machinery. Now, with something to give it scale, he was able to see how large the creature truly was. It barely fit in the area behind the engines. It seemed to have wedged or coiled itself into the hull. Pipes and fittings buckled under its weight as it rolled and twisted in the dim light that broke through from outside. Fessenden could see it moving, writhing like an eel, sliding and twisting and rolling.

It howled again—quietly, almost to itself. It made guttural gurgling sounds that echoed through the metal ship. Fessenden caught glimpses of thick limbs, but he could not see specific details. He could see its muscular back, which was leathery and scarred. Pocks, welts, and lesions covered it, reminding him of the barnacles that grow on an old ship. The captain also noticed a bony protrusion on its back. What, he wondered, was he was seeing? Did it once have wings? As absolutely preposterous as it sounded, he had to wonder if he was seeing what would have been known in antiquity as a dragon.

The creature moved and bumped into dangling pipes and fittings that snapped and bent like twigs as it howled again. It had squeezed itself tightly into the cramped space, and Fessenden couldn't figure out what it was doing. It seemed as if it couldn't get comfortable. Then it held perfectly still for a moment before it began to wretch. That was unmistakable.

Fessenden and his family had always had dogs. He'd seen plenty of his family pets throw up something that hadn't agreed with them. The creature was exhibiting the same behavior. It was violently vomiting. Fessenden could hear the splashing of liquid as it gushed out. He knew that the remains of eaten men were coming back up. He figured that the creature hadn't had such a banquet in awhile. It had gorged itself on dead men and was now paying the price.

Fessenden had once read that a wolf, if taken from the wild and given an endless supply of meat—something that doesn't happen in nature—would never stop eating. With an oversupply of food, the wolf would eat and vomit at the same time. As he watched, he could hear smacking and crunching. He could see the jerky spasms of the creature's neck. It was gorging and vomiting at the same time.

Fessenden's mind raced. It was vulnerable now. If only they had that dynamite or the petrol or a Panzerfaust, the creature might be easier to kill or perhaps the sub would collapse on it. All they had were a few rounds of bullets, and bullets had sadly proven ineffective. Fessenden even thought he had seen a few bullet holes on its side.

As it howled and retched, Fessenden started to back his head out of the hatch. Then the creature shifted again. He saw it, and it saw him. Its black eye, the size of a grapefruit, stared directly at him—or so it seemed. Fessenden held still. He felt the primal urge to flee, but he held fast. After what seemed like hours, the creature's leathery eyelid closed. The beast slid around into another position, presumably still trying to get comfortable.

Perhaps it hadn't seen him. Its black eye was featureless, and it was impossible to tell where it might have been looking. Perhaps it had seen him but in its discomfort hadn't cared, knowing that he wasn't going anywhere anytime soon.

The captain pulled out of the hatch and eased away to where Temple crouched shivering on a piece of machinery. He motioned for them to leave, and Temple didn't hesitate. They quietly worked their way through the hazardous wreck toward the nose of the ship and up and out onto the miserable island.

Once back on shore, shivering uncontrollably, they climbed back through the rocks and made for their shelter. Although Temple hadn't eaten much that day, he vomited all the same as they clambered over the rocks.

At the shelter, they stripped off their wet clothes, pulling on odd uniforms and bundling up as best they could. They laid out the tools and took stock of what they had.

"Damn!" Fessenden muttered through his chattering teeth. "If we'd had some petrol or some sort of rocket launcher, we could have taken another shot at the creature. I don't think we could have killed it, but maybe we could have blinded it or trapped it in the boat."

"What do you think it was d-d-d-d-doing?" Temple asked as he wrapped himself in more filthy cloth.

"It was sick—sick as a dog, just *like* a dog. I'm guessing food is pretty scarce for that thing, only what it can catch that happens to swim by. But now the bastard has overdone it on our men. Perhaps we're just too rich after its all-fish diet."

"Jesus Christ, this is the goddamn nightmare to end all nightmares," Temple said. "Maybe we can use the torpedo while it's inside the sub."

"No," Fessenden said. "Something must really hit the detonator. And, besides, there's no way we could get the warhead in there. And now that it's uncovered, the electronics can't get wet."

"How'd the creature get in there?" Temple wondered.

"It's obvious that the back of the sub is completely destroyed. There must be a giant hole on what would have been the deck. That's *how* it got in there. *Why* it's in there is anyone's guess. Once it had eaten all the dead on shore, I think it found a bunch of bodies in the boat and has been going back there to feed. It will return to its lair eventually."

"Well, what do you want to do?" Temple asked nervously.

"Stick with the plan. That cave is deep enough, and if we can drop the warhead right, it will go off. I know our plan has only a remote chance of working, but it might."

They sat in silence, trying to stop shivering.

"What the hell is that thing?" Temple asked.

"I haven't a clue, some sort of unknown creature. But does it breathe air or have gills? I don't know. It's one of a kind. If we were scientists and were able to capture it, it would be the scientific find of the century, maybe of the modern age. Get dressed. We've got work to do. Let's get back to its cave while we know it's temporarily detained."

15.

Temple and the captain found their way back to the deep pit and stood at its edge in the pouring rain. It smelled bad, but nothing like the inside of the submarine.

The captain wasted no time. He lashed the rope around a stone pillar and tossed the end into the black pit. Holding the thick rope, Fessenden prepared to climb down into the pit.

"Wait. Why are you doing this? Why the hell are you going in there?" Temple didn't like this.

Fessenden stopped and stood up. " I told you, if we're going to detonate the warhead, it's got to hit something solid. I've got to find the right place so that we can position it above a flat rock or something," the captain said.

"Well, how the hell are we going to do that?" Temple demanded.

"I don't know. I've got to look around. I hope there's a big flat rock right under the lip. We dangle the warhead over it, stretch the rope out, let the rope go, and—if we're lucky—boom!"

Temple watched closely. The captain had been without sleep and food for too long. Yes, it had been hell for Temple and his men, but their suffering had lasted only a few days. They'd been well fed the whole time, with some reasonable rest and the proper winter clothing. The captain, on the other hand, hadn't had a decent meal in two months. Temple had eaten so many helpings of pork chops and gravy while traveling to the island that he had almost made himself sick. That was just over a week ago.

A month earlier, Temple had stuffed himself with pancakes and sausages drowned in hot maple syrup at a USO breakfast that had turned into an impromptu eating contest at the Seabee base in Davisville, Rhode Island. At the very same time, the captain and his crew were out in the North Atlantic enjoying the last of their gray salted ham on canned, moldy brown bread.

Temple could see the shaking in the captain's limbs as he tried to position the rope.

"Let me go," Temple said. "Look, pal, you're too weak. You won't be able to climb back up."

The captain, in sturdy German form, waved him off. "I'm fine, Temple. I can take care of myself."

But Temple was already on the rope and walking toward the edge. "Just keep guard. I'll go."

Temple clung to the rope and guided himself down. He was able to use his feet on the almost vertical incline, digging into cracks and fissures running down the slimy wall. When he got ten feet from the bottom, the wall sheared away, and he slid down the rope, burning his hands and landing hard, sending shooting pains from the wound on his shin. He was still soaking wet, but he could feel the warmth of his own blood, oozing from under his makeshift bandage into his soggy boot.

The floor of the pit was uneven, and he was un-

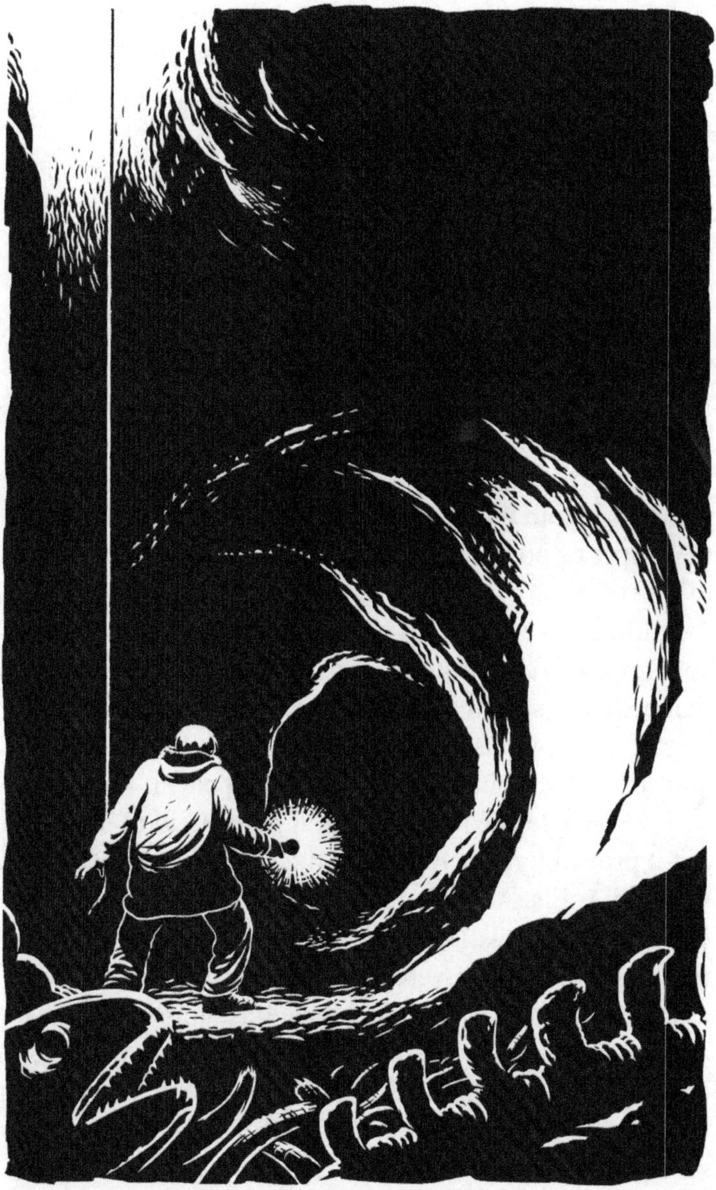

steady. The smell of dead fish and rot was overpowering. In all directions, it was pitch-black, and he could see almost nothing. Obviously, it was more than just a pit. It was a large cave that ran in two directions. One tunnel ran out toward the water, and, at a slight angle on the opposite side, the other tunnel went deep into the island.

Temple fumbled in his coat pocket until he found O'Connor's flashlight. He shivered in the cold blackness. His trembling hand finally was able to turn the flashlight on. Up top, the flashlight had been feeble, practically useless. But in the black void, it seemed bright. He was so thankful that he had been able to hang on to it.

As the light clicked to life, it illuminated the ground he stood on. It wasn't sticks or wood but a thick tangle of dried bones. He shone the light around, the vapor from his breath moving through the beam, as he studied the carpet of bones below his feet. They were fish bones of all sizes and types. Most were broken and twisted, and they filled the entire floor of the cave as far as the light could reach. Temple stood on a mass of fish bones so deep that he could see no floor below it. Whatever the creature was, it had obviously eaten them, thousands of them, perhaps millions of them, and picked them clean.

Temple tried to walk through the field of bones, but it proved too uneven. He had to steady himself on the wet rock walls. As he limped along, he felt grooves and gouges in the rock. He turned his light up to examine the markings. The walls were scraped and worn, and Temple assumed that the creature had done this, aimlessly clawing at the walls or perhaps sharpening its talons. Up above, the captain was peering into the pit. Temple waved, indicating that he was going to look around. The captain waved back.

Temple moved on into the tunnel that led deeper into the island, stepping as gingerly as possible, damaging as little as he could. He hadn't a clue what else might be down here. He found little comfort in knowing that the creature was most likely still in the sub. What if there was more than one? he thought to himself in a moment of panic. His only consolation was in knowing that a thing of such size would be unable to move through the cave of bones without making a hell of a lot of noise.

Temple rounded a corner and was out of sight of the captain. He ducked through a small crevice, a vaulted ceiling looming over him. He could feel a breeze from the sea and smell the salt of the ocean. In the distance, he could hear the pounding of the waves beyond the walls of the cavern.

He hobbled through the space and shone his light on the slimy walls. "Go back and find a big flat rock that you can drop the torpedo on," his mind demanded. "What the hell are you looking for?" he asked himself. His curiosity trumped his fear when up ahead he saw something different, something that looked like a thick wooden slab. He maneuvered carefully, falling several times as he tried to negotiate his way through the crunching bones. He climbed around the wooden slab. It was easily eighteen feet tall and at least four feet thick. He stepped back, surprised to see that the front of the rough wood was intricately carved.

The carving was old, very old, but what it depicted was clear. At the bottom were symbols—writing perhaps—but nothing he could make heads or tails of. Above the inscription, a mural or sorts was carved into the wood. Temple had not been a scholar back in high school, but it didn't take a scholar to comprehend the image. In a huge ring were intricate carvings of ships—old ships—each with a sail and a curved bow. The carvings were very detailed. Each ship had oars that cut into curvy

212

waves, obviously depicting the ocean.

The ships were arranged like the numbers on the dial of a clock. From each ship, a carved line led to a ship that was situated in the middle of the circle. The central ship was smaller. Unlike the others, it was plain and had no sail or oars. It seemed to be tethered to the others by the carved lines.

All at once, Temple heard a distinct crunch back toward the entrance to the tunnel. Something had crunched into the field of bones. Fear shot through Temple as he pulled out his pistol and cocked it. He crouched down and switched off the flashlight. His heart was in his throat, and he trembled in silence.

"Temple? Temple? Where are you?"

It was the captain calling out in a hoarse whisper. Temple sighed with relief.

"Captain," Temple called back quietly, "I'm here." He switched on his light and stepped around the wooden slab, shining the light back in the direction he'd come from.

Fessenden maneuvered clumsily through the bones toward Temple. In the dim light, he looked around his feet.

"I thought you were staying up top?" Temple whispered.

Fessenden stepped through more bones. "What the hell are you doing? Where did you go? I thought perhaps I heard something down by the shore. We need to find a rock below the mouth of this cave. We can't waste time. We have to clear—" He stopped and looked at the floor in the dim light. "These are bones, fish bones. My god, there must be hundreds of years' worth. So this is what it's been eating. Well, until we arrived. Incredible. Absolutely incredible."

"You want to see something incredible, take a look at this." Temple guided Fessenden around the slab.

The captain studied it and rubbed his stubbly beard in amazement. "Oowaa...incredible. It's Norse. Probably from Sweden or Norway. Who knows how long ago. I think this was a door—and a warning. Whoever they were must have been trying to warn anyone who happened to come here." He shook his head in disbelief.

"Look. They brought the creature here. To them, back then, this must have been the ends of the earth. My god, look at that." He counted the ships in the carving. "Eleven, twelve, thirteen ships towed our friend here. Obviously, they couldn't kill it, but they had to get rid of it somehow. One can only imagine what havoc it must have wrought before they were able to capture it. Look at the size of this, this door." Fessenden ran his hands over the aged wood. Thick, rusted metal bands and corroded hammered spikes hung from the split wood. He easily pulled one of the spikes from the rotting wood. It was about ten inches long. "What an effort they made to seal that bastard in here," Fessenden said.

"Well, it busted out at some point," said Temple. "But it was marooned here for who knows how long. I guess that was their plan." Temple studied the image and ran his hands over the carved lines.

"Well, I'm not a Norse historian by any means," Fessenden said. "But it is entirely possible that thing has been here for nearly a thousand years, maybe more." He rubbed his hands over the carving.

lower in the water and was carrying what looked like a cage. "Unbelievable. Absolutely unbelievable," Fessenden muttered.

"Some sort of creature that could live for a thousand years or more? We've discovered—or rather rediscovered—something completely unknown to science. Perhaps it's the famed Grendel creature from mythology. Or maybe it's the devil himself."

Temple was getting nervous. He shone the light around the space.

The captain continued. "All those stories—St. George and the dragon and demons and whatnot—this may be the source of those stories. Of course, something like this would live on in stories. No one would ever want to forget him." He tapped on the boat chiseled into the wood. "Maybe it is the devil. Maybe this is the entrance to hell."

The two of them moved past the huge door, further into the tunnel. The stench was overpowering, and in the dim light, they could discern a crushed path in the field of bones, obviously where the creature had crawled across the bones countless times. Beyond the trail was inky blackness. Each of them realized that he had no desire to see where the thing ultimately lived.

They worked their way back into the main chamber, and Temple was relieved to see the sky overhead framed by the pit walls. The steady rain continued as Fessenden hobbled in the bones behind Temple. The captain stopped under the lip of the cave. He looked up and then looked at his feet. He shuffled his feet and began to kick away at the thick layer of bones.

"What are you thinking?" Temple asked, looking up.

The captain stared up into the rain and then back down at his feet. He bent over and started to dig in the bones, flinging them away. "Let's try it here. We'll hoist the warhead up there. It's reasonably flat up there. We'll have it hanging straight down.

Then right here we'll clear away the debris so

that when we cut the rope, the torpedo drops and hits solid rock. My guess is this is an old lava tube. It has to have a solid floor down there somewhere. That should detonate our torpedo. But we've got to get down to the stone floor. I'm worried that all this bone will act like a cushion and the warhead won't have enough velocity to detonate. We'll only get one try if we get any at all. Here, help me dig."

Together, they dug at the bones, trying to clear a spot directly under the lip of the cavern. They dug one foot, then another. The floor was nowhere in sight.

"My god, this creature has been here so long. It's hard to imagine," the captain said as he huffed and puffed.

They continued, stopping occasionally as broken bones, spines, and teeth punctured their digging hands.

"It can stay here for all I care," Temple said as he dug. "But if we live and can blow the hell out of this creature, we'll sell the skull to Robert Ripley. It'll be in the newspaper and in *Ripley's Believe It or Not!* Do you know *Ripley's*?" Temple asked as he pulled more bones from the ever-deepening hole.

"Yes, everyone knows *Ripley's*. A column ran in our daily paper until … well … the West became our en—"

A splashing and crashing from the tunnel that went out to sea stopped them cold. They waited, hoping it was just a large wave, or something else, when they heard more splashing and could feel movement. They looked at each other and knew immediately. Temple motioned for the captain to climb the rope.

The captain grabbed on and began to pull, but he'd underestimated his fatigue and his weakness. Even with a burst of fear-driven adrenaline, he had no arm strength left. He couldn't pull himself up. Temple, his panic growing, pushed Fessenden from below, trying to help him up.

Fessenden looked up. If only he could get past the first ten feet, he could get a foothold on the rocks. But despite their efforts, he was just too weak. He dropped back down, out of breath.

Temple was brimming with fear. "We've got to go! It's coming!" he whispered frantically.

The captain hunched over, gasping for breath. His hands were burned and raw from trying to scale the thick hemp rope.

Temple wasted no time. He whispered hoarsely, "I'll pull you up. I'll go first." Temple jumped up on the rope. Temple was able to shinny easily up the rope and get his feet on the wall. He pulled himself up and out, lay down flat, and called down into the pit. "Tie it around your waist, and I'll pull you up."

The captain took the rope and began to wrap it around his waist. A series of louder crunches echoed from the tunnel. Both men could feel the thunderous vibrations of the approaching creature. The captain tried to tie the rope, but as he loosened it for another attempt, Temple yanked the rope free and pulled it up. The captain pawed wildly after the end of the rope, but Temple hauled it up and out of the pit.

The captain looked up in horror. Temple peered back down. "It's coming. It's too close. Hide, hide!"

Fessenden glanced frantically around. With three big leaps, he flung himself against the wall and slid down into a squat. He scooped and grabbed at the loose bones and pulled them around himself as camouflage. He covered himself completely. He held his breath as the crunching grew louder. From between the bones, Fessenden could see Temple's head still poking over the edge of the cave. As the beast loomed closer, Temple ducked out of sight. The captain's heart pounded in his chest as the noise grew louder and louder. Did the creature really have a weak sense of smell? He was about to find out. Fessenden held his luger flat against his chest with both hands. The captain could feel the vibrations through the mat of fish bones as the creature closed in.

Before Fessenden could see anything, he could hear the crunch of the thing shattering and snapping bones several feet thick. More bones rolled and ground under its enormous body and tail as it moved along. Its breathing was thick and deep with a rasp and a hissing wheeze following each rumbling breath. It instinctively paused in the shadows and then stepped into the light from above the pit. The captain dared not move as it lumbered past him, not ten feet away. It was enormous—like a train car. It was wet, but its skin had a thick, oily covering.

As it passed under the opening of the cavern, the creature seemed to notice the depression that the men had dug in the bones. It looked at the hole and pawed at it. Fessenden was unable to think, unable to process what he was seeing. After an agonizing minute, it began to move on. The captain could see its outline, and through his camouflage of bones he was able to make out more of its appearance. It had thick, leathery skin, like an elephant, but it was oily and slick. Its head reminded him of a strange serpent, with folds of shiny skin and strange wisps of fur. It was covered with sores, old scars, and other marks that made specific features almost unrecognizable. It's lipless mouth must have been three or four feet wide, lined with long yellow and brown teeth. Many were broken and cracked, but many were still sharp and almost a foot long.

Pieces of pink flesh and a swatch of a uniform were still hanging from its teeth and gums. The captain continued to hold his breath as it moved past him at an agonizingly slow pace. As the creature squeezed around the bend, the captain saw the strange bony protrusion that he had spotted earlier. But now, with the light from above, he was astonished to see that it wasn't a bony mass at all. Instead, it was clearly and obviously a sword. The metal blade still had spots that were shiny, and the bent handle and the finger guard were completely green with corrosion. The leather wrapping was long gone, but it was undoubtedly a sword buried deep in the monster's side. A few ribbons of seaweed were tangled where the blade went beneath the monster's thick hide. Even in his state of frozen panic, Fessenden had to wonder whose sword it was, what had happened to him, and how long it had been lodged in the creature's body. The creature lumbered on, making its strange sounds, as it wound further into the deep cave.

The captain guessed that perhaps it was still sick, but he took no chances. He held perfectly still, even though it was heading deep into the cavern.

Out of the corner of his eye, the captain saw the rope drop back down. Fessenden sat up slowly, brushing off the bones, and crept back across to the hanging rope. He began to lash the rope around his waist and then stopped.

Temple, watching from above, was alarmed. The captain waved, signaling him to wait just a second. The captain reached inside his coat and produced one of the smoke grenades. He walked carefully down the passage to the point where the creature had to squeeze past the wooden door. He wedged the smoke grenade into a crevice in the rock wall and stretched a piece of wire across the gap. He secured the wire around one of the rusted metal straps and then attached it to the grenade pin. He took a deep breath and tried to relax as he pulled the pin on the grenade until it was just a quarter inch from springing free. He removed his hands and remained still for a second to see if it was set. It was. He carefully returned to the rope and wrapped it around his waist.

Temple was relieved to see the captain down below. He positioned himself, seated on the ground. He braced his feet against a sturdy rock and waited for a sharp tug. When he got the signal, he began hauling the captain up. Once the captain was able to get a foothold, he helped Temple as much as he could, considering his pitiful condition. Temple, with the rope ripping into his palms, using all his might, was able to pull the captain to the surface. Once the captain was on top, they both lay flat on their backs, panting, as the steady rain pelted their faces.

"Sorry. I had to pull the rope up, but I knew you couldn't make it, and I didn't want you to try. I was worried that if it saw the rope, it might figure out someone was in there."

"I thought you'd abandoned me, but you were right. I would have tired, and I wouldn't have made it. Thanks."

"And where the hell did you go? Did you tuck it into beddy-bye?"

"No, I rigged up a smoke grenade with a trip wire. When it comes out again, it may give us some warning."

"Unless it comes out at night," Temple said. "And what are we going to do now? We didn't get to the rock floor, and there's no way I'm going down there again."

"It's fine. I don't thinking digging would have worked anyway, but I think we might still be able make it work." Fessenden rolled over and climbed to his feet. Near the mouth of the pit were numerous boulders. Using all his weight, he got one to rock back and forth slightly.

"These will work. Come. Let's get warm if we can. Then we'll try to spring our trap."

The two men coiled the rope, picked up their weapons, and started back toward the encampment.

The captain suddenly stopped Temple. "I saw it. I mean I really saw it. It's like nothing else. It's ancient, absolutely ancient. Who knows how old? And it's got a sword stuck in its side."

Temple realized what the captain had said. "A sword? How would a …" He shook his head. Maybe this thing is the goddamn devil."

Back at camp, the two lit their feeble fire and tried to heat a cup of instant coffee. They were only able to get it lukewarm, but it sufficed. They shared it, passing it back and forth.

Temple looked at Fessenden, who was wearing coveralls with the name "Temple" embroidered above the greasy breast pocket.

"What a crazy damn war this is! Here we sit, you wearing my uniform, trying to keep some prehistoric monster from killing us, while our two countries slug it out. No one is going to care if two sailors die, just another war casualty. They'll send a telegram to my folks saying I died while on a secret construction mission—honorably—in the defense of my country. If only they knew what we'd found."

"Well, as far as I'm concerned, there are no countries here. This is the Island of Otto Fessenden and Lawrence Temple. And that thing in there, that's the enemy."

Temple took a swig of the cold coffee. "I'll drink to that." He offered the last sip to the captain.

"It's all yours," Fessenden said.

"Maybe, since we know it's sick," said Temple, "we can use the time to get some real shut-eye. Who knows? Maybe it will curl up and feel sick for a century."

The captain shook his head to the contrary. "No, I

think we should work on the trap. Who knows when it will come out again? No, we should set up the trap, and then we can rest."

Temple was beyond any exhaustion he'd ever known, but he knew the captain was right. "You're right. OK, what next then?"

Fessenden stood up, grabbed a coat, and pulled it on. He picked up the tools. "Lunch break is over. Back to work," he said.

Temple pulled himself to his feet. "Aye, aye, captain."

Fessenden, with real tools, went to work on the torpedo. He was precise and calm. Temple was impressed. The captain removed the screws and covers and opened the controls, where the range and depth of the torpedo would be set.

"Wow, you really know your stuff, captain. Do all accountants work that well with tools?"

"Well, I got my credential in accounting, but at the polytechnic school we were required to have a second discipline. Mine was mechanical engineering. And as a U-boat captain, I had to know how everything works. We spent weeks in the shipyards in Danzig, watching as our boats and all their components were assembled. Of course, that was early on, when Admiral Dönitz believed we had a chance.

"I was lucky," Fessenden continued. "I was actually well trained. But that kind of training was short-lived. After '42 or '43, most of the sailors were rushed to sea and went straight to the bottom. Even the well-trained crews haven't fared very well. Of the thirty-seven captains I knew—last I heard—eight of us were still alive. But it's been a few weeks since I've heard any reports, so who knows? Of course, some are listed as missing, but in the submarine business, missing doesn't mean you're sitting in a military hospital unable to speak or in a coma. It means you're at the bottom."

"Wow, eight out of thirty-seven? That's pretty bleak."

"Well, that's war for you. A lot of them were good friends. My sister's husband was lost on the U-509. I never wanted this war. None of us did. It was just dumped upon us. My poor sister, she didn't take it very well."

Temple felt genuine sympathy for Fessenden as he watched the captain work quickly, dismantling the head of the torpedo. He watched Otto, with his short brown hair and his focused gaze. Lawrence Temple had one brother of his own, but Fessenden could easily have been his brother, too. They had different lives, but they were so alike. Temple even felt a bit guilty for no reason he could understand. He tried to sound comforting as the captain worked. To Temple, it looked very complicated, but Fessenden seemed to know exactly what he was doing.

"Well, maybe when this whole stinking mess of a war is over, your sister will be able to move on, find someone new. Time heals all wounds."

"Well, in Helga's case, that won't happen. When she got the news that Malcolm's sub was lost, she slit her wrists. Hand me those pliers, will you?"

Temple was at a loss for words. He handed Fessenden the tool.

"Did you know that Hitler—the mad man—and all his ... followers truly believe pure Germans are direct decedents of Norse gods?" Fessenden asked.

"I didn't know that." Temple said.

"It's true. The über-German is who we are—like our friend in that pit—descendents of some supernatural being. If that's the case, he sure doesn't treat family very well. Here, stand here and hold this."

Together they freed the explosive mechanism. Temple was relieved. The actual explosive mechanism was smaller than the head of the torpedo, but it was still two-and-a half feet long and easily sixty or seventy pounds. They kept the warhead covered with a piece of tent and put it on the litter that Fessenden had fashioned.

They staggered up and over rocks. Together, they sat panting, taking a short break. They rewrapped the explosive head in more tent canvas and carried it slowly and laboriously on the litter across the island, stumbling and slipping with almost every step. Temple's leg had stopped bleeding, but each step was painful. He didn't complain. Minor physical pain was now very low on his list of things to be worried about.

A few yards from the pit, they set the litter down carefully. Temple made a quick recon of the jagged hole to see if the creature had returned. He peered down into the shaft. The cave floor seemed undisturbed. Fessenden dismantled the litter and untied one of the long pieces of construction rebar. He handed it to Temple.

"Here's what we'll do," he said. "We'll use this to leverage one of these rocks free and drop it down into the cave. Then we'll suspend the explosive over the hole with the ropes. Then we wait. When it comes out, we cut the rope and hope it will be blown to bits. If we could set the warhead off near the creature, all those jagged bones would make excellent shrapnel. At the very least, we should be able to seal it in the cave. I don't know, scare it, blind it, anything."

Temple could see plenty of ways that this could go wrong, but he had no ideas of his own, so he did everything he could to help.

"Wait," Temple said. "Maybe we should position

the warhead first. Then if it hears us drop the boulder and comes to see what's going on, we'll be able to set the warhead off."

Fessenden looked at the mechanism covered with the tarp on the makeshift litter. "I get what you're saying, but we might have to make adjustments. I doubt we can drop a boulder down there and have it land exactly under the warhead."

"Well, at least it will be ready to go. We can just adjust it and drop it—just in case it comes out." Temple had a good point, and Fessenden agreed.

The storm was kicking up again as they struggled over the hostile terrain with their flimsy frame. They were almost comical. Each man fell every step or two. They often tripped simultaneously as they carried the litter over jagged rocks. Finally they reached the spot and set it at the mouth of the pit.

Both men gasped for breath. The two pieces were almost in place. They tied a rope around the back end of the explosive. Together they laid the warhead gently on the rock below their frame, and they stepped back. Temple hauled the warhead up, and Fessenden guided it until it was hanging vertically while Temple tied off the rope to a nearby boulder.

"OK, now we put rocks on these long planks as counterweight," said Fessenden.

The two gathered flat stones and piled them onto the back legs of the sled. Together they pushed it into place, and both were amazed to see that it was staying together. They slid it out further, until the warhead was almost dangling over the pit.

It was now or never. Fessenden lifted the tent piece and ducked under it. He studied the warhead. It had been awhile since he'd armed a torpedo, but it came back quickly. He made the adjustments to the weapon, setting the depth at zero and the distance at zero. Without the casing, Fessenden could hear the whirring of little motors and the electronic buzz of the detonation system as it came to life. The batteries were only good for about an hour. But that didn't matter; that was all for guidance. The warhead was armed, and all it needed now was a solid shot to break the nose and trigger the firing pin.

While the captain had been arming the warhead, Temple clambered up the short slope above the pit, looking for the best rocks to pry free. The captain emerged and directed Temple to a pile of rocks over the pit to their right. Temple scrambled over with the metal bar and began to pry a huge boulder. He used all his strength, and the rebar bowed as the boulder began to move. He rocked it back and forth, and finally the boulder rolled forward, then back, then forward. Temple rocked it back and forth with the lever until it finally rolled over, found the incline, rolled once more, and dropped, along with numerous smaller rocks, into the pit with a resounding crunch.

The captain ran to the edge and peered in. It was hard to see, but it seemed as if the pile was not under the warhead. Temple wasted no time. He moved up another few feet and went to work on more boulders. He pried them loose too, and they spilled into the pit, taking a bit of the cave mouth with them. The captain looked over the side again. The sled was too far from the new rock pile below.

He called to Temple. "Help me. Quick. We've got to move it!"

Temple slid down the rock but lost his footing and dropped the rebar. As he struggled to keep himself from falling in, the rebar tumbled into the pit. Temple righted himself and joined Fessenden.

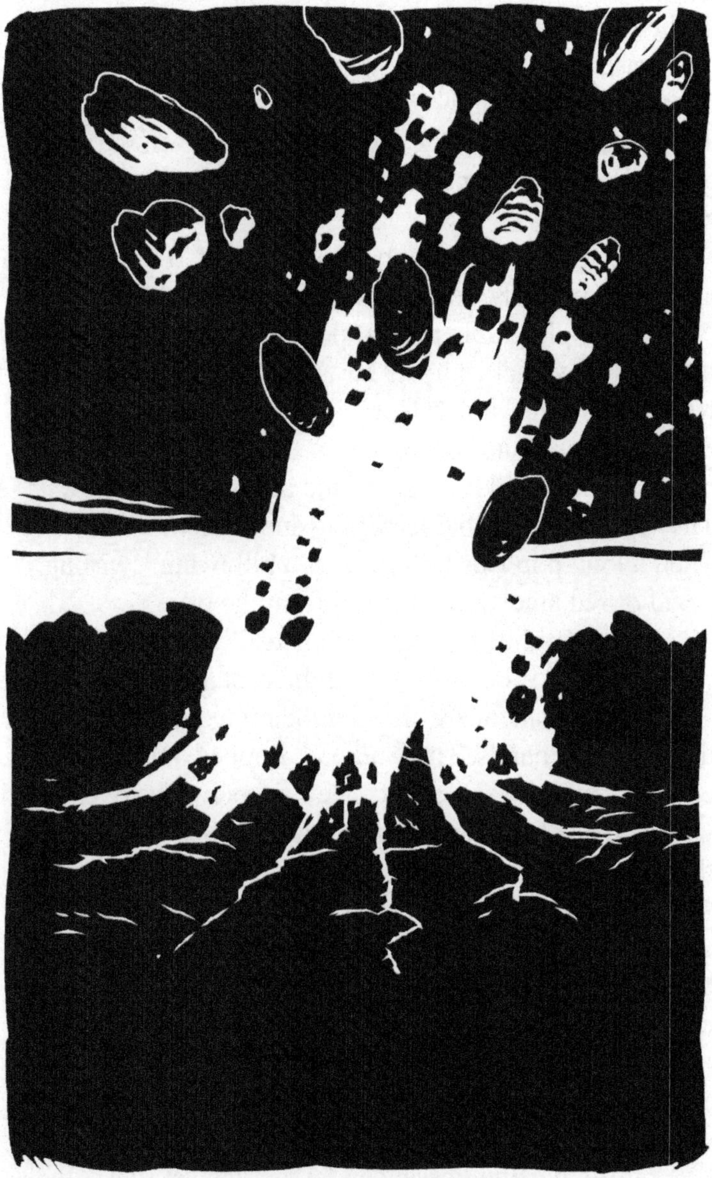

The commotion didn't go unnoticed. From deep in the cave, they heard the roar of the creature. They began pushed the sled a few feet forward. The sound of the creature crashing through the tunnel grew louder. Temple and the captain pushed their contraption more frantically, and the warhead swung back and forth, banging on the sides of the frame. The captain ran up to the edge to check the alignment.

"OK, that's it. Get back! Get back!" Fessenden ran over and untied the rest of the rope.

Temple grabbed the rope as well, and they kept it taut as they backed up as far as they could—until they were holding just a few feet of extra rope between them. Below, the creature roared again. It was directly underneath them. They knew the sound all too well by now. They shuddered at that terrifying and deafening howl. Then a loud pop was followed by a billowing, swirling cloud of red smoke that poured from the pit.

"Holy shit! It's right below us!" Temple shrieked.

"Let go! Let go!" yelled the captain.

Simultaneously, they let the rope go, and it ripped through their hands. The warhead dropped, and the wooden frame tumbled in with it. The two men dove over a wall of rocks as a tremendous kick reverberated through the island, followed by an explosion that blasted into the sky. The concussion rang their brains and punched the air out of their lungs. A huge cloud of red and black smoke blanketed them as debris rained down all over, pelting the curled-up men.

A second later, a rushing sound, the sound of an avalanche, ripped through the air as the top of the tunnel collapsed.

Temple and Fessenden lay on the wet rocks, their ears ringing from the blast. Rocks and fish bones rained down, and the acrid smell of cordite filled the air. Temple was flat on his back. He reached over, without looking, and felt Fessenden's shoulder. Each was relieved that other seemed fine.

They climbed to their feet and looked at the hole they'd made. It was now twice the size it had been. The entire wall had broken free, and a dusty mound filled the side of the pit, a complete collapse. Temple clasped Fessenden on the shoulder. There was no growling, no movement, no sound at all, except a few loose pebbles rolling down the new mountain of rocks.

"Outstanding! Otto, you're a goddamn genius!"

Fessenden wasn't as jubilant. He sat and listened, motionless, waiting to see if the creature stirred. After a full ten minutes, he was satisfied. With difficulty, they stood up and shuffled off together.

Back at the shelter, there was now no reason not to make smoke. At long last, they got a real fire going with destroyed crates and driftwood. They cooked up more of their rations. For the first time, they both felt somewhat safe—although neither of them was ever far from the pistols and rifles and the few rounds of ammunition they still had.

They sat, soaking up the heat from the fire, relishing the new feeling of warmth. The food was hot, too, and had never tasted so good. For a few hours, they drifted into and out of sleep.

Then Temple, almost unable to keep his eyes open, muttered to Fessenden, "Do you think it's dead?"

"No, I do not. Modern weapons or not, I don't think we did any better than the Vikings.

I hope it's at least trapped in there—at least long enough for us to get on your boat. Hell, I'm not sure it *can* die. Maybe it's some long-lost creature that has amazing, unknown longevity."

"Should we go down there and check?" Temple sleepily whispered.

"No, if it's alive, we'll know soon enough. There's nothing we can do about it. We've got like ten rounds left between us," The captain said almost deliriously.

Temple yawned. "And we ain't got no more torpedoes either."

Barely awake, Temple mumbled, "Should someone keep watch? Sleep in shifts, just in case?"

"I … I … I think we'll be o-o-okay …" Fessenden muttered as he fell deeply asleep.

Temple was already asleep.

Morning came, bringing with it a roaring storm, but as bleak as it was on the tiny rock, the creature did not emerge. They had burned the last of the wood so they just camped under a pile of uniforms, sleeping intermittently.

And they talked for hours. Fessenden told Temple stories of his life and of his world. Temple did the same.

That night, as the storm continued to howl, their predicament still wouldn't let them go. Exhausted as they were, they couldn't sleep for long, couldn't shake the images of the carnage they had experienced. They both knew—although they never said it—that they'd never be the same. The smell of rotting corpses was in the air. They wondered, Would it ever go away? Even If they lived, even if they got off that miserable rock, they knew that something about them would always be left behind.

In all likelihood, that smell would be permanently stuck in their noses, embedded in their brains. The absurdity of the war set against survival in these most extraordinary circumstances was something they could never shake loose.

Hours passed, and the big storm tracked across

the island. Temple and Fessenden talked quietly, with their guns drawn, as the driving rain and wind continued. Lightning flashed, and thunder boomed. The men winced at each thunderclap. The creature had always used the worst weather to attack, and they both felt sure that it would come again. But it did not. During the night, Fessenden had to pry his own gun out his hand. He had gripped the gun so tightly for so long that his hand had cramped.

Morning came, and the storm died down. The rain stopped. They sifted through the rations they had. They breakfasted on canned fruits and crackers and oatmeal. As the hours wore on, their calm and relief slowly faded. They were still stuck on the island. Their panic began to resurface.

They talked all day—politics, history, anything. Fessenden told Temple of his boyhood crushes and of the loss of his love, Elsa, who married another man. Temple told Fessenden about his life growing up in central California. They sat through a long day, alert and exhausted, as a new storm swirled outside. Fessenden found the pile of dog tags that they had collected from the dead Americans. Temple would now be their keeper.

Fessenden looked at the tags. He read each one. "Did you get them all? Are these all your men?" he asked.

"No. A couple of them were eaten. And Brenner blew his own head off. His doggies went with him. But that's OK. I'll remember."

Fessenden looked at them and shook his head in sadness. "I have nothing. I have no tags, nothing. All of them are just names in a book in the naval headquarters, just a line. Hans Burman. Heinz. Kruger. The boy—I don't even know his name."

"It's a war, Otto. We had to do what we did. I shot

some of your men dead. I had to. We were fighting for our lives, you and I. God, I wish I hadn't, but I did."

"You know, looking through a periscope was so removed from the killing. It was different. I sank tons and tons of ships, but I never saw a person, not one actual human figure. It was always just a gray blob on the horizon, a heading, a distance, and a depth. And then a blast, a terrific explosion, and down she went. I suppose, at my weakest, I rationalized it. They were sailors. They had lifeboats. They were just matériel—tanks and jeeps and guns—designed to kill my countrymen."

He studied the grimy dog tags with trembling hands. "But this, all this—and that thing down in that hole, that thing …" He closed his eyes. "It's too much to ask anyone to bear."

Temple knew exactly what he meant. In fact, Temple was the only other person who could ever come close to understanding what Fessenden had been through. Temple said nothing. He opened a can of rations and shared a cracker with Fessenden. Fessenden took the cracker and ate it, trying to move his mind elsewhere.

"Here, tell me about these men. I want to know. What kind of men were they?" He pulled up a tag and showed it to Temple. "Tell me, Temple, who was this?"

"Oh, that was Buchanan. I didn't know him that well. He was from Brooklyn, New York—or maybe it was Queens or the Bronx. He was always arguing about who made the best pizza or something. He really liked to play cards. I know he had a girl back home—I think. I didn't really know him, but he seemed like a good guy," Temple said softly.

They sat with their backs against the wall, hoping for nothing but expecting the worst. The captain told Temple about his crew, about his good friend Burman and the zealot Caspar. And Temple told the captain about the Seabee crew. Somehow they were able to find a funny story about this man or that man, and they'd laugh about some foolish prank someone had played or about some huge mistake someone had made. As the rain poured on, they realized they weren't enemies at all; they were now friends, who owed his life to the other.

By morning, the rain stopped, replaced by the thick fog. They awoke, had cold coffee, and resumed their conversation of the night before. They talked about the war, about their countries. Fessenden was in the middle of a story from his boyhood when Temple heard something and sat up straight.

"Stop! Wait! What's that?"

They stopped talking and listened. The familiar sound of rain was absent, and there was a new sound in the distance.

Temple checked his battered wristwatch. "This is it. They're here. Right on time. My god, Otto, were getting off this goddamn rock!"

They exploded with glee. They yelled and embraced.

"Quick! Let's see if we can signal them," cried Temple.

"Here, use this," the captain said, tossing the last smoke grenade to Temple.

"We were supposed to row out to them, so they'll most likely send a skiff when we don't show up. Come on!"

Temple and Fessenden scrambled up from their shelter and down to the north side of the island onto the steep cliff that overlooked the ocean. Fog filled the air, but the sea wasn't pitching too badly. Temple climbed to the edge of the precipice, and Fessenden followed.

Temple pulled the pin on the smoke grenade and tossed it a few feet away. It popped and flashed, and thick clouds of red smoke shot from the canister.

"Nope, can't see anything. Damn fog." Temple waved a swatch of yellow tent tarp anyway. "I can hear it. It's out there. It's getting louder. Can you hear it? Ahoy! Ahoy!" he yelled.

It was true. It was really happening. A large ship was out there.

"Temple, do you think I'll be sent to prison?" Fessenden asked quietly. Temple waved the cloth rhythmically.

"What? No. When we tell them what happened, they'll think at first we're crazy. But when they find whatever is left in that cave, we're going to be … well … I don't know what. It's incredible." But Temple understood Fessenden's concern. The captain was about to become a prisoner of war, no matter what. "Otto, don't worry. I'll make it clear, all right? This was *not* a normal situation. This was … There's no precedent for something like this."

Out in the mist, the ship noises grew louder. There was no question that a sizable ship was closing in. Its horn gave two loud blasts into the fog. It was the best sound Temple had ever heard.

"Yes! God, yes! Finally!" Temple yelled. He waved the yellow tarp, straining to see the first signs of the ship's silhouette emerging from the fog.

Fessenden climbed onto the rock. He stood behind Temple and put the barrel of his luger to the back of Temple's head.

"Sorry, friend," he said and fired. Temple dropped, flailing wildly for a moment on the rocks.

Fessenden didn't hesitate. He dropped down and pulled off Temple's dog tags and slipped them over his own head in one quick movement. Temple's body continued to writhe as blood pumped from his skull. Fessenden avoided getting blood on himself as he fired three more shots into the air. He dragged Temple's body to the edge of the cliff. He scooped up several large rocks, stuffed them into Temple's coat, buttoned the coat, and rolled Temple's body over the edge and into the waves below.

Fessenden dashed back to the Americans' beach, shedding the last items of his German clothing. Now wearing only Temple's coveralls, he fished out Kruger's wallet and watch and stuffed them into his shirt.

As Fessenden waited, he prepped himself. He repeated Temple's name, rank, and serial number over and over, searing it into his brain.

Thirty minutes later, Fessenden was standing on the gravel beach as a motorized skiff chugged into the cove. The coxswain steered the boat in, idled the motor, and then shut it off as they slid into the gravel. One of the sailors had a rifle, but he held it casually.

"We heard shots." the ranking sailor said.

"Yeah, I was trying to get your attention. Our boats were destroyed. That's why we couldn't meet you."

Who are you?" a boyish sailor called to Fessenden.

"Petty Officer Lawrence A. Temple, Seabees Second Division, 445-93-087. God, am I glad to see you guys!" Fessenden shouted.

"What the hell happened? What's going on? Where are the rest of the men?"

Another sailor scanned the litter-strewn beach with its burned crates and its pieces of twisted equipment rolling in the waves. "And where's the radio station?" he asked.

Two nervous young sailors with big duffle bags

and bright life jackets up to their ears sat back down in the boat. Had the shack been completed as planned, the two would have manned the radio for the first four weeks. They seemed quietly relieved to realize that they wouldn't be staying on the tiny island for a month.

"A German team landed on the island. We think maybe they saw us when we first landed. Just dumb luck. Nobody knows. We had a huge goddamn firefight. Lasted for days. The bastards outnumbered us. Blew up our supplies. But I got the last one yesterday. Shot him right in his rotten coconut."

The sailors looked at each other wide-eyed.

"All your men are dead? Where's your captain?"

"You mean Brenner? He's dead. German grenade. They attacked us, blew up our fuel dump, and then just kept hammering at us. And we hammered back—until it was him and me."

"Well, you'd better get aboard. We've got to report to someone," said the coxswain.

"This is something outta *Stars and Stripes*," another said.

The sailor with the rifle held it up and scanned the landing area. "All those guys are dead?" he asked. "Maybe not everyone is dead. Should we look? Maybe there are some Krauts in hiding."

Fessenden climbed shakily into the boat.

"There is no place to hide on this rock. I pored over it. The last of our guys died four days ago. I pitched them into the sea. I tossed the German in yesterday. Not that the bastard deserved it. I should have just let him rot, but I was tired of looking at his dead face. I got as many tags as I could." He held up the half-dozen dog tags of the American dead.

The coxswain shook his head. "Oh shit. A bunch of

dead men and a radio that ain't built is going to get somebody's balls up in a big old sling. Fubar. That is for sure."

Fessenden climbed aboard. They wrapped him in blankets as two sailors shoved off, pushing the boat past the unforgiving rocks.

"Launching the boat," one barked. The boat backed out and into the waves and mist.

"Wow, a firefight on this rock? That must have been—"

"It was the most horrific thing I've ever seen. I've never been so scared in all my life," Fessenden said, honestly and flatly.

The mood was awkward, and the sailor changed the subject. "Don't worry. We'll get you some hot chow. Where you from, Temple?"

"New Idria, California." Fessenden said.

The sailor put an orange life jacket over Fessenden. "New Idria. Where's that?" he asked. "I'm from Modesto."

The captain didn't hesitate. "Yeah, I know Modesto. New Idria's about an hour-and-a-half from there, about an hour west of Los Banos. My wife, Emily, and I used to go down to the fair in Modesto," Fessenden lied.

"Hey, yeah, me too," the sailor said. "Damn, It's a small world."

The coxswain fired up the engine, and the boat powered through the waves back toward the anchored ship. Fessenden looked back at the island—the feeble rock—slowly fading into the mist.

Past the breakers and nearing the ship, the USS Tacoma, the boat slowed down. Fessenden turned to look at the ship. It was a hive of activity. The radio squawked from the deck, and men buzzed around purposefully.

A young, freckled sailor sitting in the skiff studied the haggard Fessenden in awe. "You had to shoot a guy?"

"I did. It was him or me, and I picked him. And I got the Kraut bastard's pistol, too." Fessenden pulled out his own luger and showed it as his trophy. The sailors were impressed.

A million thoughts were racing through Fessenden's mind, but on top of all of them was the thought that he was getting away with it. He was pulling it off. He was so relieved to leave that island and that creature behind that he was caught off guard when he felt himself beginning to cry. If the sailors noticed it, they made no indication. They carried on with their duties.

The sea was rough enough that the small crew had to work to control the little boat and tie it off to the hanging metal deck. They helped Fessenden off the boat and onto the metal stairs leading up to the deck.

"Get this man to sick bay. And bring some soup or coffee or whatever the doc says. The captain is going to want to talk to—"

"Petty Officer Lawrence Temple, Seabees, Second Division." Fessenden now found himself completely out of energy. Fatigue, stress, and relief converged on him at once. He could barely stand, but it didn't matter. The sailors simply picked up the frail Fessenden and carried him up the long flight of steps to the upper deck.

Below, as sailors tethered the skiff, the stories were already flying.

"What happened?" asked one sailor.

"God, he looks so old," another said.

"That's what that kinda thing will do to you. Ambushed by the Germans, huge firefight, radio station destroyed. He's the last living guy. Even took the gun from the Kraut he killed. Shot him right in the head."

Another sailor whistled in awe.

Up above, someone yelled, "Winch coming down!"

A huge winch was lowered from the deck to lift the skiff out of the water. As the men prepared to hoist the skiff, down at the waterline, in the inky, green waves lapping at the metal hull, a distinct trail of bubbles gently rose to the surface.

"Fictionalized rendering of the factual events surrounding the Daytlov Pass. Incident. Well written and a page turner. Captures the time and setting well"

--Anthony Bonfiglio

"Superbly written, once I started this book I could not put it away until I was done. Great ending of a story that we already know the outcome."

--Hungryman

The facts: In 1959, nine Russian college students embarked on a ten day skiing expedition in the Ural Mountains. They never returned. After the disappearance, an exhaustive search by authorities and the then Soviet government began. Eventually, the first five bodies were found.
All of the bodies had died of exposure and were found outside their tent, in their underwear with no winter clothing. The temperature that night would have been well below zero.

Evidence at their camp suggested that they had cut themselves out of their tent during the night, abandoning skis, clothing and provisions. A criminal inquest was opened by authorities.

Months later, the final four bodies were recovered. All had died of massive internal injuries: broken ribs, punctured lungs, crushed vertebrae and one of the men had a completely crushed skull. The last body, one of two women on the team, had the most internal damage, including having her tongue removed.
All nine bodies were also reported to have been radioactive.

Mountain of the Dead is the fictionalized story of by writer, director Mike Wellins.
It's available in paperback and digital download.

www.mountainofthedead.com

Freakybuttrue's young adult fiction
CHECK OUT STELLA'S BIG ADVENTURES!

"Great story, great illustrations. A nice mix of humor and creep-factor, my 8-year old daughter loved it. I look forward to the next chapters!"
--Peter H.

Meet Stella Sedgewick. In the tradition of the greatest supernatural investigators, Stella can hold her own. Babysitting is just how she pays the bills and funds her passion: investigating and reporting on the things that lurk in the shadows, light up the sky and go thud in the night. Her two main goals: get to the truth, no matter how dangerous or scary, and keep her baby-sat kid relatively unharmed and alive, both of which are easier said than done.

WWW.STELLASBABYSITTINGSERVICE.COM

Available in paperback and digital download.

Mike Wellins is a writer, film maker, visual artist, oddities museum owner, and has authored several books. Among his titles are *Mountain of the Dead, Stella's Babysitting Service* for young readers, *Serious Wackos*, and a textbook; *Storytelling Through Animation*. He has always had an interest in mysteries and odd phenomena. Mike resides happily in rainy Portland, Oregon with his terrier Leonard.

www.Freakybuttrue.com

Printed in Great Britain
by Amazon